MOUNTAIN BLUES

Sean Arthur Joyce

Mountain Blues

a novel

NeWest Press
Edmonton, AB 2018

Library and Archives Canada Cataloguing in Publication

Joyce, Sean Arthur, 1959-, author
Mountain blues / Sean Arthur Joyce.
Issued in print and electronic formats.
ISBN 978-1- 988732-30- 5 (softcover).-- ISBN 978-1- 988732-31- 2
(EPUB).--
ISBN 978-1- 988732-32- 9 (Kindle)

I. Title.
PS8569.O98M68 2018   C813'.54
C2017-905222- 5
C2017-905223- 3

Board Editor: Merrill Distad
Cover design & typesetting: Kate Hargreaves
Cover photographs: Sveta Federava and Holly Mandarich via *Unsplash*
Author photograph: Juscha Grunther

NeWest Press acknowledges the support of the Canada Council for the Arts, the Alberta Foundation for the Arts, and the Edmonton Arts Council for support of our publishing program. This project is funded in part by the Government of Canada.

201, 8540 – 109 Street
Edmonton, AB T6G 1E6
780.432.9427
NeWest Press www.newestpress.com

No bison were harmed in the making of this book.

PRINTED AND BOUND IN CANADA

1 2 3 4 5 20 19 18

To the people in rural communities everywhere who find a way to make a life outside our increasingly urban-centric world. And most of all to the people who make my community great. You know who you are.

Chapter One

The cusp of the snow-bitten Valhalla range cut into the October blue with such crispness I could almost feel it, all the way down below at lake level. Ice crystals on Eldorado Glacier between the Twin Peaks glittered in the sun, as if winking at me: "Better find cover, son; camping season is over." Sapphire Lake was a mirror deepening in colour with the season change, reflecting the retreating ranks of the Valhalla Mountains. Like most of the glacier-fed lakes in this region, it was narrow but incredibly deep—hundreds of metres—and shockingly cold. The ragged granite that cradled these lakes gave the water a starkly beautiful indigo cast. There was something oddly comforting to the eye about it. Yet its clear, clean waters were profoundly energizing, a kind of holy well on the roof of the world. I wondered what saints, sinners, modern-day mystics, or just plain crazies would be drawn to it. I would soon find out.

The angular crispness of autumn light cast everything in sharp relief, prompting me to wonder what the hell I'd been thinking. It just wasn't like me to bolt from a good job in the city and wander the countryside in a beat-up '85 Toyota Corolla station wagon with Shadowcat. Sure, I'd grown up in northern British Columbia, learning the tricks of wilderness survival from my old man. So camping wasn't particularly a hardship for me. It activated an old touchstone from family camping trips. Very soon it all came flooding back in—how to build a proper campfire, how to catch trout, how to leave a campsite cleaner than I found it. And with it, the gradual lessening of urban white noise I'd carried with me so I could actually hear the subtle sounds all around me. But with the first bite of winter in the air it was time to find more permanent lodgings. And anyway, two weeks of pitching camp and then having to pile everything into the wagon every few days was starting to get old.

Leaving Vancouver hadn't been particularly hard. Fifteen years of slogging in the journalistic trenches, interoffice politics, and the whole damn clatter and grind of city life had frayed my nerve ends. Like that old saying, "I've got one nerve left, and you're getting on it." It's what I should have said to my editor Bob Lejean at the *Vancouver Daily* when I quit, though in fairness to him it wasn't his fault. Instead I half-mumbled something lame about needing a change of pace, a total break with city living. Truth was, the thanks I got for my years of faithful service was a demotion. Supposedly I was being given a "roving reporter" gig when what I really wanted was the City Hall beat. Sure, politics has a way of getting old fast. But it meant less jerking myself all over the city in rush hour traffic all the goddamn time. Hitting my mid-forties, I was getting tired. Vancouver having never designed its traffic system to handle the load it was now carrying; my new assignment meant hours per day trapped in a car, fuming. City Hall beat meant mostly phone work, a few trips a week to the iconic building for research and interviews, and the occasional ribbon-cutting photo op around the city. Whereas the 'new' job meant being basically on call daily, chasing after every news lead like a cub reporter. That could take me from Granville Island in the morning to the deepest, darkest burbs of Langley in the afternoon. The Managing Editor, Veronica Mills, had mealy-mouthed something about my years of experience suiting me ideally to the position. She was the corporate type, parachuted into the newspaper from Toronto to try and cut costs. I made it quite clear I wasn't impressed with her hiring a 23-year-old intern to cover what rightfully should have been my job, given my experience. I muttered some choice words on the way out of her office, not giving a damn whether she'd hear. I was done anyway. Christ! Some bean counter comes in and poof! Half a century of journalism practice goes out the window. No more veteran reporters, no more regular beats, just a steady stream of underpaid cub reporters straight out of journalism school.

I'd watched the downhill slide ever since the early '90s, when the corporate mergers and cost-cutting began. The first to go were proofreaders, followed by copy editors. Gradually more and more beats got melded into one. Then the steady creep of "infotainment" and celebrity "news," the insidious reach of advertisers' agendas on the newspaper's editorial slant. Science for hire, meet journalism for hire. No wonder no one trusts the media anymore. I wouldn't. But then, I never really was an apolitical reporter. Lejean had cautioned me too many times to count about mixing activism and journalism. And every time, I had to remind him: As far as I was concerned, old-school journalism was all about keeping a watchful eye out. Not for rich patrons or advertisers but for the community. I don't care who said it (since no one really knows for sure), because it's true: "News is what someone else doesn't want published. Everything else is advertising." Now with the *Vancouver Daily* buyout, I was being not-so-subtly pushed into 'dinosaur' status in the new corporate paradigm. It's a compromise I wasn't prepared to stomach.

So I gave notice on my apartment near English Bay—the one I'd managed to hold onto by the skin of my teeth through sheer tenacity as the neighbourhood gentrification spread like a virus, driving up rents. Took a last loving walk around Stanley Park's Lost Lagoon, weaved and bobbed through the masses on the Denman Street sidewalks to the beach at sunset, and watched the bizarre pageant of humanity drift past yet again. Fifteen years hadn't taken the small-town boy out of me. Finishing my high school years in the West Kootenay town of Newcombe—population 10,000—had left its stamp. I never could get used to being jostled in a crowd, or the ceaseless hum of the city even in the wee hours. Hell, I can remember the wall of silence that descended over Newcombe after the shops closed at 6:00 p.m. on Houston Street. You could literally fire a cannon down the street and expect to hit nobody. As a kid, it felt like I lived at the ends of the earth—couldn't wait to get to the Big City. But now, with the urban grit chafing under my skin, a small town has a fresh appeal. As a teenager, I used to smoke a joint at midnight and walk around the empty streets of Newcombe with my cat. The silence so palpable it was as if the oaks that lined the residential streets were listening, daring you to break the skein of quiet. Like being blind without the blindness—the heightened sense of hearing taut as a drumhead, hundred-year-old Victorian houses still as a caught breath, pregnant with stories.

And stories had become my trade, at least the non-fiction variety. Though let's face it, these days there's as much fiction as fact in the media. Probably there always was. Truth is, the real stories too often make you sick and the bullshit stories make you lose faith in your job. Your faith in humanity begins to steadily recede in the rear-view mirror. Gangland drive-by shootings in Surrey, a tragic mugging death in Stanley Park, corruption scandals at City Hall, the latest real estate or developer fraud case—*ad infinitum, ad nauseam*. I remember my grandmother in her country kitchen near Newcombe, warning me about human nature. For someone who seldom left her lush piece of Kootenay mountainside, with its gardens and chickens, she had a remarkably canny view of humanity. Maybe that took the edge off my twenty-something naïveté before I arrived in the Big Smoke, I don't know. But after a decade and a half of having my nose rubbed in grime, the trick now was to salvage what was left of my attitude. The bile of it was starting to choke me. Already it had ruined my first marriage and my last three relationships with women. Bitterness is one of those tonics that doesn't share well.

Okay, I admit it. So far, my longest-running stable relationship had been with my cat, a black Persian longhair I named Shadowcat. Felines I understand far more than humans of either sex. I believe they're a superior species—totally independent and self-sufficient in the wild or in domestication. How we ever domesticated cats is a mystery to me. I'm sure Shadowcat would argue: "It's the other way around, buddy. We domesticated *you*." Certainly feline adaptability is a marvel. Looking at Shadowcat half-buried beneath the passenger seat as we drive into the village, I have to wonder. Occasionally he pops his head out long enough to stare up at me with those ethereal blue-green eyes. It's hard to know whether it's carsickness or sheer disgust he's beaming at me. Probably both. One minute it's the expression of a guy after a three-day bender, begging for an answer to the question: "Will I *ever* feel better?" The next it's: "How could you do this to me, you bastard?" Still, he's been a helluva good sport these past two weeks as I ride around the Kootenays like a lost puppy looking for a home. When I roll up to a campsite, he leaps out of the car and disappears to reconnoitre before settling in for the night. The first time it happened I worried about him getting lost, or snatched by an owl or coyote. But his feline smarts kicked in instantly. All I had to say—once—was: "Check in with Dad, okay?" He'd make his rounds on the outer perimeter of firelight and then return to brush up against my calf every fifteen minutes or so, refusing to leave until I acknowledged him. I've lost track of the stories I had to write of people who went into the wilderness, pushed the limits, and died as a result. Not even the bloody smarts of a household cat.

But the city life was behind me now. The late autumn blue of the sky with its hard light cast everything into vivid relief, like one of those old Kodachrome slides. The jagged granite peaks thrusting up from Sapphire Lake were already contoured with snow at the highest elevations. It wasn't hard to see why Scandinavian prospectors a century ago named this mountain range the Valhallas. You couldn't get much closer to the sky gods than here, except maybe the Himalayas. Driving along the shores of the lake to the village of Elkville, population 457, it's only another five kilometres to Eldorado, population 796. This morning I'd stopped in at the Zippy Grocery in Elkville to pick up the local rag, the *Mountain Echo*, circulation 9,600: "Delivered to every mailbox in communities on Sturgeon Lake, Sapphire Lake, and the North Kootenay Lake communities." A geographical area of vast proportions sprinkled lightly with human habitation. It was a breath of fresh air, as fresh as the mountain air itself.

And sturgeon—that relic of prehistoric times—embodied reminder of subconscious fears, 275 metres down in a lake fed by glacial meltwater. Growing up on these lakes, I had a preschool memory of a neighbour coming home with one he caught, so large its tail curved up over the tailgate of his pickup truck. Years ago I'd read that the local fish and game agency was stocking some of the lakes here with sturgeon, endangered to near-extinction after the dams had come in and cut off the food supply. As apt a metaphor as any for where civilization seems to be heading. Sapphire Lake had escaped being turned into another reservoir for the dam system, making it the only lake in the region unaltered by human technology.

Circulation 9,600. Hell, in Vancouver or Surrey you could pack 9,600 people into a single neighbourhood. And the so-called headlines. Over my morning espresso at Elkville's Cracked Teapot Café I had to chuckle. This week's headline: "Goat Bylaw Has Lowery Residents in Uproar." (Lowery was the village east over the mountain pass from Eldorado, population 1,217.) It seems the urban/rural divide has even reached the backwoods of the Kootenays. Urban-minded folks were angry that they might have to share their back lanes and nostrils with goats. Farm folks just wanted to subsidize their grocery bills. And it was a helluva lot easier than having to mow the lawn every week in the summertime. "I don't understand the problem," Lowery goat-farmer Norman Dickerson was quoted as saying. "Don't these people know it's pigs, not goats, that stink?"

But it wasn't the small-print headlines I was after. I'd turned immediately to the "For Rent" section of the classifieds. Truth is, for a week already I'd been watching this space, with no luck. Vacancies around here are thin on the ground. But today I found it: "Cabin north of Eldorado at Owl Creek, 1 BDR, heat and elec. included, fabulous view, pets negotiable. $425 mo." The woman at the number I called answered immediately in a clear, businesslike but warm tone. It was something I'd forgotten about folks in the Kootenays: If they sounded friendly, they generally meant it. Here it wasn't always just about reeling you in. Her name was Irene Kasnikoff—a good local Doukhobor name—and we'd arranged to meet on Eldorado's main street at 10:00 a.m., near the Lost Socks Laundromat.

Irene was already there, seated on the bench outside the Laundromat when I pulled up. I'd described my car to her so she recognized it immediately and stood up to greet me even before I got out. She was dressed in a neatly tailored, buckskin-coloured waistcoat with a red-and-white checked shirt, a short yellow scarf knotted below her chin, and neatly pressed blue jeans. Her hair was dark brown and well coiffed, dyed to cover grey. She had a smile that easily passed the test of genuineness. I guessed her age at about late fifties, a few laugh lines at the corners of eyes and mouth but otherwise remarkably well preserved. Any lingering doubts about her sincerity were gone instantly.

Her hand was already out. "I'm Irene. Nice to meet you."

"Roy Breen. Thanks for agreeing to show me the cabin on such short notice."

"No problem at all." Looking over my shoulder at the wagon. "You always travel with your cat?"

"Uh, yeah. Well, not always, of course. I've been footloose for a few weeks now. Didn't want to leave him in Vancouver with friends. Whenever I've done that before, he won't talk to me for weeks. He actually likes camping, believe it or not."

Irene's laugh was genuine, unforced. "Well that's a story you'll have to tell me sometime. I assume he's litter trained?"

I had to smile. "Well he *is* five years old now, so he is an adult. And yes, he has me well-trained to care for his every need."

She chuckled again. "I'm sure that's true. Would you like to come with me, or just follow my car?"

"I'll follow you. If I drive somewhere once I usually remember the way."

Breathtaking. After living with a view of a streetlight shaded by oak leaves at the end of Haro Street, the view at Owl Creek was breathtaking. Though as far as I could see it was nowhere near a creek. The valley bottom at the head of Sapphire Lake sloped southward, hemlock and fir thick on the mountainside, the frosted jaw of Mount Pyramid thrust into the skyline. Its name was well deserved, looking as if it had been sculpted into three smooth sides of granite. And all framed in two sets of sliding glass doors on the side of the cabin facing the peak—Nature's TV. For a long time I just drifted, staring.

The cabin was basically a modified A-frame, just suitably Kootenay eccentric enough but neatly done, and clean. Anchoring the living room was a woodstove. It flooded me with memories of my grandmother's kitchen—the white enamelled McClary's cookstove she insisted was the *only* way to bake bread. I could never forget her girlish smile, even in her fifties, the simple delight she took in feeding grandkids. The quiet one-on-ones with her, the few words that told me she alone, of all people, understood. Here the stove was black, not white, and not designed for baking or cooking. But it would keep the frost out during power outages. That much I remembered from living in the Kootenays. The regular electricity shutdowns in wintertime thanks to poles and wires the provincial hydro corporation had allowed to dissolve in the Interior rainforest damp. Thirty years behind the urban infrastructure. But what the hell, it forced me to chop wood again, which actually felt good on a cold winter day. And the kerosene lamp was another fond reminder of earlier days. A living relic from days most of the rest of the world has long left behind. Such pristine simplicity: Cut the power and see how you fare.

Just try that in a city.

After settling in, I had my first coffee and bagel at the Blue Moose Bistro in Eldorado. I'd been up late organizing the space in the cabin. Besides, the first day I didn't want Shadowcat thinking I'd abandoned him in the middle of nowhere. I *had* to hang out awhile. The stars last night were fantastic. Stood on the back deck, my neck crooked at a crazy angle, drunk in the swirl of autumn stars, brighter and sharper than I'd seen them for years in the city. My open-mouthed face more eloquent than any poem. That is, 'til Shadowcat sidled past, giving me a look that said: "Dad, close your mouth before you swallow a bat."

So by the time I rolled up to the Blue Moose, it was already noon. The place was a small house with an addition built on one side for the public kitchen, serving bar and seating. The menu was a neon marker board. A tall, slim woman with glossy dark hair was busy behind the counter. She occasionally threw me a half-sneering look as I examined the menu options.

Half-sneering or half-leering I couldn't tell. Having decided on an espresso and a breakfast bagel, I looked directly at her. She put down her wiping cloth and came to the counter. Her dark hair was cut just below her ears, a short bob curling into sharp tips. Her eyes were dark brown and not unattractive. But her smile was an enigma. One minute it would seem warm, inviting—the next, sneering. It wasn't something I expected to see in small-town Kootenay—a Robson Avenue Starbucks, maybe. But not here.

"I'll have an espresso—short—and a gluten-free breakfast bagel please."

"Espresso—*short?*" She said it like an accusation.

Determined to start with a good impression, I smiled. "Yes please, no extra water." The espresso machine was behind her, gleaming.

She gave me an enigmatic smile, somehow warm and cold at the same time. "You said gluten-free?"

"Yes, please."

"Sorry. Don't have *that.*" She said it like it was about as appetizing as roadkill. "Think you could live with hundred percent rye instead?"

"Uh, yeah thanks."

I saw a small stack of the *Mountain Echo* on the counter so I grabbed the top one and headed to a table out front where the sun was flooding in. A heavy woman in a light jacket came noisily in, her shoe hitting the aluminum screen. Despite her weight she was quite attractive, with fine features and pale auburn hair, wavy and beautifully coiffed. The screen door was awkward, on a tighter tension compared to the main door so it was hard not to let it slap when it closed. With her was a younger woman in her twenties, thin and honey blonde, attractive but a bit over made-up. By the time they reached the counter I could hear the younger one telling her, as if she were the older sister:

"Don't you take any *shit* from Zelda today, Deb."

The woman named Deb waved her off. "Don't worry, Angie, I'm a big girl."

"Yeah, but you *know* what happens...."

The bob-haired woman behind the counter named Zelda

stepped up. "Morning, Deb. Whaddya want today?" Her tone flat as a table.

"My usual soy cappuccino with chocolate garnishes and double cream."

"Geez, Deb, you really think that's a good *idea?*" Flicking her eyes at Deb's girth.

I could see Deb sucking in her breath, holding herself. The younger woman was tugging at her angrily. "We can go somewhere else, Deb. *Come on....*"

Deb turned and whispered sharply: "No! I won't let her drive me out."

By this time, a retired couple in the corner was nervously looking in the direction of the serving counter. I was watching closely too, but more discreetly, from a distance.

Deb turned determinedly toward Zelda, put down a fiver. Without malice, she repeated: "Soy cappuccino with chocolate garnishes and double cream."

Zelda smirked, one shoulder shrugging ever so slightly. Turned her back to concentrate on the espresso machine, the steam valve, and heating the cappuccino foam. As she rotated the steel jug she threw a look back over her shoulder. "*Careful* when you come in that door. I don't want any damage."

A loud slam! and the older couple startled in unison. I looked toward the screen door but it was the younger woman, her palm flat on the counter. Deb's lower lip was loose, quivering, as she stared disbelievingly at the shorter woman. "Angie, what the hell are you doing?"

Angie leaned forward, not at Deb but toward Zelda, still busy at the machine. "I've fucking HAD it with this place! *Every* time we come in here. We give you our money and you insult us! Does nobody else *get* this?" She turned to look at the old couple, who recoiled defensively, then looked away, meeting my eyes briefly. Zelda poured the cappuccino foam, added the cream, and dusted it with chocolate. Cool as Emma Peel in *The Avengers*. Except her smirk was far more acid than Diana Rigg's could ever be.

Angie was still livid. "You can stay and take this shit if you want, Deb, but I'm outta here—permanently!" With that she pivoted on her heel and stalked out the door, slamming the

screen deliberately. Deb looked shaken but took her cappuccino to a table about as far from Zelda as she could get in such
a small place. Which happened to be the table next to mine.

I leaned toward her sympathetically. In a low voice: "Why
do you put up with that?"

Again her lip quivered just noticeably. When she looked at
me her eyes were very soft. "Because I think I understand her."

I had to suppress a chuckle. "Really?"

"She reminds me of someone in my family." She smiled
but her tone was deeply sad. She turned her gaze to the window, watching the tall cedar across the street waving in the fall
breeze. Sad, but resolved, somehow.

"Well," I thought. "Village Character Number One. Zelda
the Sarcastic Server." In tribute to Deb, I gave her a thumbs-up.
The gesture caught her eye, and she smiled at me, then turned
back to her cappuccino and her private sadness.

Clearly, village living isn't quite the idyll I'd pictured.

The building was unimpressive. A long, low rectangle that
stretched back from Eldorado's main street, with a simple roof
and a western-style wooden façade on the front, painted bright
green with yellow trim. Several of the buildings on the main
street sported this conceit, a tip of the hat to the town's frontier beginnings in a mining boom a century ago. A boom that
went bust in about ten years, setting off echoes that reverber-
ated for a century in local culture. Some of the façades were just
rectangular, giving the illusion of a second story where there
was none. Others were more obviously decorative, shaped as a
great scallop over the business door. On this building I could
read a small brass plaque on one corner: "Original Eldorado
Firehouse, 1907." Fire*house*. Not even big enough to have been
a Fire*hall*. The entry door in the centre of the façade had an
inset window running from top to bottom. Essentially the
door was just a frame with glass in it. On the glass were painted
letters that read: "*Mountain Echo*. Props. Lance Robertson and
Donna Kelly. Est. 1992." The whole main street could be a set
on a Hollywood backlot, with the critical difference that the
view at the end of the street here was no plywood scenery but

the glittering Eldorado Glacier looming above Sapphire Lake, the Valhallas receding in the snowy distance.

Pushing open the door I was confronted with a counter just steps from the entrance. Behind it was a small warren of desks with computers and a door leading to a back room. I could see a man in his forties with a thick head of hair showing only a few traces of grey, leaning back from a computer screen. His beard had grown out a little bushy from what had recently been close-trimmed and the screen was reflected in his glasses. He looked mildly annoyed that he might have to tear himself away from whatever he was doing. I got a glimpse of some freeware video game. Before I could open my mouth, he shouted: "Jane! Front counter please." The office was small enough that I could hear a chair being rolled away from a desk in the back room. An elfin-looking woman of fine features and a shock of grey in her thick, short hair poked her head out. She too looked mildly annoyed.

"Yes? What is it Lance?"

"Can you help this gentleman please?"

A disgruntled sigh was stopped short when she transferred her gaze from Lance to me. It was as if some flicker of recognition had lit in her eyes when she saw my face. It was odd. I'd never seen her before. The smile in her eyes was bright enough to banish a thunderstorm, the smile on her lips more subtle. She walked briskly to the counter.

"Uh, what can I do for you?"

"Well, I'm a reporter just new in town. Looking for work."

She smiled involuntarily, as if pleased by that information. "Oh! So what experience do you have?"

"Trained at College of the Kootenays journalism program. Worked in Vancouver the past fifteen years, mostly at the *Vancouver Daily*, doing the works—hard news, profiles, reviews, investigative pieces occasionally. Less and less of those lately though. Damn corporate mergers." Over her shoulder I could see a smirk cross Lance's face but he pretended not to be listening, intent on his game.

"So what brings you here?"

"In the last corporate merger they put a cap on all promotions except senior management staff. That meant my seniority went out the window in one fell swoop. They hired a Journalism 101 grad fresh off the turnip truck to do the City Hall beat I'd been hoping for. Decided I'd had enough. So I quit. Besides, I'd had enough of the Big Smoke after fifteen years. And anyway, I'm originally from the Kootenays."

"Oh? Whereabouts?" The rise in her voice was noticeable.

"Born in Newcombe but grew up in northern BC. Finished high school in Newcombe. Small-town boy."

She laughed. "*Small*-town Newcombe. Around here, that's a big city."

I could hear Lance's chair shift as he pushed back from his console and finally turned in my direction. "Thanks, Jane. I can take it from here."

A slight shade of dismay crossed her face. "Okay, Lance."

Jane scooted sideways as Lance stepped up but otherwise she didn't move. His face spread in a Cheshire cat grin—if you can imagine a bearded Cheshire cat. "Lance Robertson— publisher of the *Mountain Echo*." He stood slightly above my height, both of us in the medium range.

"Roy Breen."

Jane caught me noticing her stare. "Well, uh—better get back to my editing." She put out her hand—delicate and pale as a porcelain doll. I took it gently. "Jane," she said. "Jane Bordeaux."

"Really, like the wine?"

She flushed a little. "Yes, like the wine. My ancestors were among the first French soldiers to come to Canada in the seventeenth century. The family story goes that our paternal ancestor, Jean de Bordeaux, arrived without a last name, so they just asked what province in France he'd come from. Hence the name, ever since."

"Great story. Know if it's true?"

She shrugged delicately beneath a light, bird's-egg blue sweater. "Who knows? Makes a good story though. Just don't *ever* call me Jane Chardonnay," she joked. "Well, I better leave you two to it."

"Well, nice to meet you, Jane *Bordeaux*."

Lance took a cigar from a small box in his desk drawer and motioned toward the door. "Looks like the sun's still with us. Care to step outside for a smoke?"

"Never touch the stuff, but thanks."

Robertson stood outside the door, legs athwart like the captain on the deck of his ship. He had the grace to blow the thick cloud of smoke away from me. "I take it you're not a shirt and tie man," he grinned.

"Nope. Ever since the corporate bean counters took over, journalism's been going down the tubes. They don't seem to get that doing a decent job costs money. They cut and cut—except of course for executive salaries—until even the bone hurts. 'Til they cut their own throats, producing such crap no one wants to read it anyway. Or no one believes it."

Robertson was savouring the taste of the cigar in his mouth. "Yep, I get it. More stories cribbed from the wire services, more celebrity gossip, less local reporting. Shorter and shorter stories. Most newspapers aren't trusted anymore. We don't hold with that approach here at the *Echo*. People look to us as their *community* newspaper. If they want to read about the latest earthquake in China or the latest scandal in Ottawa they can get that on the Web. Or they can read it in one of the big-city dailies. No point us repeating it."

I shuffled, moving a pebble around with my toe. "Well. A true community newspaper. No celebrity gossip then?" I flashed him an arch smile.

He grinned back, laughing. "Not much call for it around here."

"I take it you're not part of the Interior Media Corp chain of so-called community newspapers?"

"Nope. One hundred percent locally owned and operated. My wife Donna and I run it together. She's the editor."

"And Ms. Jane Bordeaux?"

"Our proofreader and copy editor. She's in doing a little extra editing work to lighten Donna's load on the slew of media releases. She's very good at it."

"You still employ a proofreader? My God, I thought they'd gone extinct, judging by the sloppy copy in everything from the *Globe and Mail* to the *New York Times* these days."

"We have a surprising number of retired English professors who live here part-time, not to mention an overall high rate of literacy. And one or two grammar Nazis. You should read our letters page sometime."

"So you're back*woods* but not backwards, then."

Robertson guffawed. "I like that. If you're not careful I may just use that as a slogan."

"Feel free to. In exchange for some work."

Robertson evaded this one. "So you finished school in Newcombe? Spend much time in Glacier Valley?"

I could tell he was sizing me up as a potential employee. I could have lied for advantage but it's just not my style. "Not really. The odd day trip up the Glacier River in the lower valley to go inner tubing. But that's about it. Surprising how insular you can get living in even a small city like Newcombe. But I'm a quick study. So tell me: Why 'Eldorado'?"

"You'll have to brush up on your local history." His face-cracking grin with its tobacco-stained teeth seemed mischievous, as if he were testing me.

"Well naturally I'm aware of the mining boom in the 1890s here—the ghost town of Silverado tucked into the Lowery Pass. I remember that much."

Robertson shrugged. "Well it seems some legacies live on, although in much mutated form. In the 1890s, it was folks coming here in search of Eldorado, the City of Gold—or in this case, silver. Then it was lumber. Briefly it was orchards. Then after two world wars it got pretty quiet around here 'til the sixties."

"And then it was the draft dodgers and back-to-the-landers."

"Yep. Another kind of City of Gold—or the anti-city, as the case may be. People came here to get away from cities and the wage-slave economy. The reverse of a century ago—not seeking wealth but *avoiding* it."

"Or seeking a different kind of wealth."

"You *are* a quick study."

"Sure, but I'm not quite up to date. I've been away for fifteen years."

"Well in that time it's been another kind of lifestyle seeker—the spiritual fortune hunter. You can't swing a dead cat in the village of Applegrove in the south valley without hitting a half-dozen Tarot card readers, aromatherapists, and UFOlogists."

"I'll forgive the dead cat metaphor on behalf of my own feline. I take it you don't approve?"

A shrug accompanied his jaw-splitting grin. "I neither approve nor disapprove. We have our fair share of crystal gazers in the north valley too. As long as they take out ads in the *Echo* I don't really care."

"Fair enough."

"Then to complete the picture you have the grow-ops and the neo-Rastafarians, the white kids with dreads."

"I seem to remember something about that from my high school days here. I was a bit of a teenage hippie myself."

He flicked some ash from his cigar. "Our mayor once said if the cops ever shut down the grow-op industry the whole economy of the valley would collapse."

"Interesting culture."

"My sister Nicole once described it as 'Norman Rockwell with dreadlocks.'"

I had to chuckle. "I'll remember that one. That might even make a better slogan for the *Echo* than 'backwoods not backwards.' So what have you got for me?"

The grin subsided to an enigmatic smile. "Well as you might have guessed, with a circulation of only 9,600 we don't have a big-city budget or a big-city staff."

It was my turn to laugh out loud. "Yet you employ a proofreader!"

"Some things are worth it." He stubbed out his half-smoked cigar on the sidewalk, stuffing it into a breast pocket. "Are you busy tomorrow night?"

"You mean besides communing with Mount Pyramid outside my kitchen window?"

"My wife Donna has to drive over the pass to cover a council meeting in Lowery. But there's a big meeting at Eldorado Hall with the fat cats from the Provincial Health Authority about proposed cuts to our hospital emergency ward. We need somebody there to cover it. Our regular stringer is away for a few months—Bolivia. She told us she may not come back."

I laughed. "*Regular* stringer eh? So no salaried positions at the *Echo*?"

Robertson guffawed. "Nope. Not even for Donna and me. We just take what we need to stay alive and feed the kids. Some months that means fried chicken every other night and some months it's Kraft Dinner. Whatever it takes to keep the newspaper coming out."

I was starting to like this guy. "Fair enough. I've got some savings left over from the *Vancouver Daily* so I can hang on awhile. But I'd appreciate it if you can throw as much work as possible my way."

Robertson grinned. "Let's see what you're made of first, but yeah, sure. Happy to."

I had to chuckle. "So this is your idea of a big news story here in Eldorado? A public meeting with the Provincial Health Authority?" I'd forgotten how deliciously sleepy these valley communities could be.

"Trust me, if they shut down our hospital emergency ward, it's a major story. We lose that, the whole community starts to die."

The Eldorado Hall had a look consistent with the other buildings on main street—the pointless façade with a nonexistent upper story. An old-fashioned four-panel door in the roof peak had once been a fire escape for the projection room when the hall was used for movies during the last world war. A new portico roof had been built over the double doors of the entrance, supporting a faux deck ringed with square balusters. Otherwise the building had the same nondescript look as the *Mountain Echo* building. Apparently architects had been scarce in this town a hundred years ago. Unlike Newcombe, with its impressive brick and granite homes and commercial buildings, Eldorado had *not* originally been built to last. The fact that most of the local mine managers had built their mansions in Newcombe made that clear. The expectation in 1890 had been the usual one for outlying frontier towns—slap it up, get the ore out, shut 'er down once the pits were mined out. Your basic "take the money and run" business philosophy. Yet somehow a community had persisted here. The new portico and paint job on the Eldorado Hall reflected community pride.

I always like to get to public meetings early. It gives me a chance to size up the crowd and buttonhole officials before the fun gets started. Besides, with contentious issues, meetings can drag on for hours and who the hell wants to stay *after* a meeting to do interviews? The inside of the hall was basically one long rectangular space with a kitchen to one side and a raised stage at the rear. The walls were bare, unadorned. A portrait of Queen Elizabeth circa 1959 was hung above the entry door. I wondered if it was because no one in the village had bothered to update her portrait in forty-five years or because they liked her better as a young queen. The acoustics were awful. You'd think a box like this would be boomy, but even footsteps died with a dull thud. I was relieved to see a tall man with a full head of white hair setting up microphones at the head table. A name-plate sticker above his shirt pocket read Graham Kenwood. I asked him to point out the Provincial Health Authority officials to me. Looking around the room he said: "Sorry, mate. Not 'ere yet." His British accent came as a pleasant surprise. Then with a nudge-nudge, wink-wink grin he added: "Not eager to enter the lion's den I imagine."

The meeting was scheduled for 7:00 p.m. but by 6:50 there was hardly anyone in the seats. Suddenly, as if the gates to Future Shop in downtown Vancouver were opening on a Boxing Day sale, the place flooded with people. By 7:05 the hall was packed. Graham had set up his mike mixer on the serving counter at the side of the hall off the kitchen. "Kootenay Time," he whispered to me with a grin. "A point of principle to be five minutes late." In a decade and a half, I'd forgotten about that. I decided to set up my laptop on the counter next to Graham's rig. Standing at a meeting made it easier to pick out interview prospects from the mass of faces. Somehow the PHA bigwigs had snuck in the hall's side door and taken their places at the head table—three of them, each with a mike.

Watching the parade of locals coming in was an education in itself. As diverse in its own way as a Gay Pride parade on Burrard Street. Graham gave me an affectionate running commentary in his north-of-England accent. The Aging Hippies, in all sizes, shapes, and colours. The clothes no longer psychedelic but looking like an explosion in a thrift store—everything mismatched, much of it faded as if it hadn't been replaced in far too long. The hair still long, braided on both men and women although woven with grey and marred by men's receding hairlines. Then the New Age Mystics. Except for the age bracket, it could be hard to tell them apart from the Aging Hippies, Graham explained. You had to look at their necks and ears, usually festooned with multiple earrings and dangling chunks of quartzite crystal big enough to choke a mastiff. The other chief difference between them and the Aging Hippies was in the eyes. Many of the latter had long been on the front lines of protest and activism. The weariness of decades bled through bleary eyes. The New Agers were typically younger, the eyes still bright, like children with an all's-right-with-the-world glow. And the Loggers, with their perpetual air of barely restrained aggression. Trying to avoid eye contact with any of the Aging Hippies or New Agers for fear of ridicule from their buddies later at the pub. A few of the village public works crew wearing their check shirts, work boots, and safety vests, looking as neutral as possible. And a contingent of senior citizens with clothing bland enough to obscure any affiliations whatsoever. A few of them could have been Aging Hippies but they were beyond wearing it like a badge anymore even if their hearts still held a fondness for the era. You had to watch carefully who spoke to whom to suss out the associations.

By 7:10 one of the officials at the head table tapped a mike to see if it was working. He was clean-shaven as a billiard ball—scalp shining like it had been buffed with carnauba wax. His features were narrow—pinched nose, thin lips, slitty eyes behind narrow glasses. Graham's fingers worked the mixer knobs effortlessly. "Uh ... uh, we'd like to get started if everyone could please take your seats. My name is Wade Detwiler, Chief Financial Officer for the PHA Southeast BC Division." Turning to his left he pointed at a rotund woman in her thirties with long dark hair and designer glasses. "This is Marla Frankenheim, our Chief Public Relations Officer." Marla displayed teeth so bleached it blinded the first three rows of people in front of her. Leaning forward in his chair to get a better view, CFO Detwiler extended his arm toward the third person at the table, a youngish man of indeterminate age with carefully maintained beard stubble. "And this is Josh Denton, one of our Policy Analysts." His hipster features twitched in what passed for a smile.

"We ask that you allow us to present our case before asking questions," Detwiler began. "Your village mayor, Larry Miller, will act as moderator during question period. Please respect his direction." He pointed out a man sitting in the front row who could have passed for one of the Aging Hippies. Miller had glasses, a grey and ginger moustache, hair thinned out on top and a ponytail. Somehow I'd missed him. He turned and flashed a grin at the crowd. There was an impish expression on his face that said: "We all know what this is about but let's just play along anyhow." It was a face that managed to look both slightly conniving and warm at the same time. A politician's face, yet not, somehow.

Detwiler sucked in a lungful and leapt into the breach. "As you probably know, the PHA was formed with the mandate to ensure equal delivery of health services across the province. Our premier has gone on record affirming his support for the BC Medical Services Plan. We—"

A man's voice from the crowd cut him off. "If that's true then why do you keep raising rates and lowering benefits?" Laughter rumbled across the wooden floor.

This wasn't going to be easy. Detwiler gave a prim sigh, turning to Mayor Miller, who rose with a mike in his hand. "Folks, please save your comments and questions for later."

"As part of our year-in-review of ministry finances last year," Detwiler continued, "a few—ahem—*adjustments* have had to be made if we're to balance this year's budget. As the average age of British Columbians continues to climb upward—"

A woman's voice this time. "How can you keep charging us more and more and still claim you have to make cuts to balance the budget?"

Detwiler lifted his hands helplessly, looking toward Miller. Miller stood up again, speaking loudly but without annoyance. "Folks, please. I know you've got a lot on your minds. But if we can just let these people say their piece, we can all get home sooner. Thanks. We appreciate it."

Detwiler soldiered on. "As I was saying, as the average age of British Columbians continues to climb upward, the costs to the healthcare system also spiral upward." Muttered growls of "Bullshit!" arose from the loggers' contingent but Detwiler pressed on, keeping his voice as bland as possible. "And yes, I understand we're all having to pay more for our medicare premiums. Nobody likes that. But it means we have to make hard decisions, decisions nobody likes—not you and not us. But they have to be made."

Another male voice. "Get to the point! We don't have all night."

Detwiler seemed to wither a little. He turned to his Chief PR flack Marla Frankenheim, as if helplessly seeking rescue. She straightened in her chair and flashed her pearlies again, causing a few in the front to cover their eyes. It couldn't have been more fake if she'd cut the smile out of a magazine and stuck it on her mouth. There were more diamonds on her chubby fingers than in the rest of the hall combined. "Thanks, Wade. What Wade is trying to say is that in the interests of efficiency, and given the small population base here in Eldorado and Elkville, we think a reduction in the emergency room hours at the Sapphire Lake Health Centre is in order."

"It's a *hospital*," a woman in the front row muttered.

"Well, technically under our new definitions, it's a health centre," Frankenheim explained, still smiling.

One of the taller loggers shot up from his chair. "What *kind* of goddamn reduction?"

Miller stood up too. "Please, please folks. Let's keep this civil. You'll get your say."

"Let me explain," said Frankenheim. "We'd keep the helipad so the acute cases can be shipped out to Hannaville to the south of you or Caledon to the west, where we have full surgical facilities. Which, at present, is really no change to current services here. But as a means of preserving your ER and keeping the health centre open within current budgetary constraints, we propose seven days per week at 9:00 a.m. to 5:00 p.m. That way—"

It was as if a bomb had been set off. Half the audience was out of their seats, shouting. Many were gesticulating angrily, especially the loggers.

"Great! I'll just make sure I have my heart attack during banker's hours then, shall I?"

"Fucking logging don't work nine to five, why should the ER?"

"How will I get help if my baby runs a fever in the night?"

The New Agers looked cowed and more than a little afraid. The Aging Hippies looked even sadder than usual, if that was possible, exchanging looks that sighed: "Here we go again." Miller was on his feet again. "FOLKS! FOLKS! PLEASE! This isn't going to help anyone!" He used his free arm to wave them down to their seats again. Miller was obviously well-liked because I could see the change come over people when they turned their gaze from the PHA officials to their mayor. Except for the loggers, who only grudgingly obeyed and sat down. "Goddamn hippie mayor. Don't know how he ever got elected," one muttered. Gradually the uproar subsided to a rumble of mutterings.

Denton the policy analyst looked petrified, incapable of speech. Detwiler's shiny dome was sprouting sweat beads, which he hastily swabbed with a handkerchief. Only Frankenheim maintained her poise-perfect persona. She continued: "Naturally as part of this, uh—*modification* of the service schedule—PHA will be removing certain services from the hospital." The audience muttering began to surge again so she raised her voice, causing the microphone to squeal against the back of the hall. "Services to do with your lab testing regime, nothing to do with ER. The ER will remain fully functional during stipulated hours."

A woman in her fifties, with short-cropped wavy grey hair and glasses, wearing a jean jacket and slacks, stood up. "So you're not only eliminating 24/7 ER, you're also shutting down our lab? We supposed to drive two hours to Hannaville or five hours to Caledon every time we need a blood test?"

Miller got up again but this time whispered at Denton, who broke his rigidity to huddle with the other two officials. They all nodded and then nodded again at Miller, who lifted the mike to his chin. "Folks, since this is a controversial decision and we understand you're all upset, we're going to move right into question period. This lady has asked a question so I'm going to direct it to the panel for an answer."

Detwiler spoke and to his credit looked directly at his questioner. "We are *not* shutting down the lab, only select services."

"*What* services?" the woman insisted.

"I'm afraid I can't tell you—" More growling erupted before he could continue: "because I don't know yet myself. We're considering our options. It will depend on what's cost effective without compromising a functioning lab. In other words, probably the least used diagnostic procedures."

One of the Aging Hippies, a wiry man of medium height with a chest-deep salt-and-pepper beard and shoulder-length hair, stood up. Graham whispered "Tom Bombadil" in my ear. At my raised eyebrows, he smiled. "Seriously. His adopted name. One of our local chiropractors. He read a little too much Tolkien in the sixties." I had to suppress a laugh.

Bombadil was to the point: "So you're saying I might still be able to get a blood test but if you decide to take out the x-ray machine I'd have to go to Hannaville for that?"

Detwiler shrugged pathetically. "I'm saying what I just said: We don't *know* yet."

Bombadil persisted. He had a somewhat reedy voice capable of being assertive without aggression. "Well, is this a public information meeting or not? Or are you just going to spring it on us once you decide?"

Frankenheim leapt in. "I'm not sure how to answer that." To cries of: "Well, try!" she said: "Obviously the government is committed to keeping the channels of communication open. We'll let you know when *we* know."

Bombadil pressed his advantage. Others seemed content to let him speak, as if he were the unofficially nominated spokesperson. Even the loggers were quiet. "Let me tell you a little story. I was born in this valley. In a little cabin near Kane Creek. It was early post–World War II and my dad had come home the last year of the war with a shrapnel wound in his leg."

Detwiler gave a slight shrug. "I don't see what this has to do with—"

Miller stood up again. "I think it's fair we let Tom have his say, Mr. Detwiler."

"Thank you, Mr. Mayor," said Bombadil evenly. "As I was saying, my parents lived at Kane Creek here in this valley, the old mining camp. They raised my younger sister and me on prospector's wages. By grade three they had to move us into the village here so we wouldn't miss so much school. Dad was in pain almost all the time. He didn't show it but we knew the signs. Then Mom developed high blood pressure—the stress of worrying about Dad, probably."

"Get to the point, Tom!" One of the loggers.

Tom turned in the direction of the voice but kept composure. "I will, I will. Anyway, Mom and Dad formed the first post-war Hospital Committee in Eldorado. It was just them and a few neighbours. Mom organized the bake sales to raise funds and Dad wrote letters to Victoria explaining our needs. They managed to get a full-time doctor sent here. This was long before the days of professional health administrators getting paid six-figure salaries and expense accounts. The community got together to figure out what it needed, and mostly just got the job done. Victoria was happy with that because it meant less work for them. And we didn't have some bureaucrat from the city who didn't know shit about our needs making decisions for us. When medicare came in, premiums were affordable for everyone no matter what their income." Seeing Detwiler attempt to interject, Bombadil anticipated him: "Yeah, yeah, I know all about premium subsidies for low-income folks. My point is, the community knows what it needs and what it doesn't need. And people like my mom here"—he gestured toward a tiny, ancient woman in frizzy white hair half-crumpled in the chair next to him—"worked all their lives to make sure we had what we needed at our village hospital. Hell, half the equipment in that hospital was paid for by the Eldorado Hospital Committee at one time or another. I'm sorry to say Dad is long gone. But, I want to know—are you going to tell my mom and all the other good folks here that what they need doesn't matter anymore, after a lifetime of back-breaking work and community service?"

In a split second every person in the audience was on their feet, cheering and clapping. Graham had to crank down the mixer so the thunderous rumble didn't create a feedback loop. When the cheering finally died down, a sheepish-looking Detwiler leaned forward and said very softly: "I think we can call this meeting adjourned. Watch the pages of the *Mountain Echo* for future announcements and public meetings."

Chapter Two

The next morning, I decided to take a walk on the old logging road by the cabin, really no more than an overgrown trail now. Shadowcat wasn't about to be left inside, knowing I'd probably be gone to town the rest of the day. People laugh when I say he goes for walks with me but it's true. When I was living near Stanley Park he used to walk to the corner store with me. In typical fashion, I only had to tell him once not to cross busy Denman Street. "Just wait for me," I'd say, and sure enough he would. At first he resented not being in the driver's seat. "What, you think I'm a *dog*?" But he soon adjusted. It quickly became an opportunity to soak up admiration from passersby who stopped to stroke his glossy black fur. He's inordinately proud of his long ebony hair and spends half his waking hours grooming himself. If I even pretend to laugh at him I get the Filthy Look that could drill through steel.

The logging road, barely wide enough for a pickup truck even in its day, was by now overgrown and criss-crossed with fallen timber. Chickadees sang their inimitable song as we walked, stepping over logs furred with phosphorescent green moss. After the subliminal rumble of the city the silence itself felt oppressive at first. But hell, it grows on you fast. In fact it isn't entirely silent in the woods. It's a pregnant silence—all the muted voices of growth and greenery alive with possibility—the soft whoosh of a breeze, the nasal call of a nuthatch. A palpable sense of agelessness emanates from bracken fern and glacial slope. A silence that's there, yet not there. In typical fashion, Shadowcat acted as pilot, always ten metres or so ahead of me, slipping through the undergrowth like a whisper.

I used Irene's phone to call the *Echo* and arranged to come in and use their broadband connection, since there was none out in Owl Creek. I wanted to check the latest media releases on the PHA website just in case there were any announcements about the proposed cutbacks to the Eldorado ER and hospital lab. When I opened the glass-panelled door of the *Echo* Lance pushed back from his screen, putting his video game on pause. I wondered how he ever got any work done. It was a distinctly different pace than a city newsroom. I saw no evidence of Jane Bordeaux. Instead another woman I hadn't met was sitting at a desk staring into a laptop screen. She had hair that was a shade somewhere between sandy blonde and brunette, very fine and shoulder length. Her narrow face was almond shaped with dark brown eyes. Lance gestured in her direction.

"This is my beautiful wife Donna Kelly, our editor. Donna, this is Roy Breen, our new stringer."

I walked over to her desk to shake her hand. Like Jane's it was very fine boned but had a healthy grip. Also like Jane, she was barely over five feet tall, with a willowy build. A feather could have knocked her over but there was strength in her grip. Her smile was dazzling in a way that easily outshone the PR woman's at last night's meeting for sincerity. This was combined with an almost girlish, welcoming laugh. It was a famous laugh—the kind you'd expect to hear from a movie starlet. "Great to meet you. Lance tells me you used to work at the *Vancouver Daily*. I used to work in Vancouver too, teaching ESL."

I had to remind myself to let go of her hand. "What brought you here then?"

"Oh, Lance and I met in Vancouver. When I was pregnant with our first, Robbie, we decided we didn't want to raise a family in the city. We came here ten years ago after a camping trip the summer before, just looking for any work we could get." She laughed. "Guess you could say we caught the Spell of the Kootenay. Our daughter Jen—Jennifer—was born here."

"So you didn't start up the *Echo* yourselves?"

"No, we've only had it about a year now. Bought it from Sally Blackwood and Catherine McLachlan, who started up the *Echo* nearly ten years ago. Like most folks around here, 'til then we just made do with odd jobs—as many as we could cram into a week. I waitressed for awhile at the Rosehip Café over on the north side of the village."

It was my turn to laugh. "Oh, I'm glad you didn't say the Blue Moose!"

Lance chuckled. "I take it you've already met Zelda."

"Zelda the Sarcastic Server? Oh, yeah."

"Just one of many local eccentrics—endearing or otherwise," he added with what I was realizing was his trademark Cheshire cat grin.

I turned back to Donna. "So how DO people cobble together a living around here? I don't see any sawmill except at the little village of Bonanza Creek at the southern foot of the lake."

"Like I said," Donna explained, "by doing a little bit of everything. Cutting firewood, doing house renos and other odd-job carpentry, yard work, making and selling pottery and other crafts, providing massage services—whatever it takes to keep the wolf from the door. People come here because they fall in love with the place, not because the career prospects are good."

"Then of course there's always the grow-ops," Lance cut in, still grinning.

"Seriously? That's a big industry here?"

"Mostly it's just mom-and-pop grow-ops here, no organized crime."

"I don't imagine the pay is great for most of these jobs," I ventured.

Donna erupted in her famous laugh. "Hardly. Last I checked this region has the lowest income levels anywhere in the province outside of Vancouver's Downtown East Side."

"So you won't be paying top rate, I'm guessing."

She flashed her magic smile. "Well, no, but we try to be fair."

"So Jane is presumably a part-timer too?"

"Mostly just every two weeks when it's production night and we need a proofreader," said Donna. "And a damn good one, too. Professionally trained by the editors' association."

"Here? In a little backwoods village like this?"

"She's from Ottawa originally. And like I said—"

"Yeah, I know, the Spell of the Kootenay."

"So what else does she do for a living?"

"Works for the local environmental NGO, the Selkirk Grizzly Society—SGS. Office just down the street." I could have sworn she winked.

"Really? An NGO based in Eldorado? Next you're going to tell me you have an opera house."

Lance chimed in. "Actually in the mining boom days the ghost town Silverado had one."

I shook my head. I could see Eldorado was hardly your blink-and-miss, quasi-Appalachian backwater. "Backwoods but not backwards."

"Actually the head campaigner for the SGS, Catherine Reilly, is up for a major international conservation award for the work she did on the Grizzly Smart campaign."

I could feel my eyebrows rising. "No kidding? Next you're going to tell me Reilly trained at MIT or McGill."

"No, actually, that's the amazing thing," said Donna. "The Reillys are an old family around here. Her brother Sean is a bear biologist but Catherine was the oldest so she had to look after all the kids—big Catholic family y'know. She just has this combination of native smarts and charisma that makes her an ideal leader and public figure. She's already met and worked with David Suzuki and other environmentalists."

"I bet that goes down well in a logging community."

"In the early days of the SGS, she used to get rocks through her windows all the time. The loggers boycotted her business 'til she had no choice but to sell."

"Okay, *now* I'm starting to hear strains of duelling banjos...."

"Don't worry, it's settled down a lot since those days," she laughed. "This *is* the twenty-first century after all. I think people have more or less settled into a live-and-let-live philosophy. There hasn't been an incident like that here in twenty years."

The creak of the metal arm that held the door could be heard. I turned to see Deb, recognizing her from the incident at the bistro. Donna excused herself to go to the front counter. They spoke in soft tones but by the gestures Deb was making I could tell it was something upsetting to her. She stood a good six inches taller than Donna so it wasn't hard to see. Still, it's hard not to eavesdrop—only musicians have more sensitive ears than journalists. In this case, I couldn't quite catch the conversation anyway, so I set up my laptop and plugged it into the Ethernet cable. I make it a practice to get my stories done well ahead of deadline, although with a biweekly like the *Echo* that wasn't likely to be a problem. It would also give me time to pursue other freelance writing assignments. I Googled the government website for PHA and scrolled down the list of media releases. Nothing more recent than two weeks ago, well before the announcement at last night's meeting. Finally Deb turned and left. Donna was standing beside my desk. I hit "save" on my notes and looked up.

"You covered the PHA meeting for us last night, didn't you?"

"Yep. Just doing up my notes now. What's up?"

"That was Deb McCloskey. She's a nurse in the palliative care ward at the Eldorado hospital. She's been given a tip but we need to keep her name out of it."

I nodded. "Of course. Good old 'anonymous.'"

"Absolutely, or she could lose her job. Deb says hospital staff has been told by the PHA office in Victoria that the equipment to be removed from the lab is the x-ray machine. That'll mean shutting down the x-ray lab. She thinks they'll keep the blood-testing lab."

"Hang on a second." I refreshed the laptop screen and pulled up the browser again to the tab with the PHA website. "I don't see anything about it here."

Lance chuckled. "Why am I not surprised?"

"Deb says it won't happen for a week or two," Donna added. "They have to arrange for a crew and a big truck to take it out."

"So you want me to include that in my story and cite 'an anonymous source.'"

A delicate forefinger went to her lips as she thought about it. It didn't take long for a smile to creep in. "Actually, no. Let's keep it under wraps for now."

"Really? Judging by what I heard at last night's meeting, the good folks of Eldorado and Elkville won't be too happy about that news. They were pissed off enough about the proposal to reduce the ER hours."

"I know that. Instead I want you to take a walk down the street to the SGS office and have a chat with Jane. She can rally the troops to set up a protest, start writing letters, whatever."

I looked at her a good long time, then across the desk at Lance perched behind his screen. "Am I hearing you right? This sounds like activism, not journalism. Aren't we just supposed to report on the stories, not help *make* them?" I had to smile as I said it. It was ironic coming from me. I could hear Lejean's guffaw all the way from Vancouver.

Lance leaned to one side of his screen so he could make eye contact. "Roy, this is a small community. *Very* small. If people lose their hospital, it can be the beginning of the end for a place like this. And for the *Mountain Echo*."

I looked back and forth between the pair of them. Both were smiling like foxes. It was Donna who finally spoke again. "Deb told me that the Sapphire Lake Hospital Auxiliary raised the money to buy that x-ray machine ten years ago. In that sense, it belongs to the community anyway."

"Listen, I get it. But let me just play the devil's advocate for a minute. Something I learned from my old-time editor at the *Vancouver Daily*. He'd argue: It's just a reduction of services, not a closure of the entire hospital."

Lance shrugged, flashing his Cheshire grin. "You know how bureaucrats work if they think they can get away with something. First it's a reduction in ER hours, a slight reduction of lab services. Next thing you know, the lab is completely gone. They get to look good by cutting a few grand from the balance sheet. People here have to drive two hours to get to the Hannaville Regional Hospital as it is. Already for major operations it's five hours to Caledon General Hospital. Thin edge of the wedge."

"We've already lost our acute care beds," added Donna. "That was last year. Remember, the primary demographic here is fifty-plus."

"Death by a thousand cuts," I agreed. "Always the sign of a decadent civilization, when bureaucracy takes over. But how is it good for the newspaper to get mixed up in local politics?"

Lance guffawed. "You've been a reporter for *how* long? You

don't think newspaper owners have a political agenda?"

I must have grinned because Donna giggled, watching me. She caught the irony in my question. Lance continued: "Why else does the Interior Media chain buy up every struggling daily or weekly east of Vancouver if not to push their agenda?"

"Besides," Donna added, "if this place goes down, we go with it. For the *Mountain Echo*, good politics is good business."

"I'm guessing you won't be putting that on the masthead anytime soon."

Lance guffawed again. "Nope. But I may still steal your slogan."

The Selkirk Grizzly Society office was indeed just a couple of blocks down main street. It had originally been a trading post or hardware store and the shiplap siding on the exterior walls probably had no equivalent in modern building materials. It was painted bright white with—naturally—green trim, but the display windows that had once been used to feature new goods were two-thirds covered in reflective material that prevented anyone from peering inside. I jiggled the ancient hardware on the door handle to no avail, before seeing a sign that read: "Enter through rear door." It all seemed oddly secretive unless you knew what Donna had told me of Reilly's past intimidation. There was a small gazebo in the lot beside the building. A great tall maple tree just starting to turn gold was starting to shed its leaves. I made my way beneath it to the rear entrance.

The door was a conversation piece, practically a work of art itself and certainly an antique. There were the remnants of earlier paint jobs showing through here and there. The entire surface looked like a dry streambed in the desert—the paint raised in a caked mosaic. Strangely enough the latticework of cracks only added to the aesthetic appeal. The doorknob was one of those old cut-glass handles with faded brass hardware. Above it was a newer-looking deadbolt. A tall man with a thick head of greying hair greeted me, blocking my passage like a gatekeeper. He looked like he might have been a Sears catalogue model in a former life. A sheaf of papers hung from one hand. He introduced himself as James Kirkup. When I told him I'd come to talk to Jane Bordeaux he led me to a cramped office with two desktop computers. A copper-haired woman had her back to me, working at one of them. Jane seemed to start suddenly when she saw me but quickly composed herself.

"Oh—hi! Twice we meet in just a couple of days!"

"Yes, I've … well I've come on a bit of an errand, actually. It's kind of hard to explain."

She pushed back her chair. "Well how about a cup of tea? That usually helps." I nodded. "What kind? We have pretty much everything here."

"Jasmine if you have it, please."

"No problem! This, by the way, is my colleague Rebecca Finlay.…" The copper-haired woman turned to reveal a broad smile in a flushed complexion and pale blue eyes.

"Hi," she said. "You're in good hands with Jane."

"I don't doubt it."

Once the tea was ready I got straight to the point about the ER. Jane's fine elfin face, while not model beautiful, was compelling to look at, with just a hint of a Gallic nose. Her skin was unwrinkled, setting a young-looking face at odds with her greying hair. If I had to guess I'd say she was mid- to late forties. It was clear by her expression she was paying close attention. I could tell she wasn't somebody who wasted a lot of words. Thoughtful.

"Lance and Donna seem to think your group could help out somehow."

"Well, this is an *environmental* NGO.…"

"Yes I'm aware of that. Donna said you were the right person to talk to."

"I'm flattered, if a little puzzled. I mostly do research here for Cathy Reilly, work as her campaign assistant. Nothing too special."

"Donna told me Reilly is up for an international award. If you're her campaign assistant you must have had something to do with that."

She blushed, despite herself. "Well thank you, you're very generous." To recover composure, she sipped her tea. I waited for her to continue. "I suppose one campaign is very like another. Lance is right—we can't afford to lose the hospital. We have a pretty good database here of local activists. Use it all the time for logging protests and letter-writing campaigns. I could pull that up—get you some contact names and numbers."

"Maybe not *too* many names. I'm still new here. Who would you recommend?"

"Yes of course I see what you mean—who's a good organizer? Well let me think…. Rosanna Yale comes to mind. She's young, smart, and photogenic. A good potential leader for a 'Save the ER campaign.' Lived here all her life with her mom Diana and younger sister Holly, a hairdresser. Rosanna and her mom run the Rosehip Café during tourist season, but now that's winding down, she'll have more time on her hands."

I was starting to wonder if the male/female ratio in this village was seriously skewed in favour of the latter. I'd only met two other men besides me—so far. Eldorado: The Village of Women. Hmm…. Well that might not be bad at all, especially for the town's newest eligible bachelor. And judging by Donna, Jane, and Deb, they were all very dedicated to their community.

"Still, I have to walk a fine line. Strictly speaking as a journalist I'm not supposed to be making those connections *before* something happens."

She smiled. It wasn't the movie star dazzle of Donna's smile but softer, suffused with gentleness. A kind face, as they used to say. "I understand. Why don't you let me make a few phone calls? I can let you know what I find out. That way you're still just reporting on what happens, not making it happen." I realized it was the first time I'd noticed the colour of her eyes: emerald green, a darker shade than my own. I looked away quickly.

"Thanks Jane. You're a great help." I got up to leave, chuckling under my breath about that one-in-a-million door.

"Uh … Roy?"

I turned to see Jane looking flushed again. "You like movies?"

"Hell, yeah. Used to write a film review column for the *Kootenay Review* before that folded—years ago. Why?"

"Well, they have a foreign film night every week during the winter in Minto, just about a half hour's drive north of here."

"Yes, I drove through it on my camping tour of Sturgeon Lake."

"There's a French-Canadian friend of mine up there who runs the film night, Sophie Lariveau. Every Thursday night at 7:00 p.m. I could pick you up, I—I know the way."

"Sure, why not?"

She smiled. "You realize that's tonight?"

"Oh, uh—sure. I'm at highway number 3714 in Owl Creek. I'll wait for you at the top of the driveway. My phone isn't hooked up yet. My station wagon's still a bit of a mess, so thanks for offering me a lift."

"Say about 6:30? I have to pick up one or two others on the way."

"No problem."

She was there on the dot of 6:30, pulling up in a cerulean blue Honda Civic. It was hard to imagine fitting more than two people in it, but I could see there were already two people in the back seat. Jane looked sparkling, with a Valhalla Pure fall jacket and pale blue cashmere turtleneck sweater. Any shade of blue suited her perfectly. She turned to the couple in the back seat. "This is Bob and Lena." I reached back to shake hands. Bob had a round face, short-cropped hair, and an impish grin. Lena had jet-black hair sticking out in all directions and a generous, almost mad grin. They lived in Eldorado and had briefly run a pizza joint, Bob told me. Lena had been trained as a cook. Although he was a qualified industrial engineer, it was their way of making a life in the village. But when Lena was diagnosed in the early stages of ALS, Bob had returned to his work in engineering to support her. It meant long weeks away from home working on remote pipelines.

"So what's on the marquee?" I asked Jane as she pulled out of the driveway.

"It's the new Denys Arcand film, *The Barbarian Invasions.* Or, I suppose—more properly, *Les Invasions Barbares.*"

"Interesting that they're running a French-*Canadian* film on their foreign film night."

"I think Sophie uses any excuse she can to expose the locals to French-Canadian movies," Jane observed.

"I never saw *The Decline of the American Empire* but I loved his film *Jesus of Montreal*. A passion play within *the* passion play."

"Yeah, I loved *Jesus of Montreal*," shouted Lena from the back seat. She was one of those people who half-yelled, as if everyone else were deaf. Bob just smiled like a Zen sage.

Jane was just tall enough to see over the steering wheel. Had she been much older it might have had a comic effect, but in fact it was kind of endearing. "Well it's been awhile since he made *Decline of the American Empire*, but I imagine it won't be too hard to follow the new one. From what I read it picks up the original story, only decades later."

"I'm not sure I like French-Canadian films, but hey, always willing to give it a try," said Bob in a less strident tone than his partner. "Just don't make me take out 'distinct person' status." He returned to his standby cherub grin.

We jabbered on about movies for another few minutes before a natural pause in the conversation. I used the space to turn to Jane. "So, any news?"

"News?" She looked puzzled briefly before recognition lit her eyes. "Oh, yes! I spoke to Rosanna Yale. She's already organizing a protest to keep the ER open. They're setting up a protest and a 24/7 watch on the lab starting tomorrow."

"Really? You people can organize that fast in this village?"

She smiled her soft smile. "This valley is Protest Central, Roy. We've had to blockade logging roads to keep our watersheds from being clear-cut for years now. There are people in Glacier Valley who cut their teeth with sixties protest groups like the Students for a Democratic Society down in the States, to mention only one. Real veterans. Now some of the second generation are old enough, they're ready to protest or blockade too."

"Does that old-hat shit really work though?"

"Well once upon a time it did. But around the time of the Eldorado watershed blockade a few years ago, it seemed like we turned a corner. Or the government did. It was after that they started hitting us with SLAPP suits and court injunctions."

"Wait—SLAPP suits? What's that?"

"Strategic Lawsuit Against Public Participation. It was just a tactic to shut down environmental NGOs. That seriously raised the stakes for anyone who didn't want a police record.

And it raised legal costs considerably for NGOs. Some just don't have the funds for long drawn-out court battles and the big corporations knew it."

"So they were learning from past mistakes," I observed. "Making it harder to protest."

"And government doing industry's dirty work, yeah. At SGS we spend a lot more of our time dealing with legal issues than we ever did before. Makes any campaign a lot more complicated and a lot more time-consuming."

"You wouldn't believe the way they talk about protestors in the bush camps," Bob interjected. "And the bosses have their lawyers on speed dial."

"So wandering around with a bunch of protest signs is a waste of time," I said acidly.

Jane seemed taken aback. "Well, I wouldn't quite put it *that* way. You still need a physical presence at a disputed site, even if to some extent it's more symbolic than tactical."

"But if all they do is call a judge, get an injunction to have you removed, and then call in the RCMP to do the hauling, what's the point?"

She sighed, staring into the distance where the Valhallas cut a jagged edge into the early evening skyline. I could tell I may have gone too far. "Don't get me wrong," I backtracked. "I don't want to see watersheds and old-growth forests logged any more than you do. I just have little patience for futility."

"So what do we do, *nothing*?" It was Lena's edgy voice.

I gave her the verbal equivalent of a shrug: "How the hell would I know?"

"If it weren't for Cathy Reilly's efforts we wouldn't have Selkirk Provincial Park," said Jane. "Surely that counts for something."

"Of course, of course it does. That's amazing!" I was back-pedalling as fast as I could. "But *how* did that happen? What was done there that could work elsewhere?"

"Well it took years and years of work," Jane sighed. It was clear she knew this firsthand. "And naturally, getting a government to set aside parkland is a different kettle of fish than getting them to stop a logging company once they've already granted the permit...."

"True," I agreed. "But is there some crossover between the two?"

"Yes and no," said Jane. "With a park campaign, it's much more sexy. The element of conflict is minimized, for one thing. Almost everybody loves a park. With a park, you're mostly raising money to lobby government and corporate support. There's usually no need for any occupation tactics. And the public loves giving money for that kind of thing. With a logging blockade, you're into conflict from the start, so right away you're at a disadvantage. And you're raising money to pay legal fees, so it's a lot less sexy. Plus you find the public can be split down the middle. Half of them want to be with you there on the protest line, the other half are with the cops hauling you away."

"I see," I said, not wanting to risk upsetting her further.

"I know, I know," Lena chimed in. "Why wait 'til the logging permits are granted? Why not just *buy* all the watersheds! Think outside the box!"

I was beginning to wonder what box she was imagining. Even Bob chuckled at this one. "That's why we pay taxes, dear—to maintain public land, among other things. We shouldn't have to *buy* it to protect it. It's *supposed* to be set aside on our behalf. Although, if you apply capitalist logic, we could all spend the rest of our lives raising money to protect public land from development. Then they wouldn't have to do any work at all, just collect money from us to keep them from mining or logging." By his Zen grin I could tell he had a healthy sense of humour.

"Like a protection racket," I observed.

A silence settled in. I was too new here to start provoking people this soon, although everyone in the car seemed to be on the same page. Besides, I was starting to like Jane—a lot— and I didn't want to alienate her. I decided it was time to shift gears slightly. "So do we have a time set yet for the hospital blockade?"

"Yes, they'll start setting up tomorrow at 10:00 a.m."

"Great! I can sleep in a little. Nothing worse than early risers."

She laughed. "I take it you don't like worms, then?"

By the time I rolled into the *Mountain Echo* office it was closer to noon. In my experience, it can take a couple of hours for protest rallies to get off the ground. Nothing much happens until the media gets there anyway and starts taking pictures and doing interviews. Lance was parked in front of his screen as usual, yawning broadly. Donna was at her desk in the back corner—her usual place—with the furrowed brow she adopted while scanning text on her laptop. Putting a newspaper together is never a nine-to-five job so no doubt she and Lance had burnt the midnight oil last night. For them, putting together a small-town biweekly is an even bigger workload than a big-city daily. Here they have to handle *all* the jobs—accounting, ad sales, editing, writing, layout, with a little help from Jane and stringers like me.

"At this rate you'll soon become a regular," grinned Lance.

"That's my goal. What news today?"

He shrugged. "Not much yet."

Donna looked up from her laptop with that dazzling smile. "Yeah, but there's a *great* letter to the editor that's come in already about the hospital cutbacks."

"Wow, that was fast," I said. "I wouldn't have thought folks would be that quick off the mark here."

"Oh, yes they are. Wait 'til you get to know this place."

"Our letters page is probably the most popular part of the newspaper," Lance added proudly. "We could publish a book of them one day. Some of them are surprisingly good. Plenty of people in this valley came here with degrees."

I picked up the latest issue in the rack on the counter, thumbing to the letters page. The first thing I noticed was that—in contrast to the big-city dailies—the letters were two to three times longer. The typical average in a corporate newspaper was around two hundred words, maximum. Here some of them rambled on to well over six hundred words. I'd have to spend time over coffee reading them but I remarked on their length.

"Yeah, we get some pretty long-winded folks around here," Lance said. "But we like to give them space to develop an argument. Pretty hard to do that in two hundred words."

"And they're usually fairly intelligent, too," added Donna.

"Though very few people are actual writers, so we always have to edit their writing. Some more than others."

"Unlike say, the comment strings on websites," I suggested wryly.

"Well of course, some are just *wacky*," Lance grinned. "They seem to obey a rather different 'Five Ws' than we're taught in journalism school—Witty, Wacky, Weird, obsessed with Wilderness, and Well-informed."

"So tell me about the one you just got," I urged.

"I'll send it over to you via Mac Mail," said Donna.

I logged in to my email account and opened up the attachment. It was titled "PHA BUREAUCRAT EXCHANGE PROGRAM":

> After the public meeting at Eldorado Hall on October 8 with the Provincial Health Authority, where not one but *three* obviously well-paid bureaucrats were present to explain why we should accept reduced ER hours, I have a suggestion. You may have heard of the "Welfare Exchange Program," where a Vancouver City councillor volunteered to live temporarily on welfare income to see what it's like to make ends meet on $500 a month.
>
> Well, how about a PHA Bureaucrat Exchange Program along the lines of the international student exchanges, where Canadian students trade places with students from poorer countries for six months—live in their homes and villages, go to their schools. Only with the PHA Bureaucrat Exchange Program, instead of seeking those in good physical health, let's recruit only senior bureaucrats with a known history of poor health, preferably with diabetes, a heart condition or other major condition. Then we bring them to live in Eldorado, where they swap jobs with a local resident for six months. That may mean swapping office work for a constellation of odd jobs—woodcutting, yard work, etc.
>
> On top of that, they must rely on our local healthcare services under the reduced emergency ward regime they propose. We could train them to only chop wood between nine to five in case they cut off a finger after hours and have nowhere to go. We'd warn them sternly that it is *strictly forbidden* to have heart attacks or other health crises after hours. Naturally if they do, our excellent ER staff will take good care of them by putting them into a helicopter bound for Hannaville or Caledon. Hopefully they make it before it's too late. Then after six months of that, let's send them back to

Victoria and see what kind of budget-cutting decisions
they make.
Signed, Timber Wolf, Owl Creek

"One of my neighbours, then," I chuckled. "Yep, I'd say
that's a keeper. If your letters page is anything like this on a
regular basis I can tell I'm going to enjoy living here. By the
way, anything happening at the hospital yet?"

"I was over there this morning talking to Rosanna, but it
was too early," said Donna. "People were still trickling in—
Kootenay Time, y'know. But she's a good organizer, so it'll
come together."

"If you like I could take a run over there now, see if things
are heating up yet."

"Sure. Probably won't be much going on yet," said
Donna. "But now might be a good time to get pics and start
interviewing."

The narrow streets of the part of Eldorado known as "Orchard
Town" in the immediate vicinity of the hospital were crowded
with vehicles. The neighbourhood had originally been the site
of a Japanese internment camp during World War II and after
the war those who stayed behind cultivated gardens and fruit
trees, hence its nickname. The generally low level of income in
the area was reflected in the cars and trucks people drove—only
a few late-model vehicles and quite a few tried-and-true survi-
vors of past decades—mostly Subaru wagons, Honda Civics,
Toyota Corollas and Ford pickups. I was willing to bet the few
new vehicles were owned by hospital or school staff—the only
ones in town with decent-paying jobs. A couple of the pickups wore banners made of bedsheets stitched together, reading: "NO BANKER'S HOURS FOR THIS ER!" or: "PHA:
SAVING LIVES OR SAVING DOLLARS?"

The hospital location on the waterfront of Sapphire Lake
was gorgeous enough to make a real estate agent drool, with
snowy peaks receding southward and the uncut slopes of
Selkirk Provincial Park on the west side of the lake. The water
was crystalline blue, so clean you could see to the gravel bottom

near shore. I could see why valley residents were so fiercely protective of their watersheds. It was hard to remember the last time I'd seen water this pure.

A tall blonde woman seemed to be in charge, directing traffic and gesticulating at people still putting together picket signs. I strode straight up to her. "I take it you must be Rosanna— Rosanna Yale?" I had to remind myself to breathe—her beauty was stunning. Pale blonde hair at mid-back length, eyes as clear as the waters of Sapphire Lake, full, tastefully rouged lips. I wondered if there were brains to complement the beauty. Too often the two weren't part of the same package in both men and women.

"Yes, I am. And you are?" Her smile was cordial but businesslike.

"Roy Breen. Working on a story for the *Mountain Echo*. I'm new here." I pulled out my trusty steno pad. I had a digital recorder in my briefcase but always found the damn things annoying to work with. By the time you rewound and fast-forwarded fifteen times to get the full quote you needed you could have written the damn thing out by hand three times faster. Taking notes forced you to develop your listening and transcribing skills to a fine polish. I'd only been reprimanded by Bob Lejean a handful of times in fifteen years for getting quotes wrong.

"I gathered that, since I haven't seen you before," she said. "Everybody kinda knows everybody around here. Oh, excuse me—" She stepped aside to direct a car out of the hospital parking lot, shouting: "We have to keep access to the ER clear! Go park on Galway Street!" Returning to me, she continued: "Sorry, kinda have to keep on my toes here. What can I do for you?"

"Well you can start by explaining to me your game plan. How can you effectively blockade a hospital? Won't they just call the cops to haul you off-site?"

We stood by the steps of one of the auxiliary buildings while protestors walked in from parked cars and began exchanging greetings. She leaned with one arm draped over a wooden stair railing, the posture of someone very much in command. "It's not really a blockade. The plan is to get everybody to make a sacred circle of linked hands around the hospital, with banners and placards placed strategically around the circle. Naturally we'll let any traffic in and out; I've made it quite clear to every-body there's to be no blocking of traffic."

"Will that include PHA trucks if and when they come in to take out lab equipment?"

She smiled knowingly. "Ah, now that's another story. Our Hospital Auxiliary paid for that x-ray equipment, so it belongs to the community. We're not about to let PHA steal it."

"Really? How can you stop it?"

"We have some very dedicated volunteers here. They under-stand that without this ER ward and lab, lives could be lost."

I was scribbling furiously. "What happens if PHA comes in the middle of the night?"

"We're setting up a 24/7 watch of the lab."

"Seriously?"

"Why not? We'll keep at least two people posted outside the lab round the clock. We have what we call a 'phone tree' system. If PHA shows up to take out the x-ray stuff, one will block the door while the other starts calling the names on the phone tree. Pretty soon there'll be a lot more than two bodies blocking that lab." Clearly, this woman had far more than aver-age grey matter between her ears.

A twenty-year-old GMC pickup truck, with a hand-painted psychedelic mural on its canopy, pulled up. There were chintz curtains in the canopy's tiny windows and the thing was obvi-ously homemade. The mural had been sun-bleached and paint was peeling off in bits. A moss-bearded, long-haired face poked out of the driver's-side window. I recognized him from the Eldorado Hall meeting—Tom Bombadil. In contrast to his serious demeanour that night, he was grinning, like he was enjoying some private joke. His eyes were reduced in size by the powerful prescription of his glasses. On closer inspection, I noted that his teeth were ground down and widely spaced in the front. There was an earnestness in his expression, as if eager to pitch in. He reminded me more of a hobbit than the giant-like Tolkien character after whom he'd chosen to name himself. Rosanna wasted no time. "Can you please park on Galway or somewhere else, Tom? Then check in with me; I need to discuss some stuff with you." He put the truck in reverse and slowly backed out of the hospital parking lot.

Turning to Rosanna, I pressed on: "So do you have a public statement you plan to issue? A set of demands?"

Her pristine eyes were hypnotic. I had to fight inappropriate thoughts and concentrate. "We're working on that. That's why I want Tom's help. We need to get a media release out. But demands? Mmmm … not sure if I want to call it that. The only 'demand' we have is that they leave both our lab and our ER intact."

"Don't fix it if it ain't broke, in other words?"

"Exactly. As you may already know, the people in these villages depend on a fully functioning ER and lab. Neither Lowery nor Minto have any more facilities than we do. And it's hours to either the Hannaville or Caledon hospitals. Hours that can mean the difference between life and death without proper triage care. As it is, we've lost acute care beds and the lab is only open three days a week. That was on the first round of cutbacks last year. We probably should have seen this coming then, but…."

I had to let my note-taking hand catch up with her. "Hard to anticipate sometimes."

"Anything else?" She smiled warmly, tossing her blonde locks.

"What can you tell me about Bombadil?"

"Oh, he's been here forever, since before I was born. Harmless. A decent guy."

"What's with the truck?"

She laughed good-naturedly. "Tom never really left the sixties and seventies and we love him for it. We used to joke that we could set our clocks every spring by the fresh coat of paint on his truck mural."

"It's not looking so spiffy now."

She sighed. "Yeah, it's been a few years since he kept it up. Some of the heart seemed to go out of him when his dad died. And—you know—the decades have a way of wearing people down."

I thought it was a remarkably astute comment for one so young. I recalled the wearied faces of the Aging Hippies at Eldorado Hall. "Not to mention losing one too many battles with bureaucrats and big corporations."

She looked slightly annoyed, as if I were insinuating failure for her protest action. "Anything else?"

"No, that's great for now, thanks."

Chapter Three

It looked like it was going to take a couple of days for the hospital protestors to get their media releases disseminated. I decided to take a chance and ask Jane to my place for dinner. It was already Friday anyway, the worst possible day to try to break news. I filed my story on the PHA meeting with Donna and told her to call Irene if she had anything else for me to do. Irene's house was on the same lot as my cabin, just thirty metres away. So it was easy enough for her to get messages to me until Telco finally got around to hooking up my phone. Irene was a hard-working gal, so she'd left her front door open and said to help myself to the phone.

I walked down to the SGS office on the premise of letting Jane know what I'd learned from Rosanna about the protest plans. The paper wouldn't be out 'til next Wednesday so I'd be giving her a heads-up. James Kirkup the SGS gatekeeper met me at the rear door as usual but this time offered a faint smile of recognition. The smile I got from the red-headed Rebecca was more conspiratorial; obviously the two women had been talking about me. I could see her smiling approvingly at Jane when I rapped lightly on their open office door. Jane had been dialled into whatever computer task she was working on so at first she didn't see me. The expression on her face changed from clouded brow to surprised delight. I felt a little awkward so I suggested we go into the lunchroom to talk. Once again she made tea, remembering that I liked jasmine. She'd baked some oatmeal chocolate chip cookies to bring into the office that day so she offered me a plate. After I briefed her on the protest, I shifted gears. There was something nagging at me and I had to ask her opinion.

"Um … forgive me for asking, but is this village run by women?"

She laughed gently. "What do you mean?"

"Well, so far I've been in Eldorado less than a week and I've noticed that many of the key players here are women. Donna is the editor of the *Echo*. Irene owns real estate and runs several businesses. Rosanna seems a capable protest organizer and runs the Rosehip Café with her mom. You're the campaign assistant for an award-winning environmentalist, who also happens to be a woman. Hell, even the postmaster is a woman. I've only met a few men so far."

"Half the village council is women too."

"I rest my case."

As always her smile held not a trace of condescension. "And is that good or bad?"

"Not saying it's either; just wondering, that's all. I'm wondering if I should headline my articles on the hospital protest: 'Village of Women Blockades Hospital to Save ER.'"

"Coming from a long line of feminists," she said, "all I can tell you is, it's been a helluva long road to get this far. In some parts of this country we haven't even had the vote for a hundred years yet."

"I'm surprised you have it here. With all the mining and logging I would've expected a much more macho culture. I'm amazed you have women on the village council."

"Trust me, the gains have been just as hard-won here," she said. "Maybe harder won. Back in the day, *any* kind of difference could make you a target. When the first hippies arrived some of them were beaten up right on the street. But remember too that in frontier communities, it was usually women who brought civilization to these backwoods towns."

"You mean once they drove the prostitutes out of the mining camps."

She looked at me like I might be trying to bait her but only smiled in her soft way. There was a grace about her that was radiant. She wasn't easily riled. "Well, sure. If you read some of the local histories you'll see that the Women's Institutes played a huge role in the development of these communities. Often they were the ones responsible for raising money to establish the first hospitals. Often it was women who pushed for sidewalks and sewers. You know—all the stuff that turns a place from a squat in the bush into a town."

I grinned. "And shut down Friday night poker games...."

She laughed subtly again. "I doubt anyone's stopping men doing that."

"And you don't think there were any women beating up hippies back in the day?"

"Well, verbally, maybe, sure. No one's saying women don't have their faults. We're human beings too. That's the whole point. We're neither lesser nor greater beings."

"I imagine a lot of the women who came up with the draft dodgers were feminists too."

"Naturally. They were the advance guard. There were actually more women who came here in the Vietnam era than men."

"Really? I didn't know that."

A silence fell over the lunchroom as we sipped jasmine tea. I could tell I'd better either change topic or get to the point of this visit. I decided on the latter.

"In the name of equal rights then, how would you like me to make you dinner tonight? I mean, if you're not busy?"

She flushed slightly but it passed as quickly as steam on a windowpane. Now the smile was vaguely mischievous. "Well, I'd have to check my busy social calendar, but it looks pretty good from where I'm sitting right now."

I had to think about that one for a moment but decided not to ask. "Great! I can pick you up and drop you off again after if you like."

"No, I don't think so. That would mean you making at least four trips back and forth from Eldorado to Owl Creek and back again. I couldn't have you do that."

"Four times?"

"Once to go out and prepare dinner, once to pick me up, once to take me back to Eldorado, and then once to drive yourself home again after. Added up, that's more than an hour's driving. I could never inconvenience you that much. I'll drive myself there. What time?"

"Let's say 6:30?"

"Can I bring anything?"

"A bottle of Chardonnay," I winked, "or should I say Bordeaux?"

"Touché," she laughed. "You can have the Chardonnay though; I don't drink."

"Great! See you at the Owl Creek homestead." As I made my way to the rear door I pointed at the window, which framed a postcard-perfect scene of the Valhalla mountain range across the lake. There was a cleft between Twin Peaks that nestled the Eldorado Glacier. The peak on the north side tapered to a blunt end like a nipple. I'd noticed more than one peak like that in this range.

"See? Even the landscape here is feminine. Not that I'm complaining."

Her smile was grace itself.

Shadowcat only broke his cool on rare occasions. After all, his cool was his most prized possession next to his glorious black coat. One of those occasions was when I stepped in the door after being away all day. First it was the "flop down, roll around" dance. "Yay! Dad's home!" Then as if to recover his cool he'd throw in a few good arching feline stretches, as if to say: "But I'm cool, I'm cool. Really I am." It didn't work. His excitement always bled through. Shadowcat's priority list was eternally the same upon my return: The flop-down happy dance, then some juicy tuna in the kitchen, and finally the brushing of his coat. As I said earlier, he has me thoroughly trained to meet all his needs. The rush to the kitchen was always urgent, as if I hadn't fed him in a week and then only on dry bread and water. The meowing refrain was simple: "Now, now, NOW!" Like a little kid who can't wait for ice cream, he'd stretch himself tall on his rear legs, leaning against the cupboard as I worked the can opener. Sometimes for added effect he'd wave one paw in the air in a "Hurry, hurry!" gesture. I sometimes worried about feeding him so much tuna. But seeing the sheer gastronomic pleasure he got from it, I couldn't resist. It was probably better than feeding him commercial cat food with all the crap they put in it. Pavlov might have expanded his theory to include cats if he'd seen Shadowcat's instant reaction to the two simple words: "Tuna gravy." From the kitchen it was a quick jog to the bathroom, where he'd leap onto the sink for his brushing. Now the expression was more ardent, the look wide-eyed and almost pleading: "Please, please, *please* brush me." The very picture of adorable, like a toddler begging for a bubble bath. How could I resist? Once the protocol was fulfilled, he could return to his normal routine of resting and preening that midnight glossy fur. Preparing for the day he'd be a centrefold model for *Cats Monthly*. That meant he always had to look his absolute best.

Jane showed up on the dot of 6:30. No Kootenay Time for this gal. She had a bottle of Chardonnay and a yogurt container.

"Yogurt?" I asked.

"More chocolate chip cookies, actually. I noticed you liked them."

Shadowcat's reaction surprised me. He was after all a veteran of my last three disastrous relationships. Usually when a woman showed up at my door, he barely lifted his head from his perch on the back of the couch. "What kind of loser did you bring home this time, Dad?" I had to admit, my "femina radar" seemed to be permanently nonfunctional. But as soon as he saw Jane, he jumped down from the couch and walked over to meet her. He meowed up at her as if to say, "I don't know who you are but I like you already." I don't believe in auras but I have no doubt animals pick up on people's essential nature far faster than we do.

"Well, you certainly pass the gold standard test," I laughed.

She leaned down to stroke his back gently. He arched into her palm. I couldn't believe it. This just wasn't like him. He was looking approvingly at me now. "Finally, you bring home a good one!" Obviously he sensed something I only barely grasped.

"I'm doing a chicken stir-fry so I didn't want to start cooking before you got here," I told her. "But everything's all prepared and ready to toss into the pan. Do you mind hanging out in the kitchen while I work?"

"I'd love to. It's not everyday I get a man to cook for me."

I still had a few carrots to chop so I pulled my stainless steel folding knife out of my back pocket. The sight of it seemed to shock her. "Guess I better not get on your bad side, eh?"

"Not at all. I grew up in the north. Had a jackknife from the time I was about ten years old. My old man taught me all about knife safety and wilderness survival. I'm willing to bet a lot of men around here carry them. It's a tool, not a weapon."

She looked vaguely embarrassed. "I'm sorry, I didn't mean to imply...."

I waved her off. "It's fine. No worries."

"No, really, I shouldn't have said ... it's just that I haven't dated for a long time. Not a lot to choose from in a village this tiny. To say I was rusty would be an understatement."

"You've done just fine so far. I'm grateful for your help this week. And the tea and cookies. That's more perks than I ever got working in a Vancouver newsroom."

She laughed. "Believe it or not, my dad once sent me a book called *Dating for Dummies*."

"So was I right about the unbalanced male/female ratio in these villages?"

"Yes and no. I mean, it's partly by choice. When I left Ottawa five years ago I was coming off a train-wreck relationship with an alcoholic. I'd seen too much of that in my family and wasted enough of my own time with guys like that. I guess ... I guess I just didn't trust myself not to choose another addict."

"Well now I don't feel so bad. My last few relationships haven't been great either."

The pan made that delightful sizzling sound as I threw in the chicken strips. Soon the delicious odour was filling up the kitchen. "So what brought you all the way out to the wilds of British Columbia from the nation's capital?"

"I'd met Cathy Reilly on one of her campaigns, stopping old-growth logging on Pender Island, I think it was. She'd worked with me on the campaign in Ottawa. Told me if I ever wanted to come out west, she'd try to get me a job with SGS."

"Wow, you must be good."

"Oh, I don't know," she shrugged. "Maybe she was just being kind. Anyway, the contract I had with the Sierra Club had expired, my relationship had *clearly* expired and I was desperate for some kind of change. So I packed up my car and headed west."

"Hmm. Sounds a bit like my story, only yours was five years ago and mine is now. Still, it's a helluva long way...."

"I'd always wanted to see the Pacific Ocean. In fact I wanted to live on the West Coast. But the job market there at the time was lousy. I only spent a few weeks in Vancouver. Then I remembered Cathy's offer, so I looked up Eldorado on the map and packed up the car again. The rest, as they say, is history."

"You were able to drive right to this little village in the woods and have a job waiting for you? I don't imagine many people here can say that."

"Well, not exactly," she laughed. "When I got here, Cathy said: 'Great! We can use a first-rate fundraiser like you. You can start by writing this grant so we can pay your salary.' I was a bit put off at first, but it's what I was used to doing anyway so I just got to it. I've been doing it ever since, raising money for everything from new office computers to campaign brochures."

"Wow. Campaign assistant AND fundraiser. No wonder she lured you out here." By now the veggies were softening up in a liberal dousing of soy sauce. "Would you mind setting out the plates and cutlery?" I asked. She nodded and I pointed her to the appropriate cupboard and drawer. Once the food was laid out I lit a candle and offered her some fizzy apple cider I'd picked up on the way home. I'd loved the kitchen in this place from the moment I clapped eyes on it. I hadn't thought of it initially as an ideal spot for entertaining women but it was certainly that. The soaring A-frame ceiling with two skylights, the sliding glass doors leading to the deck, the mouth-gaping view of glacial ridges in the valley below. As darkness fell a half-moon lit the autumn sky with a preternatural indigo blue. The snows of Mt. Pyramid were incandescent. Soon the stars would be winking into existence, spreading their celestial web across the night sky.

I'd learned a long time ago that as long as one has a cat there's not much need for an alarm clock. Shadowcat had the routine worked out thoroughly. Once he's decided that *he's* slept enough for one night he does his "Captain Cat" routine. As if out of nowhere, he leaps onto the bed and then stands there in all his preened and shining glory. You can practically hear the soundtrack blaring out its triumphant horns: "Na-na-na— na—na-na!" Practising another of his *Cats Monthly* poses with the implicit message: "Admire me." He stands still as a Hollywood star posing for paparazzi, then finally relaxes and curls up while I pull the ragged remnants of my consciousness together. Mind you, during his kittenhood the whole Captain Cat routine had to be attenuated somewhat when he tried it a couple of times at 6:00 a.m. A swift kick from beneath the covers had a tendency to shatter the illusion of cool. So he quickly adjusted to my more late-morning biology.

Jane and I had stayed up late, chatting about everything from climate change to Shakespeare to the Peter Jackson film adaptations of *The Lord of the Rings*. Minto had one of the last surviving movie theatres in the area and I promised to take her to see *The Return of the King*, due out any day now. Clearly my "bimbo magnet," as an old buddy once called it, was finally going dormant. Here was a woman who could converse freely and intelligently on a wide range of topics without ever exhausting her fund of knowledge. And an original thinker, to boot. Not that there weren't plenty of such women out there, just that for some reason my radar for them was busted. Jane's finely drawn features had a refined beauty of their own—one of those faces that always looks younger than they are. It's probably a good thing she doesn't drink or we'd have ended up in bed by now. But after my last few fiascos with women, I wasn't in any hurry even if the old pocket rocket was ever-ready. I congratulated myself on finally learning Manhood's Lesson One: Not letting your pecker do your thinking for you. And it only took me 'til age forty-four. Well, better late than never.

These thoughts were turning around in my head like socks in a dryer when I heard a rap at the door. I threw back the covers—receiving an annoyed glare from Shadowcat—and struggled into my bathrobe. Through the front window I could see Irene. She had a small piece of paper in her hand.

"Oh, hi! Hope I didn't call too early!" she said.

I tried to smooth the rumple of my hair, or what was left of my hair. "No, no—not a problem." I always found myself defensive about my rising habits, especially to that self-righteous class known as early risers. Irene looked like an early riser to me, though her smile was the furthest thing from self-righteous.

She thrust out the paper. "Message for you from the *Mountain Echo*. They just called. I know your phone isn't hooked up yet so I took the liberty of asking what they wanted. I hope you don't mind."

"No, not at all. By the way, how long does it take for Telco to get a phone hooked up around here anyway?"

She smiled knowingly. "Weeks sometimes, I'm afraid. We're kind of at the end of the line here, so they don't exactly have us on their priority list."

"WEEKS? Omigod. That's going to make work a challenge."

"I know. Trust me, I've been through it."

"And no cellphone service out here yet?"

"No, like I said, we're the end of the line. Anyway, Donna says she wants you to head over to the hospital protest to check in."

"Why? Has something happened?"

"No, I don't think so, or she would have said. Just wants you to keep on top of it, I guess."

"Okay, thanks Irene."

"How are you settling in?" Her tone was friendly, not snooping.

"Great. I think Shadowcat approves. He was getting tired of the gypsy life."

As if on cue, Shadowcat hopped off the bed and poked his nose around the bedroom door. "Oh, he is adorable, isn't he?" she said.

"As long as you don't cross him. Then he might kill you with a glare."

She laughed in a way that made me think of my grandma when she joked about the antics of her chickens.

The hospital parking lot looked like a cross between a MASH unit and a farmers' market. Two pickups were strategically parked on the street with their bedsheet banners framing the entrance. A neighbour had graciously allowed the protestors to set up a marquee tent on her lawn for shelter from the occasional shower or to serve up refreshments. I was impressed by the fact that Rosanna had kept all the hospital laneways and parking spaces free of protestors' vehicles. I had to park the wagon a block away, walking past the helipad with its postcard-perfect view of the Valhallas looming over the lake. Rosanna was the picture of busyness—making sure that protestors holding placards kept the hospital entrance free, chatting with the volunteer in the refreshment tent, or directing traffic.

This was someone you had to catch in motion so I quickened my pace in order to catch her eye. When she saw me, she stopped. "Oh, hello." She made a sweeping motion with her arm. "Welcome to D-Day."

I had my steno pad out. "So how's it going?"

"Well we got our media release out Friday afternoon, and as you can see, we're pretty well organized here."

"Friday afternoon? You may have to send it out again Monday morning. Friday's not a good day to try and get media attention."

She shrugged. "Easy. But as you're our local reporter, you get first scoop."

"I've already filed my story on the PHA meeting at Eldorado Hall. I can include a photo if you've got anything set up for me."

"You'll have to wait 'til next week. Once the rest of the media gets a chance to see our blurb, we're going to do a sacred circle."

"Sacred circle?"

"It's a First Nations idea. We get everyone to form a great big circle around the hospital, all holding hands. We have a Métis woman in the village who does smudges and traditional prayers, so she'll perform the ceremony, asking the spirits for their protection of this vital healing lodge." She must have noticed my eyebrows raising, though I tried to hide it. Her smile had me utterly disarmed, for the moment. "Think we're a little crazy?"

"I didn't say that. Wasn't even thinking it. Just wondering how it might look to the media, that's all."

"Listen, *all* of this country was originally Indian land. The Sa'wyshyn people here have a documented presence going back at least ten thousand years. Every summer UBC archeologists come out to do excavations in the lower valley. At very least we're honouring their presence on the landscape by inviting one of them to perform the ceremony."

"But you said the woman was Métis?"

"Part Sa'wyshyn, part French Canadian. Marie-Louise Tremblay. She also likes to be known as Cinnamon Bear."

"Oh. Well, I suppose it makes good theatre. The media does love a spectacle."

"That they do." She smiled again. I could tell I was dealing with a smart cookie. Yet when she spoke of the ceremony there was no sense of prevarication, no lack of sincerity. I noted to myself that—once again—one of Eldorado's key citizens was a woman. Fascinating.

"Anything else planned? Letter-writing campaigns, or—"

"Yes, that's already underway and we've contacted our MP Alan Kosiancic. Then there's—"

Her attention was diverted by what was obviously an argument that had suddenly risen in volume. Near the hospital doors, two protestors were madly gesticulating at one another. The argument was punctuated by a smoker's-lung cough from the woman and her occasional gravelly chuckle. "Excuse me," said Rosanna, "it seems I'm needed."

"Do you mind if I tag along?"

She shrugged again, tossing back her golden hair. "Why not? We've got nothing to hide."

A black man in his mid-fifties with greying dreadlocks was arguing with a woman about the same age. The woman had shoulder-length, mostly grey hair and glasses and wore a wool poncho. On her feet was a pair of beaded mukluks I'd almost have killed for. The man wore John Lennon spectacles beneath a deeply trenched brow. He spoke clearly and used a forefinger to punctuate the air as he made his points. His Jamaican accent was clear but softened by long years living in Canada, though peppered with Rastafarian slang. The woman was looking a bit cowed, unable to keep up with his verbal onslaught.

"Ay, I just do my part, yeah? Okay, Cinnamon Bear?" Sweeping his arm to indicate the group forming around their argument, he added: "I an' I here to help, yeah?"

Rosanna strode up, laying a hand on his shoulder. "What's the problem, Moss?"

He turned toward her and his hands spread open in a supplicating gesture. "I tell my sistren here, I an' I—everybody—do our part, yeah? She don't think I should do *my* part. My fuckin' contribution don't *matter* to her." He had a way of ending his sentences with a question, as if it were self-evident. Turning to Marie-Louise, he added: "Dis be true, yeah?"

Marie-Louise sighed loudly. "That's *not* what I said, Moss. That's not what I meant."

"Okay, okay," said Rosanna, raising her hands in truce. "From the beginning, now."

"He wants to do his own protest," Marie-Louise began. "He wants to—"

Moss threw up his hands dramatically. "Ay, Babylon! Downpression from I own sistren! She won't even let I *say* it! It *was* my idea, wasn't it? You sayin' I not allowed to fuckin' *tell* it?"

Marie-Louise held up her palms in surrender. "Okay, okay. Sorry Moss."

He didn't waste a millisecond. "Sista Rosanna, hear I, please. You know when I young cub I study in Catholic seminary, yeah?" He let the silence drop, waiting for a response. I took notes but could feel questions forming in the back of my mind already about this man.

Rosanna nodded. "Of course, Moss. I've known you since I was a kid." Marie-Louise was busy rolling a cigarette from a handcrafted leather pouch, fingers trembling a little.

"Now I regular no more in church, but you know I never lie, yeah? I take on Jah spirit—justice—not Babylon law since I come to Canada." I could sense him making an effort to tone down his language, wrestling down the tempest inside him. "In seminary I learnt church fathers go down on dey knees six times a day to Virgin Mary. I learnt inity of all who praise Jah—Christian, Muslim, Rastaman. Jah spirit de same in all.

Some, dey smoke holy herb in praise, some, dey make holy pilgrimage, yeah?"

"Sure, Moss. I understand," Rosanna said. "How can I help?"

"So I do my own protest for I an' I." Again he indicated the group with a wave. "I go on my knees all de way to Newcombe, just like dey do at shrines, like Camino de Santiago. Ay! Dat gotta get de fuckin' government's attention—pardon I French! De Lion of Judah in de Mountains!" He smacked his fist into an open palm to seal his argument, as if it were irrefutable.

For once Rosanna looked rattled. "But Moss, that's over one hundred kilometres—sixty miles! It could be dangerous on these narrow mountain roads. What if someone runs over you because they can't see you down on your knees?"

He flashed a satisfied grin of yellowed, worn-down teeth. "Ah, Sista Rosanna, all is irie! Don't worry! I carry own banner to de walls of Babylon—" He spread out his arms like a prophet calling down fire from heaven. "SAVE OUR ER WARD, I write, in big red letters, yeah?"

"Do you have support for this, uh—tactic?" I asked.

He looked puzzled momentarily. I could see the tumblers rolling behind his eyes, searching for a plausible answer. Marie-Louise chuckled as she exhaled a long draught of smoke. He glared at her. "Never you mind, sistren. I know *somebody* help I even if you won't. Everyone knows I. Dey ain't gonna let I go hungry nor thirsty."

Marie-Louise sighed through a cloud of smoke. "I didn't *say* I wouldn't help, Moss. Don't put words in my mouth."

Rosanna reached out to hold him gently at arm's length. "Moss, we love you. Of course we wouldn't let you go out on the road unsupported."

A relieved grin spread across his face. "I'se known you since you was a kitten, Sista Rosanna. Always said you'se one o' de good ones."

"I know. And it's *great* that you want to help, to offer such a—noble gesture. But—"

Marie-Louise chimed in. "But to some people it might look a little *crazy*."

It was exactly the wrong thing to say. Rosanna flashed her a steel-cutting glare. Moss had wrenched himself loose of Rosanna to turn on Marie-Louise. "SEE! See what I say?! She don't WANT I fuckin' contribution. Ay, great for you, yeah? You got native blood, you do *all* da ceremonies, queen o' protests an' blockades round here! You tellin' I dis sacrifice useless?"

Marie-Louise had stopped chuckling and stubbed out her cigarette on the sidewalk. "Listen, Moss. I'm sorry, okay? I've done some crazy shit myself in the name of protests. Nothing violent or destructive; I draw the line at that. But crazy if you're John or Jane Suburban. So, whatever, Moss. You wanna do it, you go ahead; nobody here'll stop you."

Rosanna was trying to signal her with quick jerks of her head to shut up already. Finally Marie-Louise gave her the out she needed. "Listen, I'm just gonna go home for lunch. The grandkids are coming over so I gotta get some soup on."

I could sense weight lifting from Rosanna's shoulders. "Moss, I understand this is important to you. It's really very, very generous of you. But I hope you'll sleep on it first before you decide to go ahead. Please—"

"I mind made up, Sista. Moses on de shores of de Red Sea."

Rosanna raised a palm and made a soothing gesture. "Okay, fine. But promise me this—check in with me before you start. I want to make sure you don't die of thirst or starvation on the road. Promise me? Please?" For effect she flashed her sweetest smile at him. I had to smile at this gambit; it was clearly her last resort.

It was all he needed. He clapped a fist to his breast. "Sista Rosanna, for you, anyting. *Anyting.* I promise."

"And please Moss, get some knee pads. You may be forever young at heart but you're no young buck anymore. I don't want you ruining your knees."

He bowed to her. "Like I say, for you, Sista, anyting."

As we left him there I didn't know whether to laugh or shake my head. When we were a safe distance away, I had to ask: "You really want to let him do this?"

She shook her head, resigned. "What can I do? You heard him. He's made up his mind."

I whistled. "Man, wait 'til the big media gets hold of that. They'll have a field day. 'Protestor Goes Crazy Over ER

Cutbacks.'" I used my fingers to frame the imaginary headlines in quotes. "'Village Idiot on His Knees in Hospital Protest.'"

It was the first time she lost patience with me. "Fuck, Roy, you think I don't know that?" For once, she looked lost, out of her element.

"So what are you going to do?"

She looked at me briefly, then far past my shoulder into the mountainside. "I'm not sure. I can't let Moss go without support. But maybe I can find a way to limit the collateral damage. I'll have to think about it awhile."

"What can you tell me about Moss? Is he mentally unstable?"

She gave me an expression that was half rebuke, half despair. "I don't think I'm qualified to make that judgment. Besides, he's an old family friend. Like he said, I've known him since I was a girl. And I'm not in the habit of calling old friends crazy even if they are a little bit off the beam."

"What can you tell me about him?" I pressed.

"His real name is Lucas Brown. He came here from Jamaica in the early seventies."

"But not, obviously, as one of the draft dodgers."

"They prefer to be known as draft *resisters* or conscientious objectors," she corrects me sharply. "My dad was one."

I wince. "Oops, sorry."

"We used to call Moss 'Unlucky Luke.' He's the only person I've ever known who had two—not one, but two—winning lottery tickets and lost *both* of them. But to me he's always been Moss. He lives about as close to the bone as you can get. But I don't think he really minds."

"Seems to be the general lifestyle around here. But why 'Moss'?"

"When my sister and I were little girls we used to giggle when we saw his dreads. 'Look at the man with moss on his head,' we used to joke. That is, 'til Mom caught us one day and gave us a tongue-lashing. But he liked us, so he didn't seem to mind. We'd reach up to play with his dreads and he'd just chuckle. So the name stuck. Now, with the grey creeping in, it actually does look like the moss you see on fir trees around here."

"But a Catholic Rastafarian? Isn't that a recipe for cognitive dissonance? How the hell do you reconcile the contradictions between those two faiths?"

"Well you'd have to ask him about that sometime. All I know is, he spent a couple of years in a Catholic seminary as a young man, thinking he might enter the priesthood. But his family was Rastafarian. I guess if you grow up in Jamaica that passes for post-adolescent rebellion. He's kind of somewhere in the middle now. Like he said, he believes all religions are one."

"Still, maybe it's left him a little off the beam? And ganja as a sacred herb was just a little too hard to give up?"

"He may be 'off the beam' as you say but totally harmless. He's really a very sweet man. He'd wade through a swamp to help a neighbour and he was very kind to my sister and me. And don't make the mistake of thinking him stupid just because of his oddball English."

"Why would I do that?"

She ignored the question. "Listen, I hope you'll find a way to write about this in a sensitive manner. I don't know you, so I'm asking it as a favour. Writing about the Rastafarian eccentric who plans to crawl to Newcombe on his knees could sink us. And we really can't afford to lose this one. If the hospital goes, the community goes with it."

"Look, I never was cool with tabloid sensationalism, or reducing people to stereotypes just so they can be ridiculed. That's not journalism. I figure, if someone feels strongly enough about something to put in the time and the effort, they deserve respect. Whether that's building a better battery or standing on a protest line for something they believe in, no matter how wacky it may seem to others. As long as they don't hurt anyone." I always was a sucker for a pretty face. But I really meant it.

She grasped my hand lightly. "Thank you. Thanks so much. Now if you'll excuse me...." And with that she strode off, heading in the direction of Marie-Louise's house.

By this point in the day my espresso meter was reading dangerously low so it was time to find the nearest barista. And I wanted to take some time to type out my notes from the interview with Rosanna. I considered going to the Blue Moose but was feeling like I'd already filled my eccentric quotient for the day. Zelda the Sarcastic Server would have to practise her jabs on someone else for now. The Cracked Teapot in Elkville was only a few minutes' drive anyway, following the twisting goat track of highway along the lakeshore. I had to remind myself to pay attention; the view of the lake nestled in glacial peaks was so stunning.

The Cracked Teapot was located in one of Elkville's oldest buildings on its main drag, which doubled as the highway going through town. Like the heritage buildings of Eldorado's downtown it had a similar wooden construction with the façade rising above the roof peak. Although in this case there was a second story apartment with two windows full of aloe vera and jade plants over-spilling their pots. Vintage-style awnings swooped down over the windows that flanked the doorway, which was recessed into the building.

I had to chuckle as I walked in and the little brass bell jangled. I had an instant memory flashback to the country stores I used to frequent as a kid, now mostly gone and forgotten in the rush to giant, ugly, sterile box stores. I remembered being maybe eight years old, sent on an errand for milk and bread by my mother. It was a late summer afternoon. Dust motes like clouds of fireflies made the air softly alive in slanting sunlight. The front step of wood laths was worn concave just as it was at the Teapot now. I remember closing the screen door carefully behind me as I entered the single-room store. It may as well have been the portal to another planet. I found myself suddenly transported, unable to move. Strategically, the store owner had placed all the candy in the front row of goods nearest the door. There were jars stuffed with mini-planets of jawbreakers, squares of bubblegum, toffee, and cellophane-wrapped suckers—a rainbow splash of colours that fell across my vision like a magic spell. Next thing I know, I'm halfway home, my cheeks bulging like a squirrel's when it hits me: "A quart of milk and a loaf of bread," my mother said. "And with the *change*, you can buy one or two candies." It was as if a thundercloud had instantly blotted out the sun. I felt the spirit drain out of me, my veins filling with dread. I knew what was coming when I got home. I spent the rest of the day—if not the entire week, it's hard to recall exactly—grounded, shut inside my room. It was the last errand she entrusted me with. I've been bad at handling money ever since. In fairness to my mother, few of us with the writers' gene are financial wizards anyway.

Somehow the traumatic associations of the memory had fallen away, leaving me with my impressions of that country store and its decrepit but powerful magic. I found myself smiling involuntarily as I walked up to the counter to order. My eyes gravitated toward the glistening chrome espresso machine just behind. The man behind the counter was probably in his early forties, handsome-featured with dark wavy hair tied in a ponytail beneath a ball cap. The first hints of grey were coming in. He had a three-day growth of whiskers that shaded his jaw. The smile he offered was warm and genuine. It was something I was still getting used to after the city, where a server's smile was paper-thin—the bare minimum required to keep the job and earn tips. He seemed to want to start with conversation before business.

"Hi, how are ya? I saw you here the other day. Just visiting or—?"

I shrugged. "Not quite sure yet. I'm doing some work for the *Mountain Echo*, so we'll see how it goes."

"Oh? What's the story?"

"Donna has me covering the hospital protest."

"Yeah, I heard about that." He shook his head. "Sure hope they don't shut down the ER. We'd really be in trouble here."

"Well at this point it's hard to say what will happen. PHA says it's only a reduction of ER hours and lab services, but who knows?"

He nodded sagely. "Thin edge of the wedge."

"That seems to be the common opinion."

He held out a hand. "By the way, I'm Mark."

"Roy. Roy Breen."

At this point a woman of short stature and slim build, with her hair wrapped up in a colourful scarf, came out of the kitchen. What tufts of hair were poking out were mid-blonde and curly and her eyes were pale blue framed by pale, almost white eyebrows. She had elfin features that reminded me somewhat of Jane. The way she leaned into Mark it was obvious they were a couple. She too smiled as if she meant it.

"This is my wife Ivy."

She wiped a wet hand on her apron and held it out to me. "Ivy Jones. Cook, dishwasher, caterer, and all-round mystic."

"But not baker?" I'd noticed a well-stocked display case full of home-baked goods. Key lime pie, avocado squares, double-chocolate brownies, even gluten-free cookies. And something called Bliss Balls. I wasn't going to ask—yet.

She looked approvingly at Mark. "No, actually Mark is the better baker here."

"You two own the place?"

"Well not the building," explained Mark. "That belongs to a long-timer here who calls himself Barn Owl. People just call him Owl. Been here since the sixties. We rent the space but own the business."

"Why Barn Owl? For his annoying voice, or is he just annoying generally?"

They both laughed. "No, it's ironic," explained Mark. "Actually he's quite soft-spoken. Not very talkative at all."

Ivy smiled. "Bit of an eccentric but we love him. You should see the flowerbeds he plants outside every spring. Gorgeous."

It seemed that between the preponderance of women and eccentrics, these two little villages might just be the most unique place I'd ever lived. "Speaking of eccentrics, you seem to have cornered the market here. I've only just got here and already I've met a few. If you don't mind me saying so."

Mark grinned. "That's true. Makes life interesting."

Ivy's brow had clouded slightly. "I guess it all depends on your notion of normalcy."

I held up my palms. "Don't worry, I have no attachment to normalcy!"

She was smiling again. "People come here because they see a place where they're free to be themselves. They don't have to worry about impressing the Joneses, if you'll pardon the pun. It might look weird to the outside world, but hey, I figure, if they're not hurting anyone, more power to them." It was obvious she had an affection for the people she saw coming into her restaurant every day.

"Works for me."

"What can I get you?" Mark asked, palms flat on the counter.

"What's your espresso roast?"

He gestured at his bean grinder, which was full to the brim with shiny black beans. "Our coffee comes roasted fresh weekly from Newcombe, a local company called Black Bear Coffee. They donate five percent of their annual profits to the Spirit Bear Conservancy."

"Impressive. Dark and nutty or light and fruity?" My taste buds had been spoiled forever by Vancouver's highly competitive coffee scene.

"Dark and nutty, I'd say. If you want I can pull you a sample." He was noisily working the lever to measure out a portion of ground coffee. "The Kootenays has some of the best coffee anywhere."

I decided I'd let that one pass 'til I'd had a chance to see for myself. When I left Newcombe fifteen years ago, the coffee scene had still been nascent. Only the Italian restaurant and one or two others even had an espresso machine. Now, judging by the various signs I'd seen while driving up here, practically every village had its own coffee roaster. Definitely a good sign. I could get to like this place.

Chapter Four

It was time to check in at the *Echo*, catch up on my email, and do some Web browsing. The sky was holding fast the memory of summer's rich blue—another glorious fall day. The temperature had dropped so the breeze carried the first bite of winter. An incredible maple on the lot kitty-corner from the *Echo* was ablaze in yellow gold. Kids were running around the tree, laughing and screaming, tossing up its fallen leaves. One of those scenes lit in a warm glow that instantly takes you back to your own childhood.

Donna was at her desk near the back of the office, Lance the usual fixture at his screen behind the front counter. His bearded Cheshire grin lit up when he saw me. "Hey! How's it going Roy?"

"Great! Just came in to do a little Web surfing and catch up on emails."

He pointed to the desk opposite him. "Knock yourself out."

I plugged in the Ethernet cable and started scrolling. Donna looked up from her laptop, flashing her million-dollar grin. "So how's it going over at the hospital?"

I told her about the encounter with Moss, how impressed I was by the way Rosanna held everything together, and about meeting Marie-Louise, a.k.a. Cinnamon Bear. "I also met Mark and Ivy at the Cracked Teapot. Told them I figured this place has the market cornered on eccentrics."

Lance guffawed in his usual hearty manner. "You could say that. We don't really have criminals here, just lovable oddballs."

"Some more lovable than others," Donna said. "You do get domestic violence in the hard-drinking families here."

"Sure," I agreed. "What can you tell me about Marie-Louise? She seems like another interesting character."

"Clan mother for the Sa'wyshyn people," Donna said. "Or what's left of it. Most of them ended up south of the border in the Colville Consolidated Tribes reserve."

"Clan mother?" I asked. "Is that like a band chief?"

"No, her position is ceremonial," Donna explained. "The Sa'wyshyn chief and official spokesperson is Winona Jacks, or Salmon Mother, as she's known by the tribe. Before the dams went in salmon was one of their staple foods."

"Back up a bit—why did most of them end up in Colville?"

"They'd been declared 'extinct' by the BC government in the early sixties—conveniently enough, while Premier 'Wacky' Bennett was negotiating the Columbia River dam treaty with the States. That meant zero compensation for their land. They've been fighting the government of Canada ever since for recognition of status. But no luck so far."

"So how many are there here in the valley?"

"About a half dozen. They have a permanent camp in the south valley."

"That few? Sounds like we did a good job of wiping them out."

"For a few decades there were none of them left here, only at Colville. Then when the government tried to put a road through an ancestral burial ground about fifteen years ago, one of the older clan mothers and some supporters came up and occupied the site. Forced the government to a showdown and got their burial grounds protected. They've been a steady presence here ever since."

"What can you tell me about Cinnamon Bear—I mean, Marie-Louise?"

"Her father was a French Canadian, Yves Tremblay, who'd come west to work in logging. Met her mother on a trip south of the border. Her parents split up when she was three and her mother brought her up in Colville. She and her sister left home in their teens to try and track down their father in Quebec. Ended up living with relatives there for awhile and learning the language. Then during the Vietnam War, Marie-Louise volunteered to go over and help out with the orphanages in Saigon. You know that old newsreel footage of them evacuating the American embassy by helicopter? Well she and her sister Claudette were evacuated at the same time. The incredible thing was, the two women said: '*Jamais sans nos enfants*. Not without our children. We won't leave without them.' They refused to leave the Vietnamese kids at the orphanage. They knew genocide was brewing once the North Vietnamese took over. Somehow they managed to call on the right friends in the Canadian embassy to get a chopper load of orphans out of the country. They were in all the evening news shows of the day—CBS, NBC, the CBC, BBC...."

"My God, what a story! Wish I'd been there to break that one."

Donna laughed. "You're about fifteen years too young."

"Did she get the Order of Canada for that?"

Donna shook her head sadly. "No, I'm afraid not."

"A travesty. So what's she done since then? That was a long time ago."

"Mostly she's been an environmental activist since then. She's one of the veterans of logging blockades in the valley. The cops all know her on a first-name basis. I think they breathe a sigh of relief when they roll into a protest site and see her there."

"Why? Why her of all the protestors?"

"She has a way of grounding people so things don't get out of hand. She's absolutely against violence or tree spiking. Won't even let protestors damage logging machinery. So when cops see her it's like, 'Oh, Marie-Louise is here. This'll be fine.'"

"I guess the fact she's Métis doesn't hurt either," I guessed.

"It would if we were in Manitoba where I come from," Lance cut in. "There's been more than a few Métis women taken for 'midnight rides' in the dead of winter by cops."

"Still," continued Donna, "around here it makes her a hot potato politically. For awhile there she was the official spokesperson for the Sa'wyshyn, so that probably helps."

"Even though they don't have official status under the Indian Act?"

"Cops mostly don't want to touch anything First Nations around here with a ten-foot pole. Bad PR. Plenty of white bodies to drag off the blockades anyway," she laughed.

"You said, 'for awhile there' she was official spokesperson?"

"Yeah, they had an internal power struggle," Lance cut in. "Some of them were supporters of Winona Jacks, some of them supported Marie-Louise. When the dust settled, Jacks came out on top."

"How do you have a power struggle with only six people in the room?" I asked.

Lance chuckled but withered under the glare Donna shot him. "Before we start pointing fingers we better take a look at our own politics."

"Oh, yeah," I agreed. "I'd say ours takes the Machiavelli Prize any day."

The phone rang. Of course, it was always ringing in this office. I was amazed we'd been able to have an entire conversation without being interrupted. From the tone of Donna's urgent "Uh-huhs" on the phone I could tell something was up. I tried to get through a few emails on my list before she hung up. When she did she looked straight at me. "You better get over there. Things are heating up. The PHA removal crew for the x-ray machine just arrived."

"Mind if I leave my laptop here? I'll just take my notepad and camera."

"Sure, no problem."

"Before I go, have you seen any official PHA media releases yet?"

Donna held up a forefinger. "Just a second." She scrolled down the *Mountain Echo* inbox. "Ah! Here it is!" A brief pause while she speed-read it. "Aw, shit, nothing here really. Basically a repeat of what they told us at the public meeting."

I threw my jacket on and grabbed my briefcase. "So they've shown up with a removal truck without telling anyone?"

"Yep. Looks that way."

"Good thing Rosanna set up a 24/7 lab watch then."

I managed to find my usual parking spot on the street a block away from the hospital. I found myself jogging but slowed to a fast stride near the hospital parking lot. On the west side of the hospital complex was the lab. Its doors were now blocked by a thick throng of protestors. Two disgruntled-looking young men stood apart from the group, listening as they were addressed by Rosanna, who stood at the head of the group. As I got closer I could tell the younger of the men, who had a dark stubble of moustache and chin beard and thick unruly hair, was held in thrall by her looks. The other man, probably no more than thirty-five, was overweight and had ginger-coloured hair and eyebrows but was clean-shaven. His complexion was flushed as if in a permanent state of excitement. He seemed to be building a head of steam but was patiently waiting for Rosanna to finish.

"I know you guys are just here to do a job, I get that," she was saying. "But you have to appreciate *our* point of view. We have a lot of seniors here in the village and if they have to drive three or four hours just for an x-ray it's a major hassle for them. Some won't—or can't—do it. Besides, for the ER, it's a vital diagnostic tool. With a quick x-ray, they can tell the difference between a sprain, a minor fracture, or a major one requiring immediate surgery." She gestured to the field beside the lab building. "That's why we have a helipad here."

The ginger-haired man wasn't impressed. "Look, lady. You got one thing right: We have a job to do. Now are you gonna get outta our way and let us do it, or not?"

"Listen—what was your name?" she asked.

"Jim. Jim Milowski. And this is Warren Heinz," he said, indicating the younger man.

"Listen, Jim. We don't want any trouble. But we *can't* let you take this x-ray machine away. For one thing, it was community fundraising that bought this machine."

Several protestors raised their fists. "Yeah! It belongs to US!"

I didn't see Moss anywhere. I wondered if he'd already begun his "protest crawl."

"Save money or save lives!" shouted another, repeating one of the slogans painted on the placards bobbing above the small crowd. Tom Bombadil was in the throng, his beard and long greying hair unmistakable.

"Stop PHA thievery!" came still another cry.

Rosanna motioned for the crowd to settle down. "People! PEOPLE! PLEASE! Let's keep this civil." Tom raised his arms too, a jean-clad Moses trying to part a small pool of humanity as he moved toward the front.

"Listen, Jim. Listen, Warren," he said, his reedy voice seemingly incapable of overt rage. "I know it must be tough for young guys like you to get decent jobs nowadays. All we want—"

"Yeah," snapped Jim. "And I'm not about to screw it up. So PLEASE get out of our way."

Tom's soft demeanour recoiled slightly at the harshness of the man's tone. "Jim. Warren. Please. We don't want any—"

Suddenly Jim turned on his heel, pulling Warren behind him. They walked over to the entrance ramp to the ER and strode inside. Rosanna hustled after them but at a respectful distance. "Just stay here with everybody, will you Tom?" she said. Tom nodded. About this time, I noticed Marie-Louise sauntering up, a hand-rolled cigarette dangling from her fingers.

"What's going on?"

"They're here to steal our x-ray machine!" shouted one of the protestors.

"Fuckin' government thieves!" yelled another.

Marie-Louise chuckled in her gravelly way. "Typical. Things always get exciting when I leave." She didn't seem the least perturbed; like an old war vet, she'd seen it all before.

The group had shifted toward the ER ramp. "Everyone!" shouted Tom, moving to intercept the crowd. "We have to keep this entrance clear. Besides we need to protect the lab— we can block *those* doors. So let's move over there and just wait for Rosanna." The crowd muttered a little but shifted back into place at the lab doors.

The wait soon grew oppressive. Time dragged its heels the way it does when everyone is tense and too much is at stake. I checked my watch. Already fifteen minutes had passed. Finally the ER doors swung open and Jim stalked out with Warren trailing shortly behind. Jim's face had grown thrush-red. Warren looked nervous, completely out of his element. They swept past the crowd outside the lab doors and headed toward the utility van with the PHA logo emblazoned on each side. "Fucking protestors," I could hear Jim mutter. This was followed by the concussive slam of the driver's door as he climbed inside. Warren was careful to close his door more quietly. He watched the protestors nervously through the passenger-side window.

Now Rosanna emerged from the ER entrance. It was hard to read her expression; she was good at maintaining a blank mask in such situations. Tom stepped up, his tone wavering on a nerve's edge. "So—what, uh—what happened?"

"They wanted to talk to the hospital administrator but he's away today. So they tried to buttonhole the office manager at the front desk. Handed her their paperwork. Asked if she'd let them take the x-ray equipment out through the ER so they could avoid the protestors at the lab doors. She told them they aren't allowed to block the ER entrance to remove the equipment. The bigger guy—Jim—argued that they'd only be an hour or less getting it out. They've got air jacks, tools, and stuff in the van. She was insistent. Said no way could they block the ER ramp or reception area for five minutes, never mind an hour. He tried to say, okay, maybe a half hour. Maybe less. But she said no way—against hospital regulations. But as *we're* not blocking any vital entrances, we can stay," Rosanna concluded.

"Is that really a hospital regulation?" I asked Tom.

"I think so," Rosanna shrugged. "I don't know, really. I suspect the office manager is on our side."

A cheer went up from the small crowd. "Yeah!" "Take that, PHA!" "Woo-hoo!"

She was already lifting her palms in a cautioning gesture. "People, it's not over yet. They have the paperwork from PHA. That means, legally speaking, they have the right to take our equipment."

"Legally?" one woman chimed in. "How is it legal to steal someone else's equipment?"

"Not if I have any fucking thing to say about it," growled one man.

Tom's voice was smooth as calfskin. "Please, Fred. Take it easy."

The two PHA men seemed to be arguing between themselves. Their voices were getting louder, though not quite audible through the van's metal and glass. Finally the passenger door opened and a reluctant Warren shuffled up to Rosanna, as if being forcibly pushed along by Jim's glare. "I—uh. I'm not used to this kinda shit—uh, what was your name?"

"Rosanna. Rosanna Yale."

Warren was having trouble meeting her gaze. "See, uh. We got a baby on the way, the wife and me. I really need this job, see."

"Well then," said Rosanna gently, "you can imagine what it would be like if your wife had problems when the baby came and you lived here with no 24/7 ER."

"Yeah, I guess I can," said Warren. "But what can I do? I'm stuck between a rock and a hard place here. I guess what I'm sayin' is, if we could just please do what we came here to do we'll be gone and never bother you again." Jim had rolled down his window and was obviously listening.

"But that's just the trouble, isn't it? If it's not you, it'll be someone else PHA hires to do the job, won't it? If not this time then next time. We have to draw a line in the sand. We already lost our acute care beds last year. It's nothing personal, Warren. Nobody here wants you to lose your job. But we can't afford to lose our ER either."

Warren seemed baffled by this, mesmerized by her pale green eyes. "Well, I—uh, sure, but…."

"WARREN!" It was Jim's voice, stentorian, angry. "Get over here, NOW! This is bullshit. Waste of time. We're leaving!"

Warren shrugged so deeply his neck momentarily disappeared. "Sorry, gotta go. Sorry."

"Don't think this is over!" shouted Jim. "We have a job to do and we're going to *do* it!"

Once the van had turned around and left the parking lot, the crowd erupted in cheers. A few grasped each other by the elbows and danced around the tarmac. Marie-Louise looked amused. She was rolling another smoke. Rosanna stood beside her, watching the van leave.

Marie-Louise was grim now. "He's right, y'know. It isn't over."

"Oh, don't I know it," said Rosanna. "We'll double the volunteers on the night watch from now on." She turned to the crowd. "Listen up, everybody. I need two extra volunteers for tonight's lab vigil. Just check in with Tom and he'll sign you up. He'll be your shift foreman tonight. Please follow his directions." Next she turned to me. "Roy, you may not want to stay. This could be hours or it could be days. There's no way of knowing. As soon as we know we'll call the *Echo*. Okay?"

"Sure, Rosanna. Hang in there." I meant it. The protestors were clearly in good hands, between Rosanna and Tom.

I decided to grab an early dinner at the Teapot and then stop in at the *Echo* office on my way home. By now only one of Donna and Lance's two vehicles was still parked outside. Most likely it was Donna's; once the newspaper was sent off to press she still had bookkeeping work to do. I was just hauling myself out of the car when I saw a tall, shapely woman with short, bobbed black hair walking toward me on the sidewalk. "Omigod," I muttered. "It's Zelda the Sarcastic Server." But before I could zip inside the office, I heard her call me.

"HEY! Hey, you're that new reporter in town, aren't you?"

I was trapped. "Yep, that's me."

She strode up to me with the gait of a power walker. "I'm just closing up shop and heading home. I don't think we formally met. What was your name?"

"Breen. Roy Breen. Pleased—to meet you. Word gets around fast."

"Well as Mayor Miller says, our entire population is 796—when everyone is home." She grinned. It was hard to know if she found it funny or was sizing me up somehow. One of those kinds of grins—attractive, but sharp enough to cut paper. "I heard something today in the bistro that might interest you." She grinned again, as if baiting the hook.

"Okay ... what would that be?"

"You're covering the hospital blockade, aren't you?"

"Well it's not exactly a blockade, but yes, I am."

"And I'm not exactly a friend of protestors. Bunch of jerk-offs if you ask me. But in this case, PHA is messing with our hospital. And *that* pisses me off."

"Great! So…?"

"So, those two guys with the PHA truck came into my bistro for lunch this afternoon, after they'd been to the hospital."

"I'm sorry, but I have to take this down." I hauled out my notepad.

"Of course. Anyway, they asked to use my phone. I said, sure, just a few minutes. Don't hold up my business. The bigger guy did all the talking. Sounded like he was arguing with his boss. 'But they won't move!' he was shouting. I told him, 'Hey, keep it down, will ya? This isn't a bar!' Finally he hung up, after about ten minutes. I was some pissed, I can tell you. I heard him tell the other guy: 'We have to stay 'til the job is done. Even if it means staying all night.'" She chuckled. "The other guy damn near fainted."

I was scribbling furiously. She was already starting to walk away. "Hey, thanks Zelda."

She threw that razorback grin over her shoulder at me. "Don't worry. You don't owe me any favours. We're not buddies now. Just come in and buy an espresso and a sandwich once in awhile. But don't spend all day taking up one of my tables."

"Thanks, Zelda, I won't."

I poked my head in the *Echo* door. Sure enough, Donna was ensconced at the bookkeeping computer next to her regular station, sorting out receipts and making entries. She flashed me her smile when she saw me. "Hi! What's up?"

"Sounds like PHA is gonna make their crew push through the night to try and take out the x-ray equipment. Thing is, the poor buggers don't know Rosanna has a 24/7 watch set up."

"What do you want to do?"

"I'd like to be there when the confrontation goes down. That way those PHA guys can't pull anything fishy. Mind you, it's only the one guy I'm worried about."

"You think so?"

"Yeah. I'll have to fill you in later. Right now I need to arrange for someone to feed my cat. This could turn into an all-nighter. Any ideas?"

"Well I'm kinda busy and Lance has already gone home. What about Jane?"

I slapped my forehead. "Of course! Would you mind if I use your phone?"

She had on that smile women get when they sense romantic possibilities. "Well she only lives a couple of blocks away, and seeing as you'll have to give her your key anyway, you may as well go knock on her door. 618 Galway Street."

"Thanks Donna!"

I let the door close itself and hustled down the street. Galway intersected with main street, so I turned right and sprinted the rest of the way. It was a small cottage of a place with a compact deck on the front and a single living room window facing the street. The main door was around the back, as seemed to be the case with so many houses here. There was a roofed porch over the entrance door and firewood stacked beneath its canopy. It took only a minute for her to answer my knock, but I was still a little out of breath. She looked a little alarmed but this was soon replaced by an expression of pleasant surprise.

"Hi, how are you?" she said. "Is everything okay? You look a little flushed."

"I—I've got a story I have to cover that could take all night."

Her eyebrows raised. "Really? To do with the hospital?"

"Yeah. PHA is going to try to take out the x-ray machine tonight. Just got a tip."

"What can I do to help?"

"Would you mind terribly driving out to my place to feed Shadowcat? He's pretty fussy about getting fed on time. If I don't, I'll get the evil eye for the next three days. If I leave out dry kibble he just ignores it. Voluntary starvation is his way of punishing me. Besides, he gets lonely if I'm away too long."

She laughed in her wonderfully gentle way. "I can see how that would be tough to deal with. Sure, I'll gladly do that."

"You can take my car if you want, save your gas."

She chuckled. "No, that's fine. Once I'm done that, I'll check in at the hospital if it's not too late. I've got some cookie dough I could bake up in a hurry. I could bring some tea too."

I reached out and lightly touched her shoulder. "You are an angel. Thank you!"

"Don't be silly. Glad to do it. See you later."

The autumn darkness fell like a hammer. The irregular outline of the Valhalla range was just distinguishable from the sky above it, a shadow presence anchoring the lake. As I walked down the street from my car I could see a bonfire burning at the edge of the helipad. A few people were huddled around it drinking from travel mugs. Marie-Louise was there in her wool poncho, smoking as usual. As I walked up I could tell it wasn't her usual blend—more like Kootenay Green or whatever they were calling locally grown pot these days. She passed it around. The man named Fred held the joint up to me. "No thanks," I said. "Love to, but I may have a long night ahead of me. I just find it makes time drag out too long. And then I fall asleep. Which is great when you're watching a movie, but…."

"Have a seat." Marie-Louise indicated a folding deck chair beside her.

"Why are you guys out here? Aren't you going to miss the PHA boys if they come?"

Her gravelly chuckle rumbled. "We're the relief shift. We go on in half an hour. So it's a chance to get loose before we have to sit the rest of the night outside the lab." She held up the remainder of the joint. "Besides, I don't think they'd be too keen on us smoking this inside."

"True. But haven't you already been here most of the day?"

"Yeah I have. But I've been on a lot longer occupations than this one. I'm used to it."

"You'll have to tell me about it sometime."

"Now's as good a time as any," she chuckled.

"Okay, then. What was your longest-running protest?"

She laughed, as if at an inside joke, took a sip of her tea. "Funny you should put it that way—running. Though it wasn't so much running as *walking* across Canada. And in my shape, you can imagine how long *that* took."

"No I can't actually. Can you give me a clue?"

"Two hundred and ten days in 1997. I called it the Water Walk. I flew out to my dad's family farm in Quebec and then turned around and started walking back home. I was in much better shape then, as you can imagine." She shrugged, patting her middle. "What can I say? Middle-aged spread. I collected water samples from drinking water taps all across the country, especially on the Indian reserves. Had them tested to see how many of them actually met our federal drinking water regulations. Not that they're great as standards go."

"You must have had a support team?"

"Oh, yeah. I had my sister Claudette and her husband Jean-Remi following me in their van. Every few days they'd package up the samples and send them to the lab so the van wouldn't get too full. It rattled like a liquor store on wheels," she laughed. "We got a grant from West Coast Environmental Law to help cover the lab costs. The rest came from donations. People would stop on the highway, ask what I was doing, and offer support. 'Course, there were always a few blowhards who just stopped to scream abuse. I was glad for my brother-in-law's presence on those occasions. As soon as they saw him poke his big head out the window they buggered off pretty fast."

"What did you hope to accomplish?"

"I was trying to hold the government responsible for meeting its own drinking water standards. And in First Nations lore, water is sacred. When we pollute that, we're polluting our Mother." I could hear the capital "M" in mother as she spoke. "You'd be appalled at what we found in so many of the water samples. Some of it wasn't fit to drink, especially if you got a sample from a reserve. Theirs were some of the worst."

"So why wasn't this prime-time news, a cross-country odyssey like that? Why didn't I hear about it?"

She shrugged. "We did get some good coverage—mostly local radio and TV stations. Lots of small-town newspapers came out to snap my picture. But the big media mostly stayed away."

"Why do you think that is?"

She laughed. "Well, why do you think? To them I was just another crazy protestor. You gotta remember, Premier Glen Clark had branded protestors 'enemies of the state' over the Clayoquot protests just a few years earlier."

"A political knee-jerk reaction. Largest mass arrest of protestors in Canadian history to that point."

"And it helped save most of that forest. By comparison my lonely little Water Walk didn't rate. If they'd bothered to ask, they'd have seen I had a valid point. And we weren't waving a willow switch over the water samples either. They were all tested by accredited labs. But it's a little too close to the bone. It cuts right to the meat of the cosy relationship between government and industry. Not to mention the pathetic state of our Indian reserves. If they paid attention, they might have to actually enforce their water laws against some of the mining and logging companies. Or—God forbid—put decent drinking water on the reserves."

"Makes sense."

"There was some good news. When I got home here I took my final sample from Sapphire Lake. Not a trace of pollutants, not even septic field runoff. One of the last great pristine lakes left in the whole country."

I could see a tall feminine figure making her way toward the firelight. It was Rosanna. "We're just a few minutes from shift change. Marie-Louise, if you could please take two others and go check in with Tom? The others are welcome to stay, or not, as they please."

I stood up. "If you don't mind, I'd like to tag along."

Rosanna's hair looked preternaturally blonde in the firelight as she tossed it over her shoulder. "Great! The *Mountain Echo* is always welcome."

Tom looked tired around the eyes but his expression still glittered with the energy of commitment. He rose from the chairs lined up outside the lab to greet us. The short, round man known only as Fred had volunteered to sit the next shift with us. Like Tom he had a long beard that spread out across his chest and was threaded with grey. Even more than Tom he reminded me of a hobbit. He had the rosy cheeks, the short stature, the perpetually cheery expression, and the girth of someone who enjoys the good things in life. Tom sent the others out before conferring with Rosanna. One of them was a tall, powerfully built man with a shaved head and thick goatee. He wore a leather vest like a biker's outfit but otherwise looked harmless.

"No sign of the PHA van yet?" he asked in a rumbling baritone.

"No, not yet." Rosanna was looking tired. "I'm going to see if I can take a nap in the ER waiting room. Can you guys hold down the fort?"

Marie-Louise was grinning. "Aye, captain."

Rosanna laughed and poked her gently. "Oh, go on with you. I'm nobody's captain. Tom, you've been here all day. You should go home."

"So have you. I don't see *you* going home. Maybe you should."

She waved him off. "I'm fine. A nap will set me right."

She walked down the corridor with her long-legged stride and turned a corner toward the ER. "I think I'll catch some firelight," said Tom, walking in the opposite direction, where the double door that had been blocked earlier led to the parking lot. Fred settled heavily into a chair and started thumbing through a magazine. Marie-Louise was pulling her shawl close and shifted in her seat. "That gal is a real firecracker. A hometown daughter to be proud of."

"Rosanna? Popular, I imagine," I said.

The trademark gravelly chuckle. "Depends who you're talking about. The men all love her, of course. But not all the women."

I was surprised. "Why not?"

She was grinning. "Well, you're the scribe, work it out. She's blonde. She's beautiful. She's young. She's smart. That's more than enough for some women to hate her."

I felt stupid. "Oh, I see. But not you."

"Nah. That's one advantage of getting older. Sure, you lose your looks," she shrugged. "You can't keep the weight off. But you also don't have to deal with the sexual politics anymore. Christ, what a relief!"

I had to laugh, though not *too* hard.

Moving from firelight to the bluish artificial lighting in the hospital hallway was like entering another world. Where the mood by the bonfire had been celebratory, if not exactly in a party way, the serious atmosphere that hospitals engender dialled down the mood considerably. It was nearing midnight and I found myself nodding off. Fred was already snoozing. Marie-Louise had to poke him in the ribs occasionally when he started snoring.

I found myself struggling through a haze punctuated by voices. It was hard to tell at first exactly where I was—for a minute I thought somehow I'd slipped backward in time and was at the Eldorado Hall meeting. Voices were booming like the muffled sound of boulders driven down a streambed during spring runoff. Gradually I became aware that they were arguing and my head snapped awake. The voices were coming from outside the double doors at the end of the hallway. Marie-Louise was listening with a furrowed brow. Her hands were busy with knitting in her lap. I glanced at my watch. It was 1:15 a.m. I'd slept for over an hour.

"Listen, you idiots, I told you before, we have a work order here to carry out! Now step aside!" I recognized Jim Milowski's angry voice even through the doors.

"That x-ray equipment belongs to the community," a husky male voice was growling. "So get your fuckin' self outta here."

"How many times do I have to say it, you morons?"

Out of the corner of my eye I saw Rosanna's svelte form turn the corner and jog down the corridor toward the double doors, long hair flying like a blonde pennant. Marie-Louise continued knitting, her frown furrowing deeper. I rose and moved cautiously toward the door, switching on the recorder in my breast pocket. Rosanna pushed the panic bar carefully to open the door. It pushed against someone's back pressed up against the building. The protestor moved aside but gave little ground. There were a half-dozen protestors blocking the entrance. At the far edge of the crowd I could see Jim Milowski and Warren Heinz. Milowski was flushed like he'd been drinking. Heinz too looked a little the worse for wear from booze but kept carefully behind his larger sidekick.

Rosanna lifted her arms high. "Everybody! EVERYBODY! We need to calm down. I told you before, we need to show respect or we damage our own cause. I understand you're feeling—"

The tall man with the biker vest turned on her angrily. "Goddammit, Rosanna, these guys are trying to take away our lab equipment. Fucking government thieves!"

"Leon, please, calm down! This isn't going to help—"

Milowski shoved his way forward but was held back by

Leon. "Get this apeshit out of our way—now—or we'll call the cops. We have a job to do!"

Leon turned toward Rosanna, his powerful arm still extended toward Milowski. I caught a distinct whiff of alcohol on Leon's breath. "You're telling ME about respect?" he growled. "Listen to this asshole!"

Milowski was stabbing a stubby forefinger in the air toward Leon. "Yeah, listen to ME, you local yokels! If you don't get the fuck out of our way, I'm calling the cops. You really want that? I can have your asses hauled out of here in a nanosecond. I'm trying to be reasonable! Don't you have anything better to do than sit on protest lines? Lazy fuckers!"

It was exactly the wrong thing to say. Leon's free arm swung in a tensile arc that looked like it would break bone when it connected. It was headed straight for Milowski's face. Then as if in slow motion, I saw a thinner, jean-jacketed man's arm reach out and grab Leon's haymaker before it could connect. Leon reacted by swinging in a reverse direction, pinning what turned out to be Tom against the door. The poor man looked terrified. Heinz was anxiously backing off but Milowski was furious. "Aha! Attempted assault! That's it! I'm heading for the cop shop."

Leon snorted derisively. "Ha! Knock yourself out. They're only on call—nobody there after hours. More of your government cutbacks."

Another man I didn't recognize shoved his way into the fray. He was tall like Leon but had the build of a whippet— wiry and no less strong looking. His face too was thin, from the shape of the nose to the point of his chin, which was dark with stubble like the top of his head. "Leon!" he shouted. "We can't let them get the cops involved, or we lose!"

Rosanna held out a splayed palm. "Wait a minute! What are you saying, Carl?"

The whippet-faced man turned to her. Standing just beside Rosanna I could smell booze on his breath, too. "We keep them here 'til morning. Then we call O'Malley the lawyer."

Milowski looked alarmed for the first time. "KEEP us here? What the fuck are you talking about, you backwoods nutbar?"

Heinz was yanking at his sleeve. "Please, Jim. Let's just get outta here. Let's just leave. No cops, just get the fuck out of here. No job is worth this hassle."

For once Milowski listened to his partner and began backing away. A few more people had drifted over from the bonfire, curious about the uproar. The crowd pressed forward slightly. "Let them go, just let them go!" Rosanna shouted.

The crowd froze. Heinz and Milowski had retreated to the PHA van. Heinz slammed and locked the door, but Milowski stood on the running board with the door swung open. "FUCK YOU, you village idiots! I'm calling the cops RIGHT NOW!" With that he drew himself inside, slammed and locked the door and turned over the motor.

Leon was pulling people aside to get to the van. He leveraged his considerable bulk against the driver's side, and began trying to push the van over. Carl sprinted in a few strides to the opposite side of the van and took up the same posture. A rocking motion was established. From inside the van Milowski's screaming abuses could be heard. This seemed to set off a few more of the crowd, who crowded around the van to prevent it making any forward momentum. Tom stood at the lab entrance, looking confused, paralyzed. Marie-Louise was standing next to him, watching with a worried expression. Rosanna was yelling, "Stop, stop, STOP!" Milowski put the van in gear and lurched it forward, then backward, but wasn't willing to run anyone over. His face was a mask of frustration and rage.

"Aw, fuck this shit," growled Leon. He walked to the front of the van, pulled out a large hunting knife, and popped the van's hood latch. He reached inside, pried off a battery cable with the knife and the van's engine died as the vehicle lurched to a stop. Leon sheathed the knife and stood in front of the windshield, arms folded. Milowski now looked almost as scared as Heinz, who was visibly shaking. Milowski rolled down the driver's-side window. This time his tone was more cautious. "Okay, what now, country bumpkins? You going to attack us too?"

Carl emitted a high-pitched cackle, obviously done for effect. "Yeah, you just stumbled into *Deliverance* here. Gimme a break. All we want is for you to go away."

"I want to talk to the blonde woman, please."

Rosanna elbowed her way through the crowd to stand beside the driver's door. "You know I gotta report this to my boss," Milowski snarled.

She looked crestfallen. "Yes, I understand that. You have a choice about reporting it to the cops though."

"Oh, do I? We'll see about that."

"Because if you report it," she said coolly, "we'll tell the cops you tried to drive through a crowd of people with your work van. No one here has laid a finger on either of you." She turned toward the protestors. "And I have more people to back up my story than you do to back up yours."

I could see the colour darkening in Milowski's forehead. He knew she had him. There was a pause tight as high-tension wire while he considered. All eyes were on Rosanna and Milowski, wondering who would blink first. "Fine, fine, goddammit. All I'm asking is that you let Warren and me leave. It's been a helluva long day and I'd like to get back to my motel."

"Absolutely, Jim." She stepped back and addressed the crowd. "Everyone, please move aside so Jim and Warren can leave." She glared straight at Carl and Leon. "And I'm *warning* you, *nobody* lays a finger on these guys."

Leon shrugged. "Yeah, no problem. But I ain't letting them drive this van out of here. They can bloody well walk." He turned toward the two PHA men, who were delicately exiting the van. Leon pointed in a northerly direction. "It's less than a mile to the motel from here. Straight down the highway that runs through Eldorado. You can pick up your van tomorrow."

Warren's face flooded with relief at the excuse to make a hasty exit. He broke into a trot, with Jim keeping to a brisk stride not far behind, throwing anxious, angry looks over his shoulder every few metres. When they turned the corner of the block and were out of sight, Rosanna stepped up to Leon. Even with her considerable height he still towered over her.

"Who the FUCK made you king?" she said, stabbing his chest with a sharp forefinger. It was the first time I'd heard her swear so forcefully. Next she turned to the crowd. "And I thought I told everyone—NO BOOZE! Pot I don't mind, it actually makes people more peaceful. But booze! On a protest line! How STUPID can you get?" Her voice was cracking with her composure. Stress and fatigue were taking its toll. A few heads were hung in shame. Leon and Carl looked at one another but were unperturbed. A satisfied look of "mission accomplished" passed between them.

"You think we can just ask them nicely and they'll go away?" asked Carl. "Been there, done that. Doesn't work."

"I was in 'Nam," added Leon gruffly. "I've hardly said a word about it in thirty-five years. But I'm gonna tell ya, if it hadn't been for the grunts like me defying the command structure, we'd never have gotten outta that hellhole. You think My Lai was an isolated incident? Bullshit. We had commanders telling us every week to pull some stunt like that. If we hadn't fragged some of the bastards there'd have been a lot more My Lais happening. You wanna wait for the authorities to do the right thing? Good luck to ya."

"Leon, I asked you guys not to bring booze here," she answered.

"Booze or not, I would've done the same."

She paused. By the look in her eyes I could see she was searching for an effective counter-argument. "Leon, I totally respect your veteran status, and what you went through. And I'm grateful for your help here. But I just can't agree with any violence in protests. It puts us in direct conflict with the authorities and undermines everything we're trying to do. If this gets out, we could be in serious trouble."

"You don't wanna risk conflict, then stay home."

"Besides," added Carl, "nobody was hurt, not even the van."

Rosanna shook her head in disgust and pushed past the crowd. The lab doors closed behind her. Marie-Louise had been watching her closely and turned to follow her inside. I decided to follow. Rosanna had collapsed into one of the waiting room chairs outside the lab and had her head in her hands, long hair hanging down to cover her face. Marie-Louise was massaging her shoulders. I kept some distance between us.

"Hey, there," Marie-Louise was soothing. "It's fine, it's over now."

"Yeah, for right NOW it is," Rosanna blurted. "Don't think it's all over yet."

"Don't I know it," said Marie-Louise. "Trust me, I've been on more protest lines than you've had hot dinners."

Rosanna laughed. "And that's supposed to comfort me?"

Marie-Louise grinned. "Made you laugh, didn't I?"

Rosanna looked in my direction, hands clasped in front of her. "I hope you'll be discreet about what went on here tonight. This could really, *really* hurt us."

I felt like a fly under the microscope. "Of course. I understand."

Marie-Louise smiled at me. "I think he knows what's at stake. I also think he's a decent guy." But the look she threw me had an edge to it: You'd better not make me wrong.

"Roy, would you do me a favour," Rosanna asked, "and get Tom in here?"

I stepped outside. Most of the crowd had dispersed, some returning to the bonfire with Carl and Leon, others had obviously gone home. There were still four people stationed at the double doors. But Tom was nowhere to be seen. I walked over to the bonfire to ask but no one had seen him for the past fifteen minutes or so.

I stepped back inside. "Sorry Rosanna. He seems to have gone home."

It only took about an hour for an RCMP cruiser to arrive. It was 2:45 a.m. Milowski must have called them as soon as he got to the motel. "What a wiener," I thought. One of the protestors poked her head inside to tell Rosanna. She muttered: "Well, here goes," and strode to the double doors. A single officer stepped out of the car. I read his name tag: Constable Ron Neihardt. He wasted no time. "Who's in charge here?" he asked. Rosanna stepped forward. The constable hooked his thumbs in his gun belt as he spoke. "I've just had a complaint against you folks. Somebody named Jim Milowski, an employee of the Provincial Health Authority, called to say there was an attempted assault here tonight."

Carl and Leon had seen the cruiser pull up and were standing at a discreet distance but close enough to hear. They said nothing. Rosanna tried to look nonchalant. "Yes, officer, things did get a little out of hand. But it's all under control now. No harm done."

"So are you saying there was no assault?"

"Didn't you say *attempted* assault?" Rosanna asked.

Constable Neihardt smiled. "Yes I did, ma'am. What was your name?"

"Rosanna. Rosanna Yale."

He had his notebook out and wrote it down. "I don't suppose you're willing to tell me who made the attempt?"

"What difference does it make? Nothing happened." It was Carl. His tone was acid.

Constable Neihardt turned in his direction. "And you are, sir?"

"Carl Donaldson."

"Were you involved?"

Carl didn't miss a beat. "If you mean, was I here, then yes. If you mean, did I try to hit anybody, then no." His grin managed to somehow be both smug and honest.

Constable Neihardt may have been a young cop but he was no rookie. He guessed that Carl and Leon may have had something to do with the incident. "And you, sir—?" he gestured toward Leon.

"Leon Waruschuk." His lips were tight as a Ziplock seal.

"And do you know anything about what happened here tonight?"

"Nope." He stood with legs apart, defiant, towering over the officer. Unlike some of the other protestors, he showed no signs of cowering before authority.

Constable Neihardt allowed a brief sigh, then turned to the rest of the group. "Can ANYONE tell me what happened here tonight? Did he or did he not get assaulted?"

It was my cue to step forward. "Constable, I think I can help."

"And you are?" He had his pen ready to write.

"Roy. Roy Breen, reporter for the *Mountain Echo*."

"You're new in town, aren't you?"

"Yes, I moved here from Vancouver recently. But I'm originally from Newcombe."

"Can you tell me what happened here tonight, then?"

I could see nervous looks passing between Rosanna and Marie-Louise. Tom was still nowhere in sight. "Well, Constable, as you may or may not know, these folks are trying to prevent the loss of their 24/7 ER. On top of that, PHA has said they're going to also reduce lab services at the hospital. So they sent out Milowski and Heinz to remove the x-ray equipment, which actually belongs here. It was paid for by the Hospital Auxiliary." I could see Neihardt was getting impatient, but dutifully taking notes. "When they showed up here tonight—well after one in the morning I might add—Rosanna had already established a 24/7 lab watch to prevent the equipment being removed. As part of that effort they refused to let the PHA boys into the lab corridor. Milowski got a little excited and started yelling at the protestors. Naturally they yelled back. Then someone got the idea to surround the PHA van so it couldn't leave. It was a purely symbolic gesture as far as I can tell."

Constable Neihardt stopped writing and paced around the van, inspecting for damage. When he came to the hood, he lifted it open and saw the disconnected battery cable. He looked knowingly at Carl and Leon. "This wouldn't have been removed to prevent them leaving? Or to drive to the police station?"

Carl gave an exaggerated shrug but said nothing. I could see Rosanna struggling to keep composure. Marie-Louise watched her nervously. She stepped forward. "Constable Neihardt?" she said. "You're new here, aren't you?"

"Just posted here last month," came the curt reply.

The gravelly chuckle. "Thought so. They change you guys in and out of here faster than I change my socks. It's hard to get to know you fellas before you leave. Have you had a chance to get out on the lake fishing yet?"

Constable Neihardt looked mildly impatient. "No, not yet. What does this have to do with—"

"Oh, nothing, just making conversation, that's all. You have to understand that people here depend on this hospital. We're a long way away from anywhere. So tempers get a little hot sometimes when some out-of-town bureaucrat parachutes in and tells us he's gonna take some piece of it away. I've been on the front lines most of my life and I know a lot of you guys in the RCMP. You have a job to do the same way we do. You're good boys, most of you. I've been in the clink for logging blockades and you always try to treat a lady right. At least, in my experience." Clearly, she was buttering him up.

The constable seemed to defer to her elder status. Marie-Louise continued. "Rosanna here has done a fabulous job of keeping this protest all on the up-and-up. No emergency vehicles or patients have been blocked from getting to the hospital. We've kept our banners on our own vehicles, not on the building. We're nonviolent here. Nobody wants a conflict. Sometimes confrontations happen, like it did tonight. Just a loud argument, really. Trust me when I say there was no attack, even if Mr. Milowski got a little freaked out. I think he panicked."

"And what about the PHA van?" asked the constable.

"Is it damaged?"

"Well, no, not as far as I can see. Battery cable has been disconnected...."

"Well there you go then."

"I don't suppose you'd be willing to tell me who disconnected the cables? That could be considered vandalism of government property."

Marie-Louise shrugged. "Won't take much to hook it up again. I don't see any damage. Do you?"

Constable Neihardt took a long, hard look at Marie-Louise, then Rosanna, then back again. Finally he flipped the notebook shut. "Well I can see you've closed ranks here. And I don't see any real harm done yet. But I'm warning you—" and here he pointed at Rosanna as the leader. "We'll be keeping an eye on this protest. And if PHA gets an injunction, I'm sorry but we'll have no choice but to remove you from the site."

"Been there, many times," said Marie-Louise. "We understand."

"Fine then." He strode to his cruiser, fired it up, and wheeled it around to leave. The group watched as the cruiser exited. Rosanna's face had blanched 'til she was almost as pale as her hair. Marie-Louise laid a hand on her arm. "Shit, that was close," she chuckled.

Chapter Five

I was dreaming one of my recurring lost-in-the-city dreams. It's always the same, with variations on the theme. I'm in some unfamiliar city and I'm trying to get somewhere—sometimes home, sometimes it's some destination that remains unknown to me. The streets distort and warp out of shape, transforming into a rat's maze worthy of a German Expressionist film. Just when I think I've gotten somewhere, a new and completely unfamiliar street or maze of crooked alleys opens up before me. Often I'm also trying to keep track of a set of items—a briefcase, a pair of boots … so it's doubly disorienting because these too get lost as I go. Sometimes I end up inside a building that has me lost in a maze of rooms just as convoluted as the streets. Often there are people in these rooms, but seldom anyone I know. If I do see a friend there they seem unaware of my problem. By the way the sheets and blankets are gnarled when I wake up—and the exhausted feeling I have—I can tell I haven't had much rest.

A tap-tap-tapping sound. These dreams can be frighteningly real, but sound is often limited to the few words spoken by people in the dreams. So this sound has me confused. It doesn't seem to correspond to anything in my dream. Suddenly I feel the subtle impact of four paws on the bed. Is it time for the Captain Cat routine already? I feel like I just got to bed.… I rub the sleep from my eyes. Sure enough, Shadowcat is standing there at the foot of the bed. He walks up to my chin, purring. Something's different. Finally I realize the tapping is someone knocking on my door. I look at my bedside clock: 11:25 a.m. What? I throw aside the covers and wrap myself in my robe, sliding into my slippers on the way to the door. My heart lurches just a little when I see Jane's face through the glass. The weather above the fir and cedar skyline has gone overcast.

I swing the door wide and Shadowcat is right there to greet her. He *really* likes this "gal" as Marie-Louise might call her. "Uh … hi."

Her face registered a mild alarm. "Oh, I'm so sorry! I got you out of bed! I can leave.…"

I scratched an itchy spot on the back of my head, imagining just how sexy I must look in my bathrobe and morning face. "No! No, really it's fine. Please, come in."

She extended a cookie tin in my direction. "More cookies. Along with a few cherry tomatoes—the last ones from my garden this year." She reached down to stroke Shadowcat's fur. He arched into her palm willingly.

"Thanks, that's very sweet of you. Come join me in the kitchen," I said, padding in that direction. "I was at the hospital late last night. Didn't get to bed 'til about 3:30." I gestured at the kitchen table. "Have a seat. I'm going to fry up some eggs and bacon. Want anything?"

"No, no thanks. Maybe some tea. I'm happy to make it though."

"Okay, why not? A good pot of jasmine always sets me up for the day." I noted how easily she moved in my kitchen, how despite our relative unfamiliarity we moved in tandem, never crashing into each other. A kitchen ballet for an audience of one—a very approving cat. Once the kettle was on she sat down again.

"And thanks for driving out to feed Shadowcat. You've saved me a few days of the Filthy Look. I didn't see you at the hospital last night, though."

She blushed. "I'm so embarrassed. I hung out here with Shadowcat and stoked the fire. He seemed to be asking me to stay. He was curled up in my lap … it was heavenly. So cosy I fell asleep on the couch. By the time I woke up it was after midnight, so I just went home. I got up early this morning and went over with a tin of cookies for the gang at the lab."

I turned from my sizzling eggs and raised an eyebrow. "Shadowcat was curled up in your lap? No kidding!" I looked over at Shadowcat, who was preening. He stopped, one paw held in mid-air, as if to say: "Get over it, Dad." The look he gave me warned me not to argue. "You should feel privileged. He doesn't do that for just anyone."

She smiled down at him. "I'm honoured."

The kettle whistled and she got up. "Your tea—?" I pointed at the white cupboard door to her left. She quickly found the jasmine tea tin. She found the mugs and set two out while the tea steeped.

I set my plate next to her and sat down. "Probably just as well you weren't at the hospital last night. Things got a little hairy there for awhile."

"Nothing serious I hope?"

"Luckily, no. But it easily could've gotten out of control." I explained to her what had happened. Her brow wrinkled in concern.

"That's why I stopped going to protests," she said. "I just can't stomach the tension anymore. And like Rosanna I won't support violence."

"Actually I thought Carl and Leon showed surprising self-control. It could've been much worse."

She sighed sadly. "It's such a lose-lose game nowadays, protests. If you play by the rules they set up, they can just ignore you. If you don't, they take you away. I mean, you have to take out a permit to walk down the street carrying protest signs, for God's sake. It's hard to know *what* to do anymore."

"It's like English folksinger Roy Harper sang: 'Free speech— one each.'" We both laughed. The tea timer went off and she poured the tea. The delicate floral scent of jasmine tickled my nostrils. "Anyway, you're doing the best you can with SGs."

She smiled. "I wonder sometimes, but thanks, Roy."

"So what's on the agenda today?"

"It's Sunday—a great day for taking a drive in the country."

"A drive? Maybe a short hike too? Where do you want to go?"

She looked a little sheepish. "I'm afraid it's not entirely a pleasure cruise." She paused to sip her tea. "Rosanna phoned me this morning after I got back from the hospital."

"I'm glad to hear she got home for some sleep. What did she say?"

"Well it appears Moss has begun his protest—um, *crawl* to Newcombe."

I had to laugh. "Silly bugger. I wasn't sure he'd actually do it. What does she want to do?"

"She wants to check in on him, make sure he's got enough food and water."

"And maybe take another crack at talking him out of it. Preferably before the media gets hold of it."

"Something like that."

"Okay, what time?"

"She said just to drop by her place about two this afternoon. Marie-Louise is holding down the protest line. If she needs a break she's only a block from home, and she has help."

"Can you give me fifteen minutes or so to shower and shave?"

She smiled. "Actually we've got almost two hours yet. I thought we could take a walk in the forest first."

"Sounds great. There's an old logging road that comes by the property here. It's lovely in there."

"Perfect."

I turned to Shadowcat. "You keep her entertained while I shower, okay?" He looked at me as if to say: "I'm not letting this one get away."

On the way to Eldorado we stopped by the Rosehip Café to pick up Rosanna, who had a suite above the restaurant. She'd been doing fall cleaning to put the restaurant to bed for the winter when we arrived and promised to "just be a sec or two" while she hung up her apron and grabbed a prepared lunch. She came out carrying a small chill pack full of sandwiches and a tall stainless steel thermos. She folded her long legs up to slide into the back seat.

"Any word yet on how Moss is doing?" It was Jane, turning toward the back seat.

"News travels fast in a village. I hear he spent all day yesterday just getting down the main street of Elkville," Rosanna laughed.

"I can imagine it might take awhile on your knees," I suggested.

"No, it's not that, believe it or not. It's just that everyone around here knows Moss, so he'd go a few metres, see someone, then stop and chat. A few more metres, and he'd see someone else he knows, so the whole procedure would start over again."

We all laughed. "It's like the Post Office Social," Jane observed. "There's no such thing in this village as 'just getting the mail.' You see half the village there, coming and going. And of course everybody's got something to say, some news to share…. By the time you're done it's fifteen–twenty minutes, minimum."

"Especially if you bump into Fern the Flower Lady," added Rosanna.

"Okay, thirty minutes then," laughed Jane.

I had to ask. "Why? Who's Fern the Flower Lady?"

"Fern Monterey. She's one of the hippies who came up here from the States with her husband Joe back in the day," explained Rosanna. "Always wears flowers in her hat band. One of the original Flower Children from the sixties. But she can talk the hind leg off a donkey, to quote my old gramps."

"Doesn't that drive you crazy?" I asked.

"I admit there are days … but we all love her. She has a heart of pure gold. Always looking in on the sick and elderly. One of the most thoughtful people I know."

"For me," added Jane, "the Post Office Social took some getting used to after Ottawa. But now I wouldn't have it any other way!"

"And you haven't lived," laughed Rosanna, "'til you've had Fern's sponge cake!"

"What do you mean?" I asked.

"She brings it to every potluck—probably has done since 1970."

"Always the same and always delicious," Jane added.

We passed the gas station at the top of Eldorado's main street, crossed the little bridge over Harris Creek and followed the sharp bend toward Elkville. I was still getting used to the glittering glacial ridges, the cerulean perfection of the lake. It felt sparkling new to me every time. Finally we passed the

Teapot and began our ascent up the steep, winding grade that led to the Elkville Summit. It was a favourite stopping place for tourists and locals alike—a granite pulpit that soared nearly three hundred metres above Sapphire Lake at a point that offered equal views north and south—a stunning panorama stretching miles into the horizon.

Rosanna broke the silence as we passed the boarded-up Elkville Hotel at the foot of the hill. "I think Moss spent the first night camping by the picnic table outside the old hotel."

"How is it you can have three restaurants in these two villages and yet the hotel is boarded up?" I asked.

"The hotel's last business owner succeeded in driving off one hundred percent of the locals," Rosanna explained. "Came from Calgary and refused to pay staff except in cash, so no paperwork for Unemployment Insurance. Brought bouncers with him who were used to the rough and tumble of a big-city bar. Real losers. Their combined IQ wouldn't have matched their shoe size. Roughed up a couple of the village winos— harmless old geezers who've been regulars at the bar for ages. Between that and the shady dealings, we all just boycotted the place. It's sat empty with a 'for sale' sign for years now."

"Shame," said Jane. "Apparently there's been a hotel on the site since the 1890s. Couldn't ask for a more prime view of the lake."

I had to gear down for the steep uphill climb and the zigzag road, which would put a professional Formula 500 driver to the test. The phrase "zero margin for error" sprang to mind. Vertical granite cliffs to one side, a sheer drop to the lake on the other. As we were nearing the summit, I spotted a kneeling figure on the side of the road and had to drop-shift quickly. We rolled up to a stop just behind him. There wasn't much room to pull over—a narrow shoulder of gravel skirted by concrete berms. He'd been moving forward at a painful pace. When Moss heard tires crunching the gravel, he turned to see who was coming up behind him. He flashed us a grin that was half Daffy Duck and half Gandhi. I wasn't sure what to think. It was an odd look that blended fatigue, bewilderment and meditative determination. To a stranger, it might have appeared as a kind of dazed derangement. He was wearing a bright red backpack with a bedroll strapped to its top. He was holding a picket sign above his head but from where I was I could only see the back of it.

Rosanna was out of the car in a heartbeat, carrying the thermos and pack of sandwiches. Moss's eyes sparkled when he saw her. His tone was effusive. "Ay! Sista Rosanna! I Madonna of the Lake!"

She bent down and handed him the sandwiches, unscrewing the thermos cap to pour him a cup of steaming coffee. Jane and I stood to one side. "How's it going, Moss?" Rosanna asked.

"Irie, Sista Rosanna! Not so bad for an old lion wid gravel in de paws."

"What's that really mean, Moss?" Her tone was sincere, not mocking.

He grinned, pointing at her with his thermos cup. "Better now you be here."

It was clear he was unwilling to put down his sign. He used his free hand to sip coffee. Now that he was facing us I could read the sign. It said: "SAVE OUR ER" in red block letters, obviously hand-painted. The lettering could have been that of a child. Except that instead of writing "ER" in capital letters, he'd painted it as "Er." Jane and I looked at one another knowingly but tried not to break out in a grin. If Rosanna had noticed she gave no indication. She was examining Moss with all the concern of a mother fussing over a child.

"So how was your first night on the road?" she asked.

He shrugged. "Knees already hurtin'. Ol' Lion of Judah, he gettin' little bit outta shape."

Jane was starting to look worried. "It could get pretty cold tonight. Have you got a tent, or at least a tarp somewhere in there to keep the rain out?"

"I be set to go, yeah?" He patted the bedroll on his pack. "I been dis country tirty-five years. I been camping in bush country since before you born, Sista Jane."

Jane's palms went up defensively. "Okay, Moss. Just asking."

Moss grinned. "Ay, sistren—I guardian angel."

"How are those kneepads working out?"

He looked down at his knees. He was wearing a set of

garden kneepads. Already they were starting to look ground down by the roadside gravel. "Guess dey gonna do da trick, yeah?"

Rosanna looked dubious. "Why don't I borrow a pair from Barry the Floor Guy? He'll have some industrial-strength kneepads."

"Ay, y'know what dey say," said Moss. "Flooring guys always on dey knees, either dey be devout as hell or beggin' for a raise." He chuckled at his own joke.

A four-by-four pickup truck was making its way around the narrow curves below us. As it came into view, we could see two young guys in the cab wearing ball caps. There was a rifle in the back of the cab. It was obvious they were laughing. As they got closer they slowed to a crawl and the one on the passenger side leaned out the open window. "Hey, freaks! What does that mean? Save our Er? Some kinda endangered species? Save the Er-bird? Ha-ha-ha-ha!"

Jane recoiled visibly but Rosanna was unperturbed. "Just out for a stroll, that's all."

"On your knees? Whatsa matter? You gotta secret wish to be a dwarf or somethin'?"

Moss, to his credit, said nothing. As a black man he sensed the danger and knew better than to backtalk to white trash. I felt myself getting hot. I opened my mouth to cut these knuckle-draggers down to size, but before I could say anything Rosanna picked up the cue. She waved a forefinger in front of her lips to keep me quiet. So Jane and I pretended to be enjoying the view of the lake, making sure to avoid eye contact with the "yahoos," as my old man used to call them. As the old proverb goes, "where there's no wood the fire goes out." The driver of the truck gunned the engine into high gear, spitting a few pebbles as he sped off. His passenger leered at us through the back window.

"Bastard," Rosanna muttered. "Like to take him across my knee, teach him some manners." She was looking at Moss's sign. "Moss, maybe we can fix that for you." She turned to me. "Do you have a felt marker in your car?"

"Um, maybe. But I think maybe I'm crossing the line here from reporter to participant."

Jane nudged me playfully. "Oh, come on. Call it your civic duty. In Vancouver or Ottawa it's picking up litter off the sidewalk. Here it's helping somebody like Moss."

Moss was munching on a sandwich. Through a mouthful he said, "Tanks, brotha."

I walked back to the wagon, popping open the glove box. It was the usual chaos of insurance papers from the past decade, empty Tylenol bottles, maps, and pens. There was a Sharpie marker buried at the bottom. I took the sign from Moss. Because the marker was black I had to re-draw both the "E" and the new capital "R" over his lurid red lettering.

"As your copy editor, I must advise you to put periods between the capitals," Jane said, half-jokingly. "It'll help avoid the confusion we saw today."

I gave her a thumbs-up sign as I drew two periods. Rosanna was worried, studying the next corner on the road. "How much farther to the Elkville Summit?" I asked.

"I think it's about another kilometre from here," she said.

The sky had been gunmetal overcast all afternoon, hinting at rain. Now it came, mostly sparse but with that feeling in the air that threatened to turn into a downpour. "Moss, you don't have a hat or an umbrella!" said Rosanna.

He grinned conspiratorially. "I be de Boy Scout, mon—always prepared!" He slung his backpack off his shoulder and pulled it open. Out of it came what looked like a tiny folded umbrella but was in fact one of those miniature umbrellas attached to a hatband. It was red, blue and white. At least, I thought, it can be seen from an airplane, so he'll be hard to miss for drivers. Once again Jane and I had to suppress a giggle. But Rosanna wasn't amused.

"Moss, it could get ugly out here. Why don't you let us drive you to the top of the summit so you can set up camp early, before it really pours?"

"Ay, dat be cheatin'! I say dis before, I say again, I go all de way to Newcombe."

Rosanna sighed hopelessly. "Alright, Moss. Is that all you've got to keep yourself dry?"

Moss shook his head slowly as a Zen sage. This time he pulled a bright yellow rain poncho out of his backpack and removed the umbrella hat, pulling the poncho over his head.

"Now the ensemble's complete," I joked. Jane elbowed me sharply in the ribs. I held up my palms in wordless apology, complete with sheepish grin.

Rosanna was squatting beside Moss, an arm on his shoulder. "Moss, are you SURE? I'm worried about you out here alone. Those guys we just saw … I mean, what if the next guys that drive by get nasty? And you out here by yourself?"

Moss was serious-faced now. "Sista Rosanna tellin' I to give up?"

"Moss, you know I don't mean it that way."

"Gandhi say, 'it is a duty to resist unjust laws.' Dat's what I be doin'." He looked directly at me. "I be no ignorant Rasta, Roy. I study Gandhi in seminary jus' like de saints. Dis ol' fox, he know politricks."

I could see a slight wince cross Jane's face. "Actually I think that was Martin Luther King Jr. 'One has a moral responsibility to disobey unjust laws.'"

Moss laughed. "I be goin' daft in ol' age wid de ol' memory! I forget Brotha King! Fact is, he speak de truth."

"Yes it is," agreed Jane.

"Actually, I like Gandhi's quote about reporters," I chimed in. "'I believe in equality for everyone, except reporters and photographers.'" Jane and I chuckled.

Rosanna was looking more anxious by the second. "Moss, this ER cutback isn't a law. It's just a bureaucratic decision. And those kinds of decisions can be unmade."

Moss raised his fist in a victory gesture. "Ay, see what I mean? Sista Rosanna makes my point. I give up now, maybe dey don't change dey mind. Dis old lion hang in there, den maybe dey DO change dey mind, yeah?"

"Moss, it's not all up to you. We're all doing what we can. I've got a 24/7 watch on the lab and we've got a protest line at the hospital. You could help out there."

His usually serene composure acquired a subtle but distinct edge. It was the first time I'd seen him react that way since the confrontation with Marie-Louise. "I not helpin'? Sistren gonna tell I dis Newcombe walk stupid too?"

Rosanna sighed in exasperation—only about the third or

fourth time I'd heard her do so. "No, Moss, no. I'm not saying that at all." She stood up, towering over him. "I understand how dedicated you are and I appreciate it." He warmed to this. "We'll just make sure somebody checks in on you every day, okay?"

By his grin it was obvious he was delighted with her. "Ay, tanks Sista Rosanna—I guardian angel."

She smiled. "Madonna of the Lake, you said."

"Ay, dat too!"

When we got back to the car to leave, Rosanna gave me a long, appraising look. "You know if you write anything about Moss I'll have your testicles for castanets." It was probably the toughest thing I'd heard Rosanna say yet.

Jane giggled. "Isn't that a line from *Monty Python and the Holy Grail?*"

"Should make a fine addition to the Mexican décor in your restaurant," I joked. But Rosanna wasn't laughing. "Listen, sooner or later *somebody* will pick up on the story. But I've already given you my word it won't be me, okay? Like it or not, you'll just have to trust me on this one." I didn't mean to be hard but I didn't like people questioning my integrity.

"Okay, Roy. I'm still hoping we can talk him out of it before then."

Monday morning the damn phone still wasn't hooked up. I'd been here a week and the phone company had moved at the speed of molasses. It was a glaring contrast to the pace of political events in these two mountain villages. I reflected on the fact that in a mere seven days I'd covered a public meeting, a near-riot at the hospital protest and avoided the story of Moss's protest crawl. Not to mention getting to know Jane. I gulped down breakfast and got ready to head into the village, making my apologies to Shadowcat. He was already hunkered down on the back of the couch, head on his paws. He gave me a sour, melancholy look. "Bastard. *Sure* you're sorry. Leaving me alone all day." It was expertly done Guilt 101 but I had no choice.

Lance and Donna were at their perpetual posts. As I walked in I wondered how Donna could flash that brilliant smile and mean it every time. She either loves her job or she's one of those congenitally happy persons. Being inclined to melancholy, I envied such people. Lance was chewing on an unlit cigar. "Nice story on the PHA meeting, Roy."

"Thanks. Stay tuned—more to come after the commercial break."

"I heard about the scuffle at the hospital the other night," Donna said. "Does it look like the PHA guy will be pressing charges?"

"Not as far as I can tell. Nobody on the protest line is going to give up the guys, so it's his word against theirs. Like Rosanna said, Milowski was ready to drive through the crowd, so that wouldn't have helped his case any. And anyway, nobody *actually* got assaulted and there was no damage to the PHA van. Rosanna's crew got off with a stiff warning from Constable Neihardt."

Donna had on a sly smile. "I also heard about Moss." Somehow she had eyes and ears everywhere. But then, it was a tiny village, and she *was* editor of the newspaper. She let me tell her what I knew without her having to repeat what the "huckleberry party line"—as the mountain grapevine was known—had already passed along. I had to ask her what the expression meant. Turns out the telephone company had locals on "party lines" right up 'til the early 1990s, long after they'd become a thing of the past in the rest of the province. And huckleberry picking was a local tradition, almost a social occasion, although most guarded their special bushes jealously. Gossip traded here under many names.

"Yeah, uh … listen," I said, "she *really* doesn't want this story to get out, at least not the part of it about Moss. Rosanna seems very protective of him. She's still hoping she can talk Moss out of it. We went up the summit yesterday to bring him some coffee and sandwiches."

Donna's smile had subsided to her more serious look. "Sure, I understand. Makes the protestors look bad. What do you think the chances are of getting Moss to call it off?"

"Ummm … not good at this point."

"So it's only a matter of time before the regional or coastal media gets hold of it."

"Probably. Let's hope he puts his back out or something before then."

Lance was chuckling. "They're already calling him Moss the Crawler. Makes a change from Unlucky Luke I guess." He chewed his cigar while he watched me. "And I must say, you've certainly gone native in a hurry. Not that I think that's a bad thing." He put his fingers in quotation marks as he said "gone native."

"What do you mean?"

"Well, most guys from the city would jump all over this story. It's a great chance to gloat, show the world how sophisticated you are by lampooning the local yokels."

"I'm kinda thinking I'd like to settle here. Pissing off some of the most prominent citizens the first few weeks isn't likely to further my prospects."

"True."

"Well, if you're going native," Donna added, "you should know the best place in town to get the local gossip. Or, as we like to call it here at the *Echo*, 'wilderness tips,' with apologies to Margaret Atwood."

"Another name for the huckleberry party line? I've already been to two of your fine dining establishments—the Blue Moose bistro and the Cracked Teapot Café. You telling me there's more?"

"You mean you haven't been to the Garden Path sandwich shop yet?" Lance was mock incredulous.

"You have yet another restaurant in this tiny village?"

"The village standby," Lance explained. "Been there for years—at least since the seventies."

"That's pretty fierce competition for such a small place."

Donna laughed. "In a village this small we're all in it together. We don't really see ourselves as in competition with each other. The Rosehip serves Mexican cuisine and they don't do breakfast or lunch, only fancy dinners. The Blue Moose does breakfast and lunch only, the Teapot is still fairly new and does special cuisine nights besides their usual daytime trade. The Garden Path is where all the old-timers of the village hang out. In fact, they have their own reserved table. Rick Offenbach— the owner—calls them the 'board of directors.' They're there like clockwork every morning at seven and if Rick hasn't had time to put the coffee on yet they do it for him."

"How's the espresso?" For me this was vital information.

"Only one way to find out," said Lance.

I grinned mischievously. "Are you offering to buy me a coffee? Or better yet, lunch?"

"Sure, why not? As I always say, the pay at the *Mountain Echo* may suck, but the perks are first rate." He glanced at his watch. "It's only eleven. Let's make it noon."

"Deal," I said. "I've got emails to catch up on anyway. Oh, and that goddamn phone company still hasn't hooked up my phone. Any trick the locals know to speed that up?"

Donna rolled her eyes. "Not really. If you find one you'll have to let us know. You should see the condition of the lines and poles. Thirty years out of date and falling apart."

"With cellphones coming they're probably hoping they can defer those repairs indefinitely," I observed.

The Garden Path lived in another quirky main street building that had probably been there since the days of the mining rush. It had a canopy over the front entrance with a wooden bench to one side of the door. A small garden with an ancient, gnarled apple tree took up part of the lot on the side facing the lake. The garden was framed by a slightly decrepit white picket fence. The bower entrance was interlaced with a thick vine. A trellis on the side of the building still sported a few wilting fuchsias. There were several picnic tables arranged amongst the greenery and autumn remainders of flowers. The view of the Valhallas and Sapphire Lake made it a breathtaking setting. It wasn't hard to imagine the beauty of the place at the height of summer. But now, with the weather turning cooler, most of the tables were empty. A few hardy souls outside were munching on sandwiches and reading newspapers. Through the front windows I could see that the clientele was just about as sparse inside.

As we stepped inside I asked Lance: "Tough making a go of business in this town, eh?"

He shrugged. "After Labour Day it's like somebody pulls the plug. Plenty of tourists in the summer months. But after that it's pretty much one hundred percent locals 'til the next peak season. Businesses here have to make hay while the sun shines."

"But wouldn't it be simpler to close shop in the winter months?"

"Yeah, if you don't live here. But Rick and Rhonda live here. And just between you and me, I think they love the ritual of the locals coming in every day."

The linoleum floor looked like it hadn't been changed since the 1960s, testament to its hardiness. You could see a slight wear pattern down the middle in the direction of the order counter at the back where the kitchen was. A divider about two-thirds of the way from the front door created a small nook just off the kitchen. "The Gossip Clutch," Lance called it. A robust woodstove looked like it could kick out enough BTUs to heat a battleship. A short corridor leading to the garden door had a counter with a drip coffee machine, mugs and carafes. There was a sign on the water cooler that read: "100% Organic." Next to that was the bathroom door, which had a sign that read: "Out of Order."

Behind the counter was a tall wiry man with sandy hair sticking out in tufts beneath a ball cap that read: "Dildo, Newfoundland." I had to stifle a laugh. Lance stepped up to order. "Rick, this is my new reporter, Roy Breen. Roy, this is Rick Offenbach, owner of the Garden Path." Rick was busy buttering bread for sandwiches. He looked up through a pair of old-fashioned black-rimmed glasses. He had one of those grins that constantly hinted at mischief.

"I won't shake your hand, for obvious reasons. Welcome to Eldorado."

"Will that bathroom be out of order long?" I asked.

He grinned slyly. "It's not really out of order."

"Then why the sign?"

"It keeps the tourists in line during peak season."

I looked at Lance for clues. His whiskered Cheshire grin was on high beam. "We have no sewer systems in Eldorado," he explained. "Everybody has septic tanks and it's not cheap to get them pumped out. Locals just get used to using less paper. Tourists like to flush down massive amounts of paper or change diapers in the sink."

"Oh," was all I could say.

"Exactly," said Rick, nodding in approval. "What can I get you guys?"

"I trust you have espresso?" I asked.

"Only the finest Italian espresso roast," said Rick.

"I'll have a double. And a corned beef on rye, no mustard, no pickle."

Lance ordered and we sat down in the Gossip Clutch. There seemed to be an unwritten understanding that all conversation in this part of the restaurant was up for grabs by whoever was there. I listened in on discussions of getting in winter wood, how the squash harvest was this year, who was already having grandkids. It felt like I'd stepped back in time fifty years. It wasn't a bad feeling. Yet many of the comments were overtly political. The favoured political topic was naturally the proposed reduction of ER hours. It was clear that people in this village were actively engaged with public life. After all, it wasn't a big pond to ripple out into, and everybody felt the effects of such decisions much more quickly and intimately. This was no proto-Appalachian village; people spoke passionately but intelligently. It was obvious there were some well-read people in the room. They certainly seemed well up on current affairs. Although there was the merest hint of a drawl, the local dialect was purely Western Canadian. Not particularly colourful as dialects go. For colour you had to listen to the choice of topic and the unique perspectives that shouted out personality.

"Say, did you hear about Moss?" one woman was asking another woman.

Lance tipped his head at me, a signal to pay attention. "Oh, yeah," said the second woman. "Him and his crazy ideas. Ever seen that crazy house of his? Built out of old car grills and cement, framed with trees he cut down on his property. He even left the headlights in some of the grills so it looks like the house has eyes when the light catches it right. It can be quite spooky looking in the moonlight."

"I was at a party there once. Thought it was kinda cute, actually. Very cosy."

"You would think that. Didn't you go out with him once?"

She giggled. "Who hasn't?"

"So what's he up to now?"

"He's doing a protest crawl to Newcombe."

"A protest *crawl*? You can't be serious. Why?"

"For the hospital ER."

"Well, I'm as against them putting our ER on banker's hours as the next person, but that—that's just *weird*."

"Takes all kinds to make a world. Especially around here."

"You can say that again!" They both giggled.

"They're calling him Moss the Crawler already," Rick piped in.

More laughter. The first woman continued: "Poor Moss. First it was 'Unlucky Luke' for losing two winning lottery tickets. Now it's Moss the Crawler."

A slight woman in her early fifties walked up to the counter, long dark hair tied in a bun. Her French-Canadian accent was immediately distinguishable from everyone else in the room. Compared to Eastern Canada their numbers were fairly sparse out west. She looked as if a stiff wind might blow her away. Her face was deeply creased with worry. Rick recognized her distress.

"Everything okay, Juliette?"

"Comme ci, comme ça. 'Ave you seen Tom? 'E went fishing yesterday and din't come home last night."

"Did he say how long he expected to be gone?"

"I t'ought 'e said 'e would be home last night." There were tears welling up in her eyes but she held them back.

"Did he tell you where?" Rick had his hands on top of the counter, leaning forward.

"'E likes to go Kane Creek, maybe Silverado Creek, that way. But sometime 'e likes to go Lowery for fishing."

"Have you reported him missing?"

"Not twenty-four hours yet. But 'e don't come home last night."

"When did he leave yesterday?"

"I t'ink about tree-tirty, it was."

"Hmmm ... okay. Listen, I can call up a couple of the Highways guys, see if they don't mind taking a run up there. It's only fifteen minutes' drive."

She reached out and grabbed his hands gratefully. "Oh, merci, Rick. I mean, t'ank you."

Juliette bustled out of the restaurant. Lance spoke up. "Probably she just forgot when he said he'd be home. He's been known to tent overnight up by Silverado Creek."

Rick nodded cautiously. "Maybe. Maybe not. Better safe than sorry."

"Who's she talking about?" I asked.

"Tom Bombadil," said Lance. Rick was already on the phone to the Highways yard.

"Oh, that Tom. I last saw him at the hospital. He was helping Rosanna supervise the protest." I was remembering the confrontation with the PHA boys when it struck me. "He did leave quite suddenly that night. Seemed a little upset."

"At least we know he got home that night," said Lance. "Juliette says he didn't leave 'til 3:30 the next day."

Rick hung up the phone. "Al Braun the Highways manager says technically they can't mount a full search with the Search and Rescue guys 'til it's twenty-four hours. But he'll radio one of the crew and see if they can take a look. The Lowery Pass is on their route anyway."

"Juliette does look pretty worried," I said.

"I have an idea," Lance said. "Tom and Moss are buddies, right?"

"Yeah, they go fishing together sometimes," Rick said.

"What if somebody takes Rosanna back up the summit to see Moss?" Lance suggested. "If we tell him his buddy Tom is missing and we need his help, we might be able to get him off his protest crawl. Plus, he probably knows all Tom's favourite fishing spots along the creeks. So it should cut down on the search time. Kill two birds with one stone, if you'll pardon the brutal metaphor. That way we also don't have to wait twenty-four hours to get started, which I'm sure Juliette will appreciate."

I was grinning. "I like the way your mind works, Lance. Wish I'd thought of it myself."

"Best of all, we find Tom before he dies of exposure—if he's lost," said Lance.

"Well, knowing Tom," said Rick, "he'd have sense enough to pack the right gear, especially if he was thinking of camping overnight."

"Then again, maybe not," said Lance. His face was serious. "You'd be surprised how many people don't, even in this country."

"Oh, yeah," agreed Rick. "Just talk to the Search and Rescue boys about that."

I walked Lance up the street and poked my head in the *Echo* door long enough to tell Donna the latest developments. There was no answer at Rosanna's number so I drove over to the hospital. I found her in a rare moment of repose, seated outside the lab with Marie-Louise, who seemed to have little need for sleep. This time she was working on cedar bark weaving to pass the time. Jane had told me her basketwork was legendary, though little known outside the Kootenays. Apparently the traditional native practice was to harvest cedar bark at a certain point in the spring when the bark was softest, avoiding damage to the tree. This was sometimes supplemented with birch bark to give added texture and variety to the baskets. I'd seen one of them at Jane's place and it was a true work of art, expertly woven and artfully festooned with pale green lichen and a crow feather. At a fancy Vancouver native crafts store it could have fetched hundreds of dollars. Jane told me Marie-Louise had refused to accept any money for it, offering it in exchange for a few hours of editing Jane had done for her.

"What's up, Roy?" Rosanna looked tired. No wonder.

"Tom has gone missing—well, for now let's just say he's gone fishing. But his wife is worried. Says he was supposed to be back last night."

Rosanna's hand reflexed to her mouth. "Oh my God, poor Juliette. I hope he's alright."

Marie-Louise put a hand on her arm. "I'm sure it's nothing. You know how guys are when it comes to communicating with their wives," she chuckled. "Probably he muttered something on the way out the door and she misunderstood."

"I agree," I said. "But Juliette is too worried to wait twenty-four hours."

"What do you want to do?" Rosanna was on the edge of her seat, ready to launch into action.

"Well Rick at the Garden Path called up the Highways yard. The manager there says he'll radio one of the guys to have a look out the Lowery Pass. But Lance had a better idea."

Marie-Louise smiled at me knowingly. "Moss and Tom are fishing buddies."

"You read my mind!" I said.

Rosanna got it too. "You want to talk Moss into helping with a search?"

"Exactly."

"I don't know," said Rosanna. "Moss can be pretty stubborn once he gets an idea in his head." She put a finger to her chin—thinking. "But you know, it just might work!"

We wasted no time driving up the summit. Although another day had passed, Moss had only made it another two kilometres or so past the Eldorado Summit. He was looking frayed around the edges—dejected as a rain-soaked cat. Fortunately the rain had only been intermittent but enough to dampen his enthusiasm. At least this part of the trek had been mostly downhill after the arduous climb up to the summit. But he still had another ninety-two kilometres to go to get to Newcombe.

"Sista Rosanna! I guardian angel!" His voice was weak. "You bring sandwiches? I belly startin' to talk back."

"I'm sorry, I didn't this time. But I have a good reason." She looked at me hopefully before continuing. "Moss, Tom has gone missing."

Alarm registered in his eyes. "Ay, ministers of Babylon! Missin'?"

"Well, Juliette says he went fishing yesterday and didn't come home last night."

"Ay! Dis be true?"

"The truth is, we don't really know exactly what happened. Roy says he kind of disappeared the night we had that fracas with the PHA boys. But he hasn't been gone twenty-four hours yet."

Moss's considerable brow knitted itself deeply. He appeared to be debating with himself. It was unusual for him not to have much to say. "Dey check out Kane Creek? Silverado Creek?"

"Not yet," said Rosanna. "The Highways crew will take a look up that way, but those creeks meander for miles into the mountains in that pass. If you know his favourite fishing spots you could save everybody a lot of time."

A look of sudden insight came into his eyes. "Sista Rosanna, you be tryin' to get I off de road, yeah?"

It was another of those rare moments where Rosanna's usually firm grip on her temper faltered. She actually stood up and looked down at him from her considerable height, like a mother admonishing a child. "Moss, you really think I'd lie about something like that, just to get you off the road? Actually lie to you? You really think that? I admit I'd do a lot to talk you out of it, but lie about Tom going missing? Never!"

And like a child, he couldn't bear to meet her eyes. "Sorry sistren! Forgive I, scriptures say, for I know not what I do. You overstand—dis means a lot to I, yeah?"

She squatted back down to his kneeling height. Her tone was warm again. "Moss, I totally get how important this is to you. Really I do. But there's no shame in calling it a day when an emergency comes up, is there? Tom's a buddy, after all."

He looked uncertain, but I could see him coming round. "Dis be true."

"And I *suppose*," she sighed, "once we find Tom, you can come back to it."

This seemed to perk him up. "Sista Rosanna, I be grateful. Just … give I de holy minute." Gesturing to us as a group, he continued: "I an' I take dis moment to tank de forest spirits for dey protection on dis journey."

Rosanna flashed me a warning look that said: Don't even go there. I gestured a subtle surrender, drawing a "zipper" across my lips. It was definitely a conversation for a later time. Moss shifted on his knees toward the lake, which at this point along the road could just be seen through a break in the thick forest cover. He had his hands on his knees, his eyes closed while he mouthed a wordless prayer. Rosanna and I stood behind him, careful not to interrupt. As we stood in silence, a bald eagle soared into view above the treetops, then circled on an updraft, hovering. I hadn't seen one for years. I found myself with my head thrown back, gaping. Rosanna was watching the eagle too. Sensing the moment, Moss looked up and saw it too. He touched his forehead with two fingers, then his chest over his heart, finishing up with the four points of the Catholic cross. It was a unique blend of esoteric and conventional spirituality.

The gesture prompted a memory I had of being in the forest when I was five years old. I'd stumbled onto a ruined cabin, logs overgrown with moss, its roof caved in. A chill on the breeze had blown in, as if some malevolent spirit haunted the place. My little boy imagination had gone into overdrive, conjuring the outdoor equivalent of the monster under the bed. Suddenly the chill lifted, as if some angel had wafted in to flush out the evil spirit. Though I saw nothing, the hairs on the back of my neck told me it was true. For a long time I communed there, hoping to catch a glimpse. It was the closest thing I'd ever felt to God in all the years my parents had made me go to church. But something far more alive and mysterious than God.

Finally Moss finished his communion. He twisted himself to face us and lifted a knee to get up. Shakily he rose, but then his knees gave out. Luckily we were close enough to catch him by the armpits. Even the industrial-strength kneepads Rosanna had borrowed for him were nearly worn through already. He stood between us, wobbling slightly.

"I be fine," he insisted.

"Here, let me take that pack for you," I offered.

He allowed me to slip it off his back and we walked him back slowly to the car. About every third step his knees buckled from the strain of his three-day crawl. We settled him in the back seat and he took a long pull from his water bottle. There were so many streams and rivulets coming off the mountain he could easily keep the bottle filled with clear, clean water. Rosanna turned to face him as I shifted out of park.

"Where should we go first, Moss?"

"Ay, where dis brotha be gone? Kane Creek an' Silverado Creek both be de best fishin' pools for Tom de fishin' fool. I camp dere with him plenty o' times. Jah and all de saints willin', we find 'im dere."

"Juliette says he likes to go over Lowery way to fish too," she suggested.

"Yeah, yeah. But Kane Creek de closest."

"Okay," I said. "Kane it is then."

"We can stop at the Garden Path and pick up some sandwiches before we head out," suggested Rosanna.

A stop at the Garden Path served double duty: filling station and central information depot. As the sandwich board sign on the sidewalk outside read: "Secrets kept. Stock tips. Gossip shared. Free marital advice." But sometimes—as it was today—"gossip" was more than just trivia. And it was a hell of a lot faster than going through official channels. Rick said he'd call Al Braun and let him know we were heading up the Lowery Pass.

The mountain pass east of Eldorado was as narrow and meandering as the highway along the lake. It was almost impossible to speed, despite our urgency. Take one corner too fast and you might find yourself careening into a granite wall, or plunging over a steep bank into the evergreen. About ten minutes out of Eldorado the road made a winding descent to where Kane and Silverado creeks merged to become Harris Creek, which emptied into Sapphire Lake at Eldorado. It was one of those narrow, rocky canyons so dreaded in the days before good roads—a steep and dangerous descent to the creek. And then the "S" climb up the other side, where a gravel road branched off to the ghost town of Silverado. During the silver boom the place had actually been large enough to cram a half-dozen hotels and as many brothels into a tight gulch. Predictably, Silverado's buildings were washed away by spring floods once every decade or so. Now only a handful of the mining-era houses and shops remained. Incredibly, the place was still inhabited by about a dozen people—presumably only the hardiest stock. Prospecting was pretty much a dead art by now. That left small-scale forestry and construction work to keep the locals sustained. Once every few years some mining corporation would get it into its collective head to do a little exploration. But all the best veins had long since been mined out. So mining exploration here was mostly a shell game designed to impress investors and manipulate stock prices. Locals had long since learned not to get excited every time some mining company made a big splash in the *Echo*, promising new mining exploration and jobs, jobs, jobs. Jobs that seldom materialized.

And when they did, they often vanished as quickly as they appeared.

There was a decommissioned forestry road at the bottom of the canyon where the highway switchbacked to take you up the Silverado hill. I shifted down to avoid taking the bottom out of the wagon, which wasn't really designed for logging roads. It's a tough little car though, one of the best Japan ever designed. Pushing a quarter million kilometres and the engine still tight as a drum. After only a few hundred metres there was a trench cut across the road by one of last spring's freshets. That meant walking from there, which suited me fine. We'd brought a bag of sandwiches from the Garden Path in case Tom hadn't brought enough food along.

The air above the old rutted road was refreshed by a steady mist from the creek, which we could see through the trees only about ten metres away in most places. It was an ideal nursery for cedars and a reminder of why the terrain here was known as "inland temperate rainforest." Not nearly as moist as the West Coast, but enough to support a dense forest of evergreen, a thick carpet of moss and some ferny undergrowth. The creek had washed down boulders of all sizes from the ridges above. In places the water spilled over granite in a foaming, crystalline cascade as delightful as any fountain. Where the creek water pooled, it was so still you could see the cobbled bottom as clearly as though you were looking through highly polished glass. As we walked I took advantage of opportunities to step down to the creek's edge, cup a handful of icy clear water and drink deeply. There was something different about this water. It was so pure, so clean it was somehow alive. A rejuvenating thrill went through my body as I drank, a gentle shock of energy. To me it didn't matter whether that was due to negative ions or Moss's forest spirits. Either way, there was something precious, even holy, there. I began to understand why Irish holy wells have been revered by pagan and Christian alike for millennia.

Moss broke the silence. "Dis place in spring be holy. I call dis Butterfly Alley. All de butterflies come out—mourning cloaks, swallowtails, anyting. Dis holy fool only have to hold out I hand like de body o' Christ an' one will land on it."

Looking through the cathedral-like stand of trees, the afternoon sun cascading through in dirty gold beams, it wasn't hard to imagine how this place could be a haven for such creatures. I could see why Moss and Tom favoured it as a fishing destination. Who cared if you caught any fish, as long as you could hang out here?

We'd walked for about a half hour when Moss suddenly turned toward the creek, where the bank sloped gently downward. I could see a deep pool nestled amongst several large boulders—an ideal place for trout to rest and feed on their way downstream. Well before we got there, it was obvious no one else was here, or had been recently.

"Rass, mon," Moss muttered.

Rosanna had a hand on his shoulder. "Don't worry, Moss. We'll find him."

The walk back to the car seemed shorter somehow, maybe because of the urgency we felt. It was nearly 4:00 p.m. and we had at best an hour and a half before dusk fell between the high ridges. If I'd been thinking more clearly, I would have backed the car *into* the forestry road. As it was, I had to back it out. If it had been spring, one tire-sized muddy pothole is all it would have taken to bog us down. Luckily there was little water on the road and we made it out without incident. I drove up the Silverado hill and took the gravel road at the top leading to the ghost town. Because the place was inhabited, the Highways crews kept the road cleared and graded year-round. We were racing the clock now so having a clear road meant we'd get to the next fishing hole before sundown. Here as at Kane Creek there were only ten metres or so between the road and creek in most places. Rosanna and Moss were glued to the creekside windows. Late afternoon sunlight strobed between the trees, impairing visibility. Finally Moss pointed to a steep hollow sloping into the creek, lined with fallen snags buried in mossy overgrowth. The late afternoon sun could be seen glittering on the creek.

Sure enough, there was a figure at creekside. We tumbled out of the wagon and half-slipped, half-jogged down the hollow. Already I could recognize the wiry, jean-jacketed figure of Tom, long salt-and-pepper hair loose in the breeze. He was casting into a pool much smaller than the one on Kane Creek but every bit as clear through to the bottom. Moss was already calling out to him. He'd hiked shakily ahead of us, his weakened knees causing him to slip occasionally.

"Brotha Tom! Ay, whaddya doin', brotha?"

Tom turned jerkily, startled by the sudden voice in the wilderness. When he saw Moss he smiled. "What do you think I'm doin', Moss? You've been here enough times with me. What are *you* doing here?"

Rosanna and I caught up to Moss, causing a puzzled look to cross Tom's brow. Moss had a hand on his shoulder. "Brotha Tom, I an' I be worried—Sista Juliette, she be worried too."

"Why? Why did you all come out here?"

"Juliette told us she thought you'd only be gone 'til nightfall," I explained.

"I told Juliette...." A look of realization hit him. He slapped his thigh in self-rebuke. "Aw, dammit. It's my pidgin French again. I tried to tell her in French I'd be gone *overnight*, not just 'til nightfall. It's one of the last chances I get before the season turns ugly. I said, '*je serai de retour ce soir....*'"

It was one of the rare opportunities to show off my high school French, or what little I remembered of it. "'I'll return *tonight*' was what you said. When you should have said, 'je ne serai *pas* de retour ce soir.' I will *not* be returning tonight."

Tom looked mildly offended. "Yeah, I get it. I've lived with Juliette for twenty-five years, so I do know *some* French. I just wasn't thinking clearly, that's all."

"Why didn't you just tell her in English, Tom?" Rosanna asked.

He looked sheepish. "I do try to make an effort for Juliette, you know. Her English isn't much better than my French. Usually we manage to communicate fairly well."

"As well as men and women *can* communicate," I chuckled.

Rosanna flashed me a "not helping—please shut up" glare. "Tom, why are you out here right now? Is there something you aren't telling us?" She was probing his eyes deeply.

Tom fell silent, reeling in his line meditatively. It was hard to tell if he was steeped in contemplation or embarrassment. Maybe a bit of both. But a chest-emptying sigh suggested something more like world-weariness. "You know, I've been in protests since the sixties. Sure, I've seen people lose it before. I've seen cops beating down kids, watched hurt and angry protestors lash out. Then for a lot of years I just tried to stay out of it. Got tired of the angst, the almost constant disappointment as yet another judge granted an injunction against people trying to protect their watersheds...." His voice meandered to a trickle.

Moss was about to launch into the breach but Rosanna sternly signalled him against it. If it had been anyone but her he probably would have objected. "But when Carl and Leon pulled that stunt with the PHA van...." The sadness in Tom's voice was palpable. "I just froze. It was like some part of me was flashing back to Kent State. I was there, man. It was like the whole thing was about to go off the rails, and everything we were trying to do was gonna unravel. All because of a couple of boozed-up pricks. Sure, it was *nothing* like Kent State, I get that. I'd never belittle the memory of those dead students by saying that. But it triggered something in me—PTSD maybe. Not sure if I'm more ashamed of my reaction—my *inability* to react—or the cretins that threatened to ruin our peaceful protest. I just thought: Man, I'm no use to anyone here. So I went fishing. I needed time alone to think." He threw another fly cast as he spoke.

"Don't be so hard on yourself," Rosanna urged. "Just by being there you helped us create a sense of calm. It's not your fault those jerks brought in booze. I told them not to but obviously, some guys are just thick as planks. That's not on you, it's on them."

"Rosanna, I wasn't there for you at a critical moment. There, but *not* there. I froze—"

"Ay, you be one fine brotha," said Moss. "I know dat, Rosanna knows dat, everybody knows dat. Dis be true like gospel, stop beatin' up on yourself. Why you don't call me, Brotha Tom? We coulda gone fishin' *together*, yeah?"

Tom grinned at him. "You were a little busy, Moss."

"Dis be true. But nothin' be too much for a brotha."

"Thanks, Moss. I appreciate it. And I'm sorry my stupidity put a crimp in your plans."

"Ay! When I hear Brotha Tom be missin' I answer de call, de same as de word o' de Lord! Brothas is brothas, yeah?" Tom smiled, reeling in his cast.

"Besides, there's a new ray of hope for the hospital protest," Rosanna said. I caught her eye sharply. This was news—news she hadn't told me. "You know Bob Williams?"

"You mean the retired guy on the edge of town who used to work for Immigration Canada?" Tom asked.

"That's the guy," said Rosanna.

"I heard he helped a lot of draft resisters get their immigration papers back in the day. Around the same time I came up here from the States. Thank God for Trudeau. If it had been today the border would have snapped shut like a bear trap."

"I was only a kid then," I said, "but I remember hearing Trudeau say, 'Canada should be a refuge from militarism.'"

"It was one of the most enlightened things I'd ever heard from a head of state," Tom agreed. "Especially considering what I was hearing in my own country. Between that and Mark Satin's book *Manual for Draft-Age Immigrants to Canada*, it saved a lot of us American college kids from ending up in body bags. That book was a bestseller for damn good reason."

"Dis be true," added Moss. "Canadian industry back in de day be supplyin' Vietnam War. Tanks, bullets, guns—anyting. Not many brethren an' sistren know dat. Dis I only learn after I emigrate to Canada."

It wasn't exactly what Tom needed to hear. Rosanna cleared her throat. "*Anyway*, as I was saying. Bob Williams worked in the finance department for the Immigration service the last ten years before he retired. So he knows all about number crunching. He's going to write up a cost comparison that will contrast the benefits of keeping the ER ward open versus the added expenses of sending people to other hospitals under the banker's hours scheme. He thinks he can make a damn good case that it'll cost PHA more to do that than just keeping it open 24/7. Same thing with the x-ray lab. He and Mayor Miller are working on it now."

At that instant, with the last rays of autumn sun cresting over the ridge above us, casting Rosanna's hair in an even more golden light than usual, I recalled Moss's name for her:

Madonna of the Lake. I'm not one for putting women on a pedestal—or anyone for that matter, from pop stars to prime ministers. We all have to put our pants on the same way. And it's ludicrous to suggest women can't be as unscrupulous as men. But we all have our shining moments, and for Rosanna this was one of them. And of course—if the plan worked—for Bob Williams. I'd interviewed far too many bureaucrats in my career and it was probably the first time in my life I actually looked forward to meeting one. Even if he was a *retired* bureaucrat.

As we climbed up the hollow back to the car, I caught up to Rosanna. "You never told me that. Don't you trust me? I know you don't know me that well yet, but...."

"No, it's not that at all. I only just found out this morning when Bob called me. He was at the Eldorado Hall meeting but he didn't want to say anything until he'd had time to work out some preliminary budgets, see if it could work."

"You must have been born under the sign of the Golden Horseshoe."

She smiled. "What do you mean?"

"First you manage to get Moss off the road before big media gets hold of it, and now this. Golden Horseshoe lucky."

She actually blushed. "Just trying to stay on the side of the angels...."

"Good job."

The production schedule for the *Mountain Echo* meant that the week of distribution was mostly a week off for editorial staff, though not for Donna, who still had to do the books. After the excitement with Tom and Moss, I felt I needed a couple of days just to decompress. And in addition to Shadowcat I now had another person in my life to give attention to. Although my Feline Overlord was overjoyed to see me finally return home, the happy dance was followed by an implicit message: "You owe me some quality time." I decided it was the perfect opportunity to invite Jane out for another dinner. She was usually bushwhacked by the end of a busy day at the SGS office, but didn't hesitate. Cathy Reilly had another campaign on the go, an attempt to add a further 2,000 hectares of forest to Selkirk Park. If she hadn't been so busy with environmental issues, I'd have suggested Rosanna draft Reilly for the hospital protest.

This time Jane insisted on cooking. I was struck again by how easily we moved together in the kitchen. Her tilapia in mayonnaise sauce with wild rice, roasted yam and steamed green beans was worthy of a Robson Avenue restaurant.

"Your French is showing," I said. "This is superb."

"My dad was a way better cook than I'll ever be," she said. "I learned everything I know from him." It was typical—she was always deflecting compliments. In an age of narcissism, I found this pleasantly refreshing.

"Not like my Anglo upbringing," I chuckled. "Veggies cooked practically to mush, mashed potatoes, and a two-inch steak big enough to feed a whole crew of lumberjacks. Mom was a superb baker though. Her pies and cookies were to die for. And her chicken dumplings … mmm…." I told Jane about the escapade with Tom and the misunderstanding caused by what he called his "pidgin French."

"I'm afraid I lost most of my French," she said. "I was only seven when my parents moved from Montreal to Ottawa on one of my dad's job transfers. He was bilingual so getting government work wasn't too hard."

"I'm sorry, I don't even know his name. Or his occupation."

"Jacques. He was a civil engineer."

"Was?"

"He passed away a couple of years ago."

"I'm sorry. And your mom? Was she French Canadian too?"

"No. Her name is Jill Taylor—Anglo-Irish. Jane was a family name. They split up when my sister Molly and I were only teenagers. Mom got a job as a fashion photographer and magazine illustrator in Toronto but by then the marriage was on the rocks, so she took us with her." She paused. I could see how it still saddened her after all these years. "Anyway, we didn't have much use for French where we were living in Toronto. Back in the sixties, if you were in an English neighbourhood and spoke French, the other kids tormented you mercilessly, so I lost most of it."

"I'm sure it would come back to you quickly. They say you never lose it if you've learned it at any early age."

"So they say. And what about your family?"

"Nothing exciting," I shrugged. "Dad and Mom both still together, both reasonably healthy."

She was smiling. "Dad? Mom? Who?"

"Oh, sorry. Cyril and Jeanette Breen."

"Hmm … interesting. Very old English name, your dad. Go on."

"Dad worked thirty-six years for the BC Forest Service, took an early retirement. Started young—just out of high school. You could do that in those days back in the fifties. Now you have to have a degree in forestry just to apply. Anyway, the old man was working as the District Ranger in the Prince Rupert district at the time. There was a dispute with head office in Victoria at one point that almost derailed his whole career."

"Oh? What happened?"

"A permit application came in from one of the big logging corporations, I forget who exactly."

"Was it MacMillan Bloedel, or Mac Blows the Forest Down as we used to call them? I think they've gone belly up now, or were bought out in some corporate merger deal. Cathy had to deal with them when she was doing the Meares Island campaign. I don't think their public image ever recovered from the Clayoquot arrests."

"As I say, I don't really remember. Anyway, whoever it was wanted to clear-cut a fairly large area somewhere northeast of Prince Rupert. As District Ranger, my old man's word was final say for all permits and he did a scrupulous job of assessing every application. He'd done all the flyovers, assessed all the mapwork, the hydrology, soil, everything. In the end, he had to turn it down. Well, you should have seen the shit hit the fan."

"He sounds like a man of integrity. Not just another government yes-man."

"Absolutely. Next thing you know, he's getting a phone call from Victoria, the minister's office. 'What the hell are you doing up there? I've been getting angry calls all day about this permit application.' Dad explained to the minister's assistant that he'd done all the appropriate assessments and his decision was no. Well, the guy on the other end of the line just lost it. 'Look, Breen, you wanna keep your goddamned pension, you better play ball. Think of how many jobs we could lose in the district....' Blah, blah, blah. The usual bullshit."

Her smile acquired a mischievous twist. "Well, this may sound odd coming from the assistant to a major environmentalist, but if I were to play devil's advocate for a second, he might have been right on that point."

"Yeah, okay. But in all the stories I've done in this province on logging disputes, it's always the same set of spurious arguments. The company trots out the same tired excuses for needing to cut more, more, more.... It's always 'jobs, jobs, jobs' but when it comes to actually hiring, that's a different story. Let's face it, for any business the easiest costs to control are generally labour. It's always labour that's the first to go when things get tight. Then with the rash of corporate mergers most of the money goes out of the country anyway."

It was clear she'd been testing me. "My points exactly. So what happened to your dad?"

"Well no bloody way he was going to sign that cutting permit. So they offered him a compromise. Take a demotion, a cut in pay, and a transfer out to another district. That way he could keep his pension. So that's what he did. I think he only worked another five or six years before retiring."

"And where's that?"

"Kimberley—they have a little place with some horses in the St. Mary's Valley."

Shadowcat leapt into my lap, insisting on being part of the conversation. He was watching Jane with a mixture of intense curiosity and admiration. I wanted to keep the conversation rolling. "So how's the park campaign going? Or should I ask?"

She made a subtle gesture of exasperation. "Oh, you know how it goes. Resistance from the logging industry is fierce and the government usually takes their side. It doesn't seem to matter whether it's ten acres or ten thousand. They mount the same objections."

"So how much parkland do we actually have in British Columbia?"

"Well, it depends on what sources you consult. But officially it's a little over thirteen percent of the total land base of the province. That leaves eighty-seven percent available for logging. But if you eliminate inaccessible terrain, private property, and areas with poor timber growth it takes it down to about a third of the land base. Only about 22 million hectares of the total 60 million was ever suitable for logging, most of it already logged by now. We actually have a pretty progressive parks system here compared to some places. BC's park system is third largest in North America, after the Canadian and the US Parks system."

"All the more reason to protect it then, and even expand it. They certainly show no signs of slowing down on logging."

"That's Cathy Reilly's argument and the position SGS takes. The old growth in the province is pretty much gone. We're looking at mostly second-growth timber now."

Shadowcat was looking at me disapprovingly: "Dad, just how rusty ARE you on the dating scene? You two going to sit here and talk politics all night?" Jane seemed to enjoy watching this communication pass between us, even if she could only guess at its meaning.

I gestured toward the living room. "I'll get the fire stoked up. We can plug in a movie or something."

Her eyes shone. "Or something."

Chapter Six

The phone company truck showed up at my door the next morning. Apparently they had to do a repair on the line before they could hook up my phone. The phone tech said that's why it had taken them so long to get someone out to Owl Creek. He was suitably apologetic so I avoided venting my frustration. Why shoot the messenger? I had no other stories assigned me by Donna yet so I thought I'd take advantage of the opportunity to get caught up on emails. Lance had already given me a key to the *Echo* office. Both of them would be out of the office doing newspaper drops.

I'd sent an email request to the Ministry of Health Public Relations Coordinator Mike Hoyson a week ago, asking for any updates to plans for the Eldorado Health Centre. Since last year's removal of acute care beds it could no longer be referred to in bureaucratese as a "hospital." But old habits die hard, and so far no one I knew here called it a "health centre." Knowing the locals, that was probably as much an act of defiance as of habit. It was impossible to tell when ministry officials would get around to responding to the community's concerns. And just as unpredictable when they'd get a media release out, although often they liked to do that on a Friday afternoon. That way, ministry officials would be off for the weekend, with the hope that by Monday morning something else would be bigger news anyway. It was a carefully worked out system.

What the bureaucrats often didn't count on was the tenacity of small-town BC. After all, it's their ass on the line, not somebody sitting in an office in Victoria. Their ass, their hospitals, their schools, their roads and bridges. When you live in a tiny, close-knit community, it's much harder for these issues to fade into the woodwork. You can no longer take such services for granted the way you might in a city the size of Vancouver or Toronto, where they can just send you to another borough. It's right there in your face and in your next-door neighbour's face. It affects you much more directly, regardless of political stripe or personal belief systems. It's one reason why volunteerism in villages the size of Eldorado and Elkville is often at a far higher per capita rate than in the cities.

I scrolled down my inbox. There was something marked MoH/Hoyson. Aha! The media release was on standard ministry letterhead and had come in yesterday. It read:

> Victoria, October 14, 2003. Provincial Director of Health Services Penny McClellan today announced revisions to budgetary restraints proposed for the BC Southeast Interior, West Kootenay region. As announced previously, no change will occur to services and hours of operation at regional hospitals such as Hannaville and Kelowna. Major surgeries will continue to be referred to these hospitals. The Ministry of Health intends to maintain its commitment to these regional health services.

> Smaller health centres in the BC Southeast Interior, West Kootenay region, however, will continue to be audited for structural adjustments aimed at streamlining costs. Among these is the Eldorado Health Centre, which serves the North Glacier Valley communities of Elkville, Eldorado, Owl Creek, and Silverado. Minister McClellan is pleased to report that a planned reduction of x-ray lab services in Eldorado will not be pursued at this time.

> However, the Ministry regrets that it must streamline the operating hours of the Eldorado Health Centre Emergency ward, effective November 15, 2003, to 9:00 a.m. to 5:00 p.m. Monday to Sunday. No staff layoffs will occur though naturally this will mean downscaling staff shifts.

So there it was—a compromise of sorts. In plain English: You can keep your x-ray lab but it's banker's hours for the ER. As a writer I almost had to admire the craft it had taken to employ weasel words like "streamlining" and "structural adjustments." There's a reason plain, clear language is taboo in government media blurbs. Nobody wants to admit to being the hatchet man or woman who brought you "cutbacks" or "drastically reduced lab services" or "closed hospital wards." I knew a lot of former reporters at the West Coast who'd left their jobs to take up public relations jobs in the government or corporate sector. In a way, I could understand it. The pay was better, and you at least got benefits. You weren't subjected to the daily barrage of bad news and then expected to stick your nose in it, drill down, and come up with a story that didn't stink of despair. All you had to do was check your integrity at the door and strap on the mouthpiece. Which, unfortunately for my retirement prospects, was never something I could bring myself to do. My old man during my rebellious teen years used to say I had an "addiction to telling the truth, usually at the worst possible time." For a long time this really stung. Then when I got to college and studied journalism, I realized: Without our truth-tellers, without a strong independent media, democracy becomes a pathetic shadow of itself. Sometimes the worst possible time to say something that needs to be said IS the best possible time.

I doubted the hospital's front desk would want Rosanna plugging in her laptop to search for the latest media releases, so I hopped into the wagon. She'd want this information ASAP. It would mean having to refocus her protest campaign. As I drove past the hospital entrance to find parking, I noticed new signs that read: "Save an ER, Save a Life." So morale was good then. As I walked up to the lab entrance, Rosanna and Marie-Louise were seated on the steps beneath the entrance canopy. They were flanked by two protestors holding picket signs. I saw no sign of Carl or Leon. I'd printed out the PHA release and waved it above my head for effect.

"What is it? Good news or bad news?" Marie-Louise had the ever-present hand-rollie trailing smoke between her fingers. Her tone was guarded. Rosanna was looking worried.

"Let's just say I don't see you dancing in the streets when you read it. Classic good news/bad news scenario. But at least there is good news."

Rosanna took the paper, her eyes darting across the page. "Fuck." She was one of those people who rarely swore, so when she did, it had the impact of a sledgehammer.

She handed it to Marie-Louise, who by now looked just as worried. As she read it her trademark good humour returned and with it the gravelly smoker's laugh. "One hand giveth, the other taketh away. Well, it's a victory—of sorts. We get to keep OUR x-ray machine. How kind of them."

Rosanna stood up and was scanning the terraced ranks of fir and cedar receding toward the mountaintop above the highway. It was as if the news had drained her of all energy, even the will to speak. Her well-defined eyebrows arched as her concentration pushed deeper into the evergreen heart of darkness. Marie-Louise and I watched her, waiting for a reaction. Without a word she turned and began walking toward the lake. I started to go after her but Marie-Louise grabbed me by the sleeve.

"Let her have some space," she said. "She's under a lot of pressure."

"Think she's okay?"

"Sure. She'll figure something out."

I was at the Echo office when Rosanna's call came in. "Line one, Roy," Lance said, putting the call on hold. I had to smile—the office phones only had two lines. The voice I heard was more like the in-command Rosanna I was most familiar with.

"Okay, Roy, this you *can* report. On Day Seven of the occupation to protest PHA service cuts to our ER, a group of citizens are planning a sacred circle around our hospital. This circle will be repeated once daily until PHA backs down on its decision. Marie-Louise will be our clan mother and lend the proceedings an air of ritual and native tradition. She'll lead us in prayers for the saving of our healing lodge."

"Day Seven?"

"Tomorrow."

"What time? Think you can get enough people out on such short notice?"

"We've got the phone tree, so yeah, I think we can get people out that fast."

"What about using email?"

"There are a lot of folks living out here because they don't *want* email. They come here to get *away* from so-called civilization. I can send out a few notices but the time-honoured phone tree works pretty well once it's activated."

"What time?"

"I'm shooting for 5:00 p.m. so we can get folks just coming off work to support us. Some will probably be happy to get off work early to help out."

"Mmm … better make it 4:00 p.m.," I suggested. "By five the light's already starting to fail at this time of year. That is, if it's a photo op you're looking for."

"Oh, right. Good idea. Can you come down with a camera?"

"No problem. You aren't planning to maintain the prayer circle 24/7 are you?"

"No, there's no need. Once daily should do it. Naturally we'll keep the occupation going round the clock."

"I've got a fairly good wide-angle lens. It would be better from the air, but…."

"But at the moment we don't have a plane or helicopter handy," she said. "So we make do with what we have. I'll get busy drafting a media release and get that out to the *Echo*."

News travels at lightning speed in a small village, with or without Internet. As one local wag put it: "Who needs a cellphone? If I just stand on main street and shout loud enough, half the village can hear me." And if that wasn't enough, the Gossip Clutch at the Garden Path sandwich shop had all the capacity of a computer virus to spread the news. Jane had volunteered to use the SGS email database to get the word out too. But as Rosanna said, many people here still didn't have email. Even for those who did want it, remote communities tend to be bottom of the list for technology upgrades. Still, one way or another all the bases were covered. Our modern addiction to technology has made us forget: Throughout history, people have found effective ways of communicating, one way or another, from the Roman slave revolt led by Spartacus in 73

BC to the Tolpuddle Martyrs labour protests of 1834. It may not have been instantaneous but close enough to get the job done. The human impulse to improvise is as deep-rooted as the impulse to innovate, with or without the latest gadgets.

Luckily the weather held—overcast but minus the heavy feeling that inevitably means rain. Which was actually good news from a photographer's point of view—no deep shadows to worry about. I was at the hospital site by 3:00 p.m., watching Rosanna marshal the troops. It was like festival day in the village. I could see Tom in his trademark jean jacket, chatting earnestly with Marie-Louise, who nodded in her sage manner. Moss the Crawler was there too, chatting up a much younger woman, his hands cutting shapes in the air. There were plenty of people I'd never seen before. The refreshment tent was being staffed by middle-school boys and girls, handing out tea and coffee. Another tent had been erected to allow kids to use their talents to produce new protest signs festooned with flowers and peace symbols. I learned from Rosanna that their teacher Kate Ross, a wiry slip of a woman with straight black hair and a perpetual smile, had made the hospital protest a part of their Social Studies assignment. The kids clearly adored her. There was lots of embracing going on as old friends met one another.

The *Newcombe Daily* had seen fit to send a reporter up the valley—a young lad in his twenties who introduced himself to me as Jeff Levinkoff, from an old Glacier Valley Doukhobor family. I'd been away so many years he was probably only a toddler when I left. He was either somewhat unsure of himself or of a taciturn nature. After a brief introduction, he had little to say. Maybe he viewed me as competition. I had to admire his porkpie hat; it made him look vaguely like a Beat poet. It seemed wisest to stick close to Rosanna, the calm at the centre of the vortex and the director of all action. She was like the nucleus of an atom, with other people constantly intersecting and then bouncing off her.

"Where should I set up for the photo shoot?" I asked.

She was just finishing up with one of the protestors. "Walk with me; I'll show you a good spot."

We walked toward the lake, which curved around to the west and south of the hospital site. Holding up her hands like a film director framing a shot, she said, "Here. That way you can still get some of the lake in the picture. And hopefully enough of the circle so that it still at least gives people the *idea* of a circle."

"I'll need at least a couple of people to hold up signs," I said.

"The kids are making more signs as we speak."

At this point an RCMP cruiser rolled into view at the edge of the helipad. She started to move in that direction. "Mind if I tag along?" I asked. She nodded.

It was Constable Neihardt. Most police all look the same to me in uniform but he had a baby face that contrasted oddly with the grey creeping in at his temples. I remembered him from the lab blockade incident. He managed a weak smile. "Hi Rosanna. Just checking in. I wanted to remind you that you're welcome to express yourselves so long as the hospital entrances and exits aren't blocked, or the helipad. If they are, I'm sorry but I'll have to remove people."

"Don't worry," she said. "I'll look after that. I've been quite specific on that point."

"Well I'd rather it was you moving your people than me."

"Absolutely. If you want we can take a walk around. I'll explain the plan."

The two of them walked off toward the lake and the rear of the hospital. I decided to get a coffee. I saw a dark green pickup truck pull up with a vaguely familiar face. It rolled to a stop beside me and the face of Graham Kenwood leaned out the window, thick grey hair ruffling in the breeze. "I see they haven't managed to drive you off yet," he said with a wry grin. I found his north of England accent pleasing to the ears.

"Nope. Not yet anyway. What brings you down here?"

"Rosanna asked me to set up a PA and microphone."

"Wouldn't cheap walkie-talkies work better?"

"Well, no. She wants to give a bit of a speech." He grinned. "I assume that's why you're here—to take down her inspiring words."

"Marie-Louise is going to add her fifty cents worth too, I think."

"Or fifty dollars, depending on your point of view," chuckled Graham. "Anyway, I'm off. Got some setup to do." He put the truck in gear and rolled ahead slowly.

"Need a hand unloading gear?"

"Nah. I'll recruit one of those strong-looking youngsters over there."

A circle was beginning to form. Constable Neihardt had left, apparently satisfied with Rosanna's reassurances. People were chatting and jostling one another as if it were a party. Picket signs were carefully spaced at about every third or fourth person. Graham was unrolling microphone cable toward the mike stand he'd set up for Rosanna. Having decided this was the focal point of the circle she'd brought Marie-Louise, Tom, and Moss to stand on either side of her. It struck me how like children with their teacher they were, meekly obeying her instructions—shifting a little to the left, a little to the right.

At this point I noticed a woman I'd never seen before. She had shoulder-length jet-black hair and wore an outfit that was part gypsy chic, part Salvation Army retreads. She wore a belly dancer's gold chain around her waist and bright, multipatterned fabric of her blouse and dress. Her lips were painted an unnatural shade of bright red. But it was her eyes that really struck me. They were preternaturally aware. As she spoke her eyelids continually raised to expose the entire pupil, giving her a slightly crazed expression. She had the intensity of someone who believes she has the inside track on just about everything. She'd managed to collar Rosanna and was pressing some point home. Rosanna was looking put out, her eyes darting toward an escape.

"Look, Lynette, I hear you. But we've kinda got things organized now."

The woman took this as a signal to lean in closer, although Rosanna was several inches taller. "It's Moonglow, remember? I legally changed my name."

"I'm sorry. Moonglow. The point is, it's a little late in the program now."

"All I'm asking is to boost the healing energy by placing crystals around the circle. That will amplify everyone's intention to save the hospital. It'll also amplify the cosmic energies. It won't take me a minute to set up."

Rosanna glanced at her watch: 3:45. There was probably enough time but I could tell it was the last thing she wanted.

She might have a soft spot for people like Moss the Crawler and Moonglow, but she knew what such stunts would look like with the Newcombe media here. We'd only narrowly avoided having the media pick up on Moss's crawl. Moonglow was drilling her with those intense, dark brown eyes. It occurred to me she might be useful in an interrogation room with eyes like that. Rosanna's sigh suggested a collapse of resistance. "Okay, you can set your crystals out. But *please* wait 'til you hear from me before performing any ritual. Now, if you'll excuse me, I need to confer with Marie-Louise."

Moonglow grabbed her by the arm. "But setting out the crystals is just *part* of the setup if we're to attract the cosmic energies we need."

Marie-Louise had walked up beside Rosanna. Seeing Moonglow, she looked away. It seemed they might have had a history with each other—and not necessarily a good one. "What are you up to *now*, Moonglow?"

Moonglow shot her a look that could wither crops before turning her full attention back on Rosanna. "I need to get the circle to do a chant. I'll lead the chant using the mike."

Rosanna just managed to stop herself short of a full eyeball roll. "Listen, Moonglow. I appreciate you wanting to help, I really do. But Marie-Louise is our ceremonial leader here today. After I do my introduction, she'll direct us in a First Nations ritual prayer."

"You're saying I'm not good enough?" Moonglow's eyes eloquently added, "compared to *her*," with no need for words. Marie-Louise was pulling in a long draught of her hand-rollie.

Rosanna sighed loudly. "No, I'm NOT saying that, Moonglow. It's just … there's a lot of people here, there's media here—"

"Oh, I see. So you don't want people to see you let the crazy woman out."

Rosanna winced as if stung. Her brow darkened, as if to say: "Girl, you just went too far."

"I'm sure lots of people probably think that about *me*," said Marie-Louise, trying to ease the tension. "That crazy half-native woman. I don't think that's what Rosanna is trying to say, if you'd just let her."

Moonglow's arms were firmly crossed. "She's saying she doesn't want me to do this. That's what she's saying."

Graham had been fitting up the microphone stand and was speaking into the mike to test the volume levels. The sound amplified across the lawns surrounding the hospital. Suddenly Moonglow grabbed the mike stand and pulled it to herself. "Everyone! EVERYONE!" she shouted, causing the PA system to squeal. "Can I please have your attention?" I could hear Graham's urgent warning that she didn't need to shout—the mike would do the work. The PA system was howling. Graham sprinted to his amplifier to push the levels down. Marie-Louise grabbed the mike stand and tried to pull it away from Moonglow, who resisted, causing a tug-of-war. The thumping sounds caused by their struggle amplified until Graham shut off the mike. People were starting to laugh and all eyes were turned toward the scuffle. The two of them were locked around the chrome mike stand, the mike cord wrapping around Moonglow's ankle 'til she tripped. Marie-Louise came down on her heavily, causing an expulsion of breath from Moonglow.

Rosanna was pulling her own hair. "Stop! STOP! I mean it, stop it right NOW!"

It was no use. The two women were intertwined, wrapped in mike cord as they rolled on the grass. Finally Rosanna turned in desperation toward Tom and Moss. Her eyes were wide, her hands open in a helpless gesture, appealing for help. The two men rushed forward, each grabbing one of the women and pulling them to a standing position at a safe distance apart. Moonglow's eyes were fierce but Marie-Louise mostly looked embarrassed. Graham walked calmly up and set about disentangling them from the mike cord. Moss looked confused, a look that said, "This isn't how this was supposed to go." Tom laid a hand on both the women's shoulders. "Now, breathe," he said softly. "Breathe. Let it all pass over. Namaste."

What almost no one had noticed was the presence of Jeff Levinkoff, busily taking notes. This was going badly, and there was no guarantee Rosanna would be able to talk him out of writing up this embarrassing incident. Tom had noticed Levinkoff and leaned to whisper urgently in Rosanna's ear. She nodded and stepped up to the mike, which Graham had put back in order. He winked at me as he walked back to the sound desk to adjust the volume. Graham had a way of seeing the humour in every situation.

"Everyone," said Rosanna. "I'm sorry, I ... I'd like everyone to please get into final formation—we're about to begin the sacred circle ceremony. I just want to say a few words before I call Marie-Louise to the microphone." People shuffled into position. I set up my tripod and checked my camera settings. "To start with, we're going to face in toward the centre of the circle, where Marie-Louise will perform the First Nations sacred circle ritual. We'd like everyone to link hands. Once that's done, we'll turn back to face outward so the photographers can get some pictures."

Moonglow was glowering in what could hardly be described as a shiny, happy manner. Rosanna ignored her. "Once the photos are done, Moonglow has offered to lead us all in a chant. You're welcome to stay for that if you like, but the program will officially end once Marie-Louise is finished." Moonglow's eyebrows lifted in dismay.

Marie-Louise was chuckling. I was standing close by, camera at the ready. "That gal's a born diplomat," she whispered to me.

Rosanna stepped away from the mike and leaned close to Moonglow. "You can set up your crystals AFTER the photo shoot," she hissed. "I mean it. Don't mess with me on this one." Moonglow's Rasputin glare wilted beneath Rosanna's authority.

Rosanna turned back toward the encircled crowd and grabbed the mike again. "Okay, everyone—"

There was a deafening roar overhead. A shadow passed over the grass in the shape of a broad wingspan. All heads were craned upward. A small-engine aircraft with float pontoons had done a flyby and was circling back toward the lake. It swung out in a graceful arc, its engine blatting as the pilot began throttling down. We watched as it headed first south down the lake toward Elkville, then banked and turned back toward the hospital. The pilot throttled down further, the engine noise bouncing loudly across the water as he brought the craft down on the lake, sending plumes of spray cascading off either pontoon. It taxied into the shallows and the pilot hopped out onto one pontoon, tossing out an anchor. He leapt into the shallow water and jogged up the gentle slope toward the hospital. He was wearing a red, black and white plaid wool jacket and a ball cap, his radio headset still on, the mike pushed to one side. His lace-up work boots were wet but not soaked—I recognized the sheen of Dubbin, the waterproofing grease my old man taught me to use on family camping trips. The circle disbanded as curious onlookers made their way toward the lake.

Rosanna strode out to meet him, Tom and Moss at her side. The pilot was lean and tall, about Rosanna's height, clean-shaven with the dark shadow of whiskers colouring his jaw. He had curly dark hair and bushy sideburns with a few grey hairs. It occurred to me that—except for the sideburns and curly hair—he looked a lot like my old man, who himself often reminded me of that old-time movie star Gary Cooper.

He stretched out a hand in greeting. "Jack—Jack Wingarde. I got the email about today's protest for the hospital from Jane Bordeaux. Thought I'd see if I could help. I do flyovers of logging cuts for the SGS folks sometimes."

After the melee of the medicine women it was like a gift dropped from heaven. Rosanna looked at me, as if to ask: Is this your doing? I shrugged innocently. It had nothing to do with me. But I made a note to thank Jane for her emails. Rosanna barely skipped a beat. "Would you be willing to take our reporter up with you to take a picture?"

Levinkoff made his way to the front of the crowd. He held out his hand to Wingarde. "And me too, if you don't mind. Jeff Levinkoff, *Newcombe Daily News*."

"Sure," said Wingarde. "But only one at a time. That's all I really have room for besides myself."

I stepped forward. "Roy Breen, *Mountain Echo*. I'll gladly let Jeff go up first—on one condition." I turned toward Levinkoff, who looked puzzled. "That he consider *very* carefully what he writes about today's event."

The look in Levinkoff's eyes said: "Well, *maybe*." But I wasn't about to let him off that easy. "I mean, that you stick to reporting on the actual *protest*, and forget that little scuffle you just saw." I winked at Wingarde conspiratorially. He got it immediately.

"Sounds fair to me," said Wingarde.

Levinkoff shook his head. "Hell, I don't need an aerial photograph. I can just—"

"Let us here at the *Echo* scoop you on the story with the best photo? Sure, I'm okay with that if you are. Think about it, Jeff. The real story is the symbolic action of protest, not some minor altercation before the main event."

He was considering his options. I could see this hit him where he lives. I was no cub reporter fresh out of journalism college. I knew how these guys think. The *Newcombe Daily News* had been bought out by the Interior Media Corporation and they were nothing if not fiercely competitive. Getting scooped by a two-bit independent like the *Echo* would be more than his publishers could probably stand.

Finally Levinkoff nodded. "Okay. You win."

A cheer went up from the protestors. People were hugging and dancing around in circles, including Rosanna and Marie-Louise, Tom and Moss. It had an unintentionally comic effect, with the height differences.

"So it's settled," said Wingarde. "Jeff goes up first, then I come back down for you, Roy."

"If you don't mind, Jack," said Rosanna. "We'd like to start the ceremony first. Then once Marie-Louise is done, we'll face outwards again and you can take the plane up."

He gave her a thumbs-up. "You betcha. Just give me the signal."

She turned toward the crowd. "Okay, everyone. Listen up! We need to get back into a circle around the hospital just like we did before. Please do it in an orderly way...."

People were already moving back up the slope to the main lawn. Tom and Moss moved in opposite directions around the circle, gently moving protestors forward or backward in an attempt to create an evenly rounded circumference, turning the outward-facing ones back toward the centre. After about five minutes of jostling one another it fell into place. Rosanna stepped up to the mike. "Thank you everyone. I also want to thank our local reporter, Roy Breen, who brought me the latest news from PHA. It's a good news, bad news story. I wish I could say it's all good news, but it's not. So I'll start with the good news. They've agreed to let us keep our x-ray machine!"

As if choreographed, all the joined hands went up in the air with a loud cheer. It went on and on, punctuated by loud whistles. Jeff and I were madly snapping pictures. It's one of the things I've always found toughest about being a reporter—having to remain in the observer role when you want to jump for joy with everyone else. Always standing on the outside looking in—simultaneously a blessing and a curse.

Rosanna raised her arms above her head. "Quiet! QUIET! Remember, this is a hospital, so there are patients here, and they need quiet." She needn't have bothered—I could see faces pressed against the windows on the backside of the hospital. Many were clapping at the news.

"And now, the bad news. They're going ahead with the cutback to our ER hours. If they get their way, it'll be banker's hours for the ER ward."

As if on cue, the crowd raised a loud, continuous "BOOOO...."

Rosanna was motioning for calm again. "That means we have to keep a presence on the hospital site for as long as it takes for PHA to back down." A few "Yeahs!" went up but she waved them down. "So today we begin with a sacred circle around our hospital, which we hope to do once a day, every day, until they back down. As you all know, wherever we live in Canada, we live on First Nations land. That means we owe them respect and gratitude. We owe them the honour of having a voice, and what better way to do that than to ask one of their people to conduct us in the sacred circle ceremony. I've asked Marie-Louise Tremblay—Cinnamon Bear—to conduct the ceremony." With that Rosanna stepped aside from the microphone.

Marie-Louise looked a little put-on-the-spot but recovered quickly. Graham was there in a flash to adjust the mike down to her level. "Thank you, Rosanna. First things first," she grinned. "As a veteran protestor, I can tell you, it's like herding cats sometimes to get us all on the same page." She paused for the crowd's laughter. "I think Rosanna deserves a big round of applause for keeping all us wayward cats in line, don't you?" Linked hands were dropped as people clapped enthusiastically. Cheers were raised but faded out quickly as people remembered Rosanna's admonition for quiet.

"In native tradition the circle is everything," Marie-Louise continued. I had my steno pad out, as did Levinkoff. "The teepee is based on a circle, the dances are always in a circle. It's symbolic of the circle of creation, the circle of the Earth. The sweat lodge is based on a circle and women's healing circles take the same form. We offer tobacco and incense to the four points of the circle of creation where the spirits of our ancestors live. By honouring them, we seek their guidance and protection. This place is a place of healing, so it's fitting we encircle it with our hearts and spirits today."

She stepped out of the circle toward the centre and two protestors joined hands to close the circle again. She pulled a pouch of tobacco out of the handbag at her side. Taking a generous portion, she held it above her head and let the wind carry it from her fingertips. "The circle reminds us that no matter where we are, when we stand at its centre, we stand at the centre of all creation. It's a reminder: We must treat it with respect and care. In native tradition, we offer a gift such as tobacco to the *Manitou*—the Great Spirit that lives in all creation."

She took out a bundle of incense and lit it, placing the bundle in a shell in the palm of her hand. With her other hand she drew an eagle feather from a pouch and fanned the smoke into the air. "The incense is made of four sacred herbs," she explained. "Tobacco, sweetgrass, cedar, and sage. The shell is a feminine symbol associated with water. The feather is masculine, associated with air or sun. The medicine comes from combining the two, neither one without the other. With it we honour all the four directions of creation."

She faced north, took the shell and feather and fanned the sweet, sharp incense into the air as she moved, turning next south, west and finally east. "The east is where everything begins and where everything ends. Everyone, please take a few moments of silence. Let's thank the ancestors for their gifts and ask their help in saving this place of healing...."

Silence descended in a weightless cloud over the assembled protestors, underlined by the occasional gust of wind in the treetops or the swish of tires on the nearby highway. After about two minutes Rosanna stepped up to the mike. "Everyone, if you could please now turn around and face outward for the photo. That way, when Jack—"

Wingarde leaned into her, whispering. She nodded. "Jack has said that when he does his pass over the hospital, he'll dip his wings when it's time to shoot the picture. If we all look up at the plane at that moment, it should make a fantastic shot."

As Levinkoff climbed into the floatplane I felt a pang of jealousy. Being fair isn't always easy. But a deal is a deal, and if it reined in the *Newcombe Daily* even a little bit, it was worth the wait. I watched as Wingarde taxied south on the lake, lifted off the water and executed a flawless arc to bring himself back on course for the hospital site. I had my telephoto lens trained on his plane—that too would make a great shot to go with the story. As it turned out, Rosanna's instructions were unnecessary. Everyone in the circle was intently watching the plane's progress. As it glided overhead, Wingarde dipped the wing and everyone was facing the sky. I could actually see Levinkoff's porkpie hat above his camera lens as he furiously snapped away. A shiver ran down my spine imagining myself in his place, with nothing more than a seat belt and a flimsy door between me and the Earth a hundred metres below.

Wingarde made a quick second pass so Levinkoff could make doubly sure he had the shots he needed. Already the light was pearling into dusk. The floatplane taxied back up to the shoreline and Levinkoff hopped out. Someone had placed a driftwood plank between the shore and the pontoons so I didn't have to wade out to the plane. As I swung myself into the passenger seat I could hear radio chatter punctuated by the occasional hiss and crackle of static or poor reception. "Buckle up!" Wingarde said.

I hadn't been in a small aircraft since childhood, when my old man had taken me with him on one of his forestry fly-overs. We were living up north near Fort St. John, which to a young teenager may as well have been the end of the Earth. As Wingarde taxied down the lake and lifted off, I felt something drop in the pit of my stomach. It was as if just being in the plane had triggered a memory. I remembered being in a Twin Otter aircraft with the old man when we hit a pocket of bad weather. I'd had inner ear infections since I was a child, leaving me with problems equalizing pressure behind the eardrum. Somehow on that day my ears wouldn't equalize, making my head feel like a pumpkin about to burst. Painful to say the least. Added to that was the sudden terror that we might not make it out of the storm alive. The Otter was buffeted as if some capricious god was batting us around the sky for play. Dad could sometimes be hard, though it was usually a surface act. I was always a sensitive kid. If I fell off my bike and scraped a knee, I'd get the tough act from the old man. "Oh come on, it's not that bad." But on this occasion, he realized I was in serious distress. I recall having his calloused, warm hand gently on my shoulder the whole time. Somehow, it helped. But to this day I'm terrified of small airplanes.

Liftoff is always the hardest. My stomach wants to stay firmly rooted to the ground. Luckily I have strong control over my gag reflex. Wingarde had the confident air of a seasoned pilot and had no doubt noticed the whiter shade of pale I was becoming. "Hey, how ya doing? I'll try to keep it as smooth as possible."

I gave him a shaky thumbs-up. "I'm okay...."

Seeing the lake surface from the air, I had to hold down my sense of vertigo. I hauled out the camera and made sure my settings were right, scanning the water surface below as we swung back around toward the hospital. We were gliding into position and Wingarde dipped his wing. I was ready, snapping madly. I had to admit to myself it was an amazing perspective being able to see the human chain encircling the hospital, faces upturned—like children with tongues out to catch raindrops. Wingarde spoke into his mike, his voice coming through on my headset. "How's that? I can do another pass if you're not sure."

"Why not?" I answered. "A few more shots for insurance wouldn't hurt."

We overshot the hospital grounds as Wingarde piloted the plane back toward the lake to prepare for the next run. As we headed south, there was a burst of garbled talk on the radio. I recalled how hard it could be trying to make out radio conversations. Wingarde fiddled with the squelch knob and managed to clear the signal. "Police channel," he explained.

"... get Search and Rescue out? Over," a voice crackled.

"What you got? Over," said another distorted voice.

"Uh, lost hiker and his kid. Tourist. Over."

"Yeah ... be ready to go in an hour.... SAR crew here is first rate. Over."

Wingarde turned down the volume. "After this pass, I gotta go see if I can help out."

My stomach was still dancing up and down but my journalist's radar was telling me this was a story I had to follow. A Search and Rescue mission would be great front-page material. I had to overcome my fear and see if he'd let me tag along. "Do you mind if I come with you?"

"Well I don't mind but it's probably not up to me."

"Who then?"

"Usually the RCMP or the Incident Commander on the SAR crew. The marina is just a half-kilometre or so from here, so we can be there in about two minutes. You might as well come with me and take it from there."

Chapter Seven

Wingarde flew us across the municipal park, playground and ball field known as Confederation Park. The park had probably been a ball diamond since early in the twentieth century but had been officially christened on the occasion of Canada's centenary in 1967. It was a prime spot reaching to the lakeshore, with campsites on either end of the park. The ball field was some of the rare level ground in the village. Eldorado had essentially been built on an alluvial fan—layers of rock and gravel that had been washed down from the mountains over thousands of years. Without that, there would have been nowhere to build but the steep mountainsides. Adding to the challenge of creating a habitable location, Harris Creek cut the village in half as it fed Sapphire Lake with glacial melt.

Wingarde headed north, passing diagonally over Confederation Park so he could swing out toward the Valhalla range and then taxi down toward the marina. As we descended I could see activity below—pickup trucks converging at the marina, men on the dock checking equipment in a rescue boat. The wind had picked up so our glide toward shore was rough this time, buffeting the plane's pontoons. The lake's reputation for going from dead blue calm to bone-rattling inside an hour was well deserved.

"What do you do if it gets too choppy?" I asked.

"Circle a few more times, look for a soft spot," his voice crackled over the headset. "If that doesn't work out, I just go in and roll with the punches. Lots of pilots don't like this lake for floatplanes though. I think our days are numbered. It's mostly choppers in the mountains these days. That's pretty much all the cops use anymore."

The plane taxied up to the docks like a truck skidding along a corduroy road. Wingarde leapt out and tossed the anchor into the shallow water. I unbuckled myself and stepped out carefully, uncertain of my feet. I could see a man walking toward us. As he got closer I recognized Don Houghton, owner of the Eldorado Hardware Store. He had on his reflective emergency vest. The light was fading fast. The two men obviously knew each other.

"Hi Jack, how's it hangin'?" Don's tone was light but his expression was serious. He wore glasses, well-trimmed hair and a stubble-length moustache and goatee. In another life he could have been a GQ model. I suspected women here secretly lusted after him.

"Great, Don. What's the scoop?"

"Oh, another lost tourist and his son. One of my clerks sold them some camping gear but unfortunately she doesn't remember whether that included flares or an emergency beacon. My guess: probably not."

"How long have they been missing?"

"They were supposed to be back this afternoon from an overnight camping trip across the lake. My clerk said the guy was talking about heading over to do the hike up the glacier."

"So probably they landed at White Sands Creek to take the trail from there," Jack guessed. "Where's Lonnie Harrison?"

"He's on his way from the Highways yard. Should be here any minute."

"Who's Lonnie Harrison?" I asked. It was like an unwanted dance partner cutting in. They both looked at me blankly. "Sorry. I'm Roy Breen, reporter with the *Mountain Echo*." I held out my hand and Don shook it perfunctorily.

"Lonnie is the Fire Chief and Search and Rescue crew Incident Commander," Don explained. He grinned mischievously. "You here to help? I'm sure they can use another body to haul equipment up the glacier trail."

"Sure," I said. "Anything I can do."

He shook his head. "I doubt Lonnie will want you along."

"Well I can't say I have your training, but I'd like to help if I can."

"We'll have to wait and see what Lonnie says. We're losing the light already, so that means a ground search will have to be postponed 'til tomorrow morning at first light."

"Is there anything you can do before then?"

"Our crew can take a run across the lake and see if they're close to shore," said Don. "We've got some powerful searchlights—they'll start by scanning the shoreline. But if they got lost or injured somewhere on the trail above, we'll just have to try again in the morning."

"I can do a quick flyby," offered Jack. "See if any flares or distress fires have been set."

"Let's see what Lonnie says," Don advised.

A pickup truck pulled into the marina parking lot followed by the slam of a door. A man of medium height, slim build and dark wavy hair under a ball cap stepped out. By the way Don and Jack stiffened slightly and turned in his direction, it was clear this was Fire Chief Lonnie Harrison. Harrison strode up to the docks, a sense of urgency in his stride. His face was grave, his manner brusque.

"Situation report," he said directly to Don, while nodding a greeting at Jack.

"A guy and his teenage son not reported back when expected."

"What time was that?"

"They were supposed to be gone overnight, back today by late afternoon."

"Late afternoon?"

Don gave a slight grimace. "They wouldn't say exactly. He was in my store buying some camping gear. Connie talked to him but I wasn't in the store that day."

"When was that?"

"Day before yesterday. Right after I opened up at 8:30. Said they were taking a fishing boat over to White Sands Creek to hike the glacier trail. He told Connie they were leaving straight from the store."

"Have the RCMP been called?"

"Yeah, Constable Neihardt is on his way. Should be here any minute."

"Were they carrying any emergency beacons or flares?"

"Don't know."

"Make a point of asking next time."

Don bristled at this. "Am I supposed to quiz every tourist that comes into my store?"

Lonnie put a friendly hand on his shoulder. "Well it's kind of convenient one of our crew just happens to own the local hardware store."

Don laughed. "So you're willing to pay me double time for double duty?"

Lonnie's serious face cracked with a grin. "Don't talk to me about that—talk to the Provincial Emergency Program folks. We've been asking for on-call pay for years."

I was taking notes. "No pay for on-call emergency crew members." This would bear following up. Lonnie strode over to the rescue boat. "Everything in order here?" he asked a crew member. I was just out of earshot so I couldn't hear everything that was being said. The crewman was pointing at various pieces of equipment tucked into the boat: back board for immobilizing injury cases, first aid kit, ropes, a long aluminum pole with what looked like a lasso on the end of it for pulling people out of the water. Dusk was coming down fast, the sky a deep indigo above the shadowy V of the ridges that cradled the snow-crowned Eldorado Glacier. The searchlight was snapped on, sending out a beam so intense it carved a path across the waves halfway across the lake. The outboard engines were already idling with that guttural chuckling sound so typical of boat motors.

The headlamps of a car swung into view in the parking lot. As it got closer I could make out the markings on the RCMP cruiser. Constable Neihardt walked briskly onto the dock. I nodded at him but he ignored me and went straight to Harrison by the boat. They conferred briefly then walked back to where I was standing with Jack and Don. Now that Neihardt was here, he was clearly in charge.

"Okay. Here's what's going to happen," he said. "Lonnie and two crew are going to take the boat across, scan the shoreline. Jack, do you mind taking the plane up for a quick pass to see if there's any distress fires lit?"

"Already on it," Jack nodded.

"I hate to ask you to do it with the light failing, but until we can get some of our own choppers out tomorrow, it would sure be a big help."

"When will that be?" I interrupted.

"Not 'til morning. We'll see how you guys do with the ground search first. If they'd managed to get themselves lost a few hours earlier we'd have had a chopper here by now from Newcombe. But it seems we can't schedule rescues to suit ourselves."

The men chuckled at this. There was an edge to the laughter, like graveyard humour. I took my opportunity. "Any chance I might come along? I'm reporting for the *Mountain Echo*."

He shook his head. "You'll just get in the way. We'll let you know what happens as soon as we know."

"What about if I rode along with Jack?"

Neihardt shrugged. "That's up to you, Jack." Jack nodded. Neihardt was unimpressed. "I don't think you're going to see much at this hour from up there. Jack's doing us a favour, going up at all in this light."

"I've got my regular lights, so I'm not exactly flying blind," said Jack. "And an extra pair of eyes should come in handy."

"We appreciate the help, Jack," said Lonnie. Turning to Neihardt, he asked: "You want to come along? We're ready to push off here."

"No, you guys know what you're doing. You're Incident Commander so you might as well pick your own crew."

Lonnie nodded. "Okay, let's get moving. Don, I'm leaving you here to coordinate. Better contact the hospital. Let them know we may have some work for them soon. They'll need to be ready to airlift somebody tomorrow morning if we manage to find them."

"Hopefully it won't come to that, but yeah," said Don.

Lonnie and two crew members got into the boat and revved the engine, sending out a bubbling trail of froth in the boat's wake as they sped off.

"Looks like you're restricted to base camp," I said to Don.

He chuckled. "Don't feel sorry for me—I've been on plenty of these rescues. The novelty wears thin after awhile. We just do what we have to do to save lives. But hey—Jack's getting the plane fired up—better move it if you want to go along."

Sure enough, the plane's engine had spat and burbled to life. I gingerly stepped onto the pontoon at dockside and climbed inside. Jack handed me the headset. "If it makes you feel any better you can also be a second set of ears, not that I need them. I'll have the police and emergency band on."

The lake had smoothed out somewhat since our earlier landing but it was still like riding a massage chair on overdrive, at least until we got into the air. I was beginning to see the appeal of a helicopter in country like this. The sky retained its late afternoon glow so the receding ridgelines were still visible, not yet plunged in black. There was a dusky rose glow on the mountains to the north, reflecting off the high alpine snow-pack. Being in an airplane always gave me an odd feeling of near-weightlessness, threatening to tip me into stomach-dropping vertigo. We could hear Lonnie on the radio. "Heading straight across to White Sands.... Be there in ten minutes or so. You there, Jack? Over."

Jack grabbed the radio mike, clicked it on with his thumb. "Here, Lonnie. Over."

"Don't get yourself in trouble, Jack. A quick pass, maybe two. Over."

"Roger that. Over."

I recalled flying with the old man in a Forest Service heli-copter—the old Bell choppers with the glass bubble—as a kid. Maybe that was another reason for my exaggerated sense of vertigo. To this day, I can recall sucking in my breath as I looked down at my feet to see the tops of trees below. The small window in the door of Jack's Beaver wasn't the greatest for vis-ibility but I was grateful for the extra metal between me and the lake. Dusk was spreading its blanket of shadows over every-thing, so unless the lost hikers had built a fire, it was unlikely we'd see anything at all. Jack was flying us toward the glacier in another of his graceful arcs, so we could swing above White Sands Creek where the rescue boat was headed. The unnatural sound of Jack's radio-amplified voice sounded in my ears.

"We'll split it up into quadrants. You take from centre front to the right, I'll take from centre front to the left."

I didn't bother to remind him that from my perch that meant scanning mostly the lake, but then, he was the man with experience, not me. I could see the rescue boat carving its plume of spray; it was two-thirds of the way there. "Should be at shoreline in a few minutes, Jack. Over," Lonnie's voice burbled over the radio.

"Not seeing anything yet, Lonnie. Over," Jack answered.

The topography of the mountainside—even in the dim light—was coming into soft relief. The sharp tips of twenty-metre firs were softened by the muddy early evening light. From the Eldorado side, it appeared as if the mountainside leading to the glacier was a single slope, but in fact the forested hump of a ridge extended diagonally from the peak down to the lakeshore. That meant hikers would have to crest this ridge and then descend the other side before climbing up the next slope leading to the glacier. It made the advantages of air surveillance in rescue operations obvious. If the hikers were behind that ridge, they'd never be seen from shore even with a campfire. Jack's voice broke into my headset again. "I'm going to gain altitude, see if maybe they're higher up the trail. Maybe they made it as far as the glacier."

As we gained altitude the glacier asserted itself into our field of vision, a sloping bowl that remained covered in deep snow year-round. Its reach down the mountainside had steadily diminished with climate change but still retained its glacial supremacy over the peak. As if alive, the ice and snow held the phosphorescent remains of late afternoon sunlight, a natural beacon on the roof of the world. It made for a stark contrast between the snowline and the deepening darkness of the forest below. But no matter where we looked, we could see no evidence of campfires.

"I'm taking her back out for another pass," Jack said.

He swung northwards, still at high altitude. I felt a stabbing pang of vertigo, as if I were at the top of a Ferris wheel trying to avoid looking down. He must have noticed the look on my face: "Everything alright?" I nodded vigorously. The last thing I wanted was to let my weaknesses get in the way of the search. As he curved eastward he began dropping altitude so that we made a spiral back toward the far side of the lake. Looking down, I could see the rescue boat had reached the shoreline and was scanning it with its powerful searchlights. I nudged Jack and pointed downward. He saw it and nodded, picking up the radio mike. "What's it look like down there, Lonnie? Over."

"Nothing yet," the radio crackled. "We'll scan a hundred metres either side of the creek. But most of that is forest so don't expect to see much there. Over."

"I'm making another pass overhead now. Over." Turning to me, he said: "I'm going to take us lower this time, buzz that lower ridge. If they got past it, I'm sure I would've seen a fire on the trail up to the glacier. Keep your eyes peeled."

I felt a lump the size of a golf ball rise in my throat as he banked down toward the lake. Treetops seemed to be rushing up to meet us head-on. At about twenty metres above treeline he levelled out the Beaver, keeping its nose on an upward incline to follow the rise of the ridgeline from shore to peak. Again I had the sensation of being strapped into a carnival ride speeding to the crest of its track. I shoved it down, keeping focus on the ground beneath. My night vision for driving had always been excellent so this at least was an advantage.

"See anything yet?" Jack shouted.

"No, not yet!"

"I can't hold us here too long before we pass the peak, which is the wrong direction for the glacier trail anyway. I'll have to break off—"

My heart leapt in my breast. "Wait! I see something!" There was something that looked like the red-orange glow of a single ember that had caught the edge of my vision as we skimmed past. Not much to see at this height but it was definitely there.

"You sure?"

"I'm sure, I'm sure!"

"Okay, I'll bank us out over the lake again and we can try to pinpoint it." He picked up the mike. "Beaver 201-X-A Daniel calling SAR-052, over."

"SAR-052 here, over."

"Lonnie, I think we spotted a fire. I'm going to see if we can pinpoint it for you. Over."

"Roger that. Don't push it too hard, Jack! Over."

Jack looped us out over the lake and followed his previous trajectory so closely it was uncanny. I knew about the legendary bush pilots of the north but here was living proof right in the seat next to me. Once again he plunged us toward the treeline before levelling out and pushing the Beaver toward the peak. I had a pretty good idea where I'd noticed the glow. It had been just short of the ridge that bisected the range heading up to the glacier—on steep terrain but not lost somewhere in the hollow behind the ridge. I kept my eyes trained on the treetops. Jack too was looking in that direction while regularly checking his angle of ascent. It seemed only a fraction of a second we were above the spot and I couldn't make anything out in the shadows below, congealing now into fully-fledged night.

"Damn!" I blurted.

"I can't see it either."

"It was there, I know it!"

"I believe you, Roy. Think you can remember well enough to point it out on a map?"

"Yeah, probably. I mean, yes, I think so."

He had the mike in his hand. "Lonnie, I'm going to put down. Roy thinks he saw something. Over."

"Can you see it now? Over."

"Negative, Lonnie. You guys see anything? Over."

"Negative. Not a thing. Over."

"I'll meet you back at the marina. Over."

"Roger that."

The wind had settled down on the lake so this time our landing was much smoother. It would take ten minutes or so for the rescue boat to return. After tying the pontoon to the dock, Jack motioned toward a picnic table on the shore. "Let's wait over there." He pulled out a pack of cigarettes. "I could use a smoke."

While we waited, there was time to ponder the situation. Even at night the lake was starkly beautiful. The Valhalla range tore a jagged edge into the sky. I wondered: If this mountain could speak, what voice would it use? The answer was obvious once you were out of the city long enough and got your "country legs." The mountain spoke in the scree of a bald eagle, the whoosh of a gale trapped between ridges, the subliminal thrum of granite in the moonlight—below hearing but not beyond comprehension. In part, it took shutting off the constant yammer in one's head. But this country had a way of *imposing* its presence on you—its voice—if you just stayed out in it long enough. What would it say to someone lost in its evergreen labyrinth? "Calm. Stay calm. Help is coming." Does the mountain speak differently to those it knows won't make it? "Here is peace. Prepare yourself." Or does it turn its face away from us—insignificant ants on its vast hemlock- and fir-clothed spine? Was the idea that it should speak to us at all merely a sign of our arrogance? Still, I had to wonder what that lost hiker and his son might be thinking right now. Barely-controlled panic, threatening to open up like a crevasse. Rock scree making one's steps greasy, unsure. And those too careless to avoid stepping over the edge, making that fatal mistake....

Finally the rescue boat chugged alongside the dock and one of the crew leapt out to tie up. Lonnie came striding down the dock to where we were sitting. He was grinning. "Well, Roy, looks like you just made yourself useful. I won't have to use you as a boat anchor after all."

"Gee, thanks—I think."

Jack slapped me on the shoulder. "Trust me, Roy—coming from Lonnie that's a compliment."

The grin had subsided and Lonnie's face was poker-straight now. "Think you can point out where you saw the campfire on a topographical map of the ridge?"

"I can certainly try. I'm no expert with maps, but—"

"That's okay, we're the experts. As long as you can put us within a kilometre or so we can do the rest. They can't be far off the trail anyway."

"I'd say near the first summit—just below where the ridge drops into the hollow on the other side," I offered.

"Good, that's good," said Lonnie. "Less than an hour's hike from the shore then. If we get going at first light we'll have them out of there in no time."

"And when is first light?"

"About 7:00 a.m. this time of year. We'll be suited up and ready to go well before then."

"Not sure I will be." It felt stupid coming out of my mouth, knowing what these guys were prepared to do.

He grinned again. "Ah, you soft journalists."

I held up a palm. "Me—maybe. But not all of us. Talk to a war correspondent sometime. On a per capita basis those guys have a higher mortality rate than most troops."

"Gotcha. I'll get a map from the truck so you can give me an approximate location."

"You said Don would be monitoring radio communications. Since I can't go with you, I'd like to know what's going on. You got a command post set up?"

"You can check in with Don at the hardware store. He keeps a radio there and he'll be carrying a walkie-talkie. If I know Don he'll pick up an early breakfast at the Garden Path next door. Then when we head across the lake he'll keep the radio on 'til we get back. You can tune in that way."

"Maybe I'll join him for breakfast."

He laughed. "Oh, you will eh?"

If nothing else, I thought, it's an excuse to pick Don's brains about Search and Rescue for my story. The next twenty-four hours could prove interesting—and exhausting.

Chapter Eight

In my mostly-asleep state it took me ages to realize that goddamn awful noise wasn't some beast in its death throes but an actual alarm. Shadowcat looked up at me from the foot of the bed with a half-lidded glare that said: "Are you crazy? Do you *know* what time it is?" I'd set the alarm for 6:30, an ungodly hour for me. I could work 'til 2:00 or even 3:00 a.m. but mornings were always torture for me. When we went camping I literally had to dump Shadowcat out of the sleeping bag every morning so I could pack up the gear. This followed by his standard-issue Filthy Look. When it came to mornings, it was like father, like son. Luckily this morning all I had to do was splash water on my face, dress, and get going.

Garden Path owner Rick Offenbach was known to open early so the rescue crew could get breakfast in time for first light. It would still be dark when he arrived to light the wood-stove, fire up the gas kitchen range, and begin his meal prep. It would only take me fifteen minutes to drive from the cabin in Owl Creek to Eldorado. That should give me time to catch Don Houghton for a little pre-search interview.

I dragged my ass a little getting out of bed so by the time I pulled up outside the Garden Path it was nearly 7:00 a.m. Light was breaking over the Valhalla range, suffusing the sky with blue. That meant clear weather—good news for Search and Rescue and good news for the lost hikers. As the door closed behind me I could see Rick already busing tables of dirty breakfast dishes. The crew had come and gone.

"I take it you heard then," said Rick.

I smiled proudly. "Actually I was up in the floatplane with Jack Wingarde. Pretty sure I spotted a campfire just below the ridge."

He grinned. "Who knew there were so many uses for a journalist?"

"Yeah, yeah, wise guy. You've been talking to Lonnie. Can you get me a traditional special, eggs over easy, bacon not too crispy?"

"You betcha."

"Have you seen Don Houghton this morning?"

"Yep. Already been and gone. But you can probably catch him next door after breakfast. He'll be monitoring the radio."

"Have the cops been in yet?"

"Yep, they were here with Lonnie and the gang."

"Is Neihardt going out on the search?"

"Don't know. You'd have to ask Don about that."

"Is Neihardt on his own here?"

"No—there's a Constable Murray here too. They transfer them in and out so fast it's hard to keep up."

"So much for community policing then."

"I guess so."

After breakfast I went to the hardware store. The building looked like it had been there since the silver rush days of the 1890s, with grey wooden siding that could well have been milled right on site by the village pioneers. There was a small upstairs apartment with a single window facing onto the main street. The sagging roof above the entrance looked as if it might give way under a heavy snow load. The door had a heavy brass handle with a latch on top you squeezed to open. A bell clinked as I stepped inside, reminding me of that long-ago afternoon in a country store. This and the Cracked Teapot must be just about the last shops in the world that still had brass bells on the door. It made me smile.

Inside, the linoleum on the floor showed wear patterns around the front counter where people stood to pay—or chat-and-pay as was more likely the case. This was no place for the cattle lanes of superstores with their blinding fluorescent lights and impersonal checkouts. Don was scrolling through an inventory list on his computer monitor when I came in. When he saw me he flashed me his GQ grin. It had a boyish quality to it, as if he were contemplating some rich practical joke that would set the whole town laughing. And in fact he and Rick Offenbach had been known to pull jokes on one another. One morning, Don had arrived at work to find a "For Sale" sign not only on his own store but on Offenbach's restaurant next door. Other shop owners had picked up the stunt and before long it looked like the entire main street was for sale. Luckily it was all done during the off-season so there were no serious offers. Offenbach had told me in his typically sardonic way he'd happily have taken an offer—if it was at least 5 million.

The radio was spitting and crackling in the background. The ceilings were high, with paddles and fishing rods suspended from fishing line. The walls were jammed with shelves, the aisles pushed so close together you almost had to turn sideways to walk through. The back wall—the paint wall—was piled high with paint cans on the bottom several rows, spray cans layered on top of that, and paint samples spread across the wall like wallpaper. Another relic from my childhood memories presented itself in the revolving metal nail trays that partially blocked one aisle. Again, I had to wonder if this was one of the last places on Earth you could buy nails and screws by the pound. It was a welcome relief from the mountain of plastic packaging that invariably accompanied purchases in stores these days. The crazy logic of capitalism seemed to dictate that even something as bomb-proof as a hammer had to be encased in hermetically sealed plastic.

There were at least two nooks tucked into back corners, crammed with stuff. If indeed the way we organize our space is a reflection of how organized our minds are, then Don must have one chaotic brain. Yet you could ask him for anything and as long as he had it in stock he knew exactly where to find it. What was even more astounding, his staff also seemed to acquire this ability after working there awhile. As a buddy once told me, "People are either pilers or filers." Different brains, different organizing systems.

"What can I do for you?" he asked.

"Just thought I'd check in to see how things are going with the search across the lake."

"Not much happening yet." He checked his watch. 7:35. "They should be reaching the first summit pretty soon. They left bang on the dot of seven and it only takes ten minutes to get across the lake in the rescue boat in good weather, fifteen if it's rough or dark. But if the hikers got off the trail it could still take awhile to find them. You were of some help with Jack."

I shrugged it off. "Just an extra set of eyes. Lonnie made some crack about journalists. Said he wouldn't have to use me as a boat anchor after all."

He laughed loudly. "Yeah, I heard. That's just Lonnie's way of easing tension. These rescues can be pretty damn stressful."

"You've been on quite a few then?"

"Yep. Started with the volunteer fire department eight years ago. In the early days, we'd be lucky to do a dozen call-outs a year. Now it's twice that, sometimes more."

"You think people are becoming more careless?"

He tilted his head side to side in an equivocal gesture. "Maybe. Maybe we just have more tourists coming than we used to, so more incidents."

"So is there any debriefing, any counselling, for the crew?"

"Never used to be. In the old days, you'd go out to an accident on the highway, scrape up the remains and it was just, you know: Suck it up, get over it."

"But now?"

"Lonnie does a debriefing after every event. Checks in with each of us to see whether we think we need a counsellor. Pretty much standard procedure these days. He comes across tough but he's actually a thoughtful guy—well-liked. He's what holds the team together."

"How about you? Ever felt like you needed help to debrief from a traumatic rescue?"

He looked at me without answering, smiling thoughtfully. "On or off the record?"

"Either way. Your choice."

He turned toward the window looking out at the Eldorado Glacier. His usually cheerful face clouded over. "*Off* the record, there was one—a house fire—one of our old miners. Wild Bill Conrad we used to know him as. Must've fallen asleep with a cigarette in his hand. At least, that was what Lonnie wrote on the incident report. By the time we got there the fire was fully engaged. Not much chance of saving the place." He paused again, staring off at the glacier. I realized it would be pointless to rush him, so I waited.

"Anyway, it was a Sunday and the only coroner for miles around was in Kelowna at the time. Standard procedure when there's a death is that you report to the coroner. They call the shots, even if someone dies at home in bed. It was going to take him over four hours to get here, so he gave Lonnie the go-ahead to remove the body. He never forces anyone on the crew to do anything they don't want to, so he asked for volunteers. I stepped forward along with another guy—Tom Brown—who doesn't live here anymore. We'd hosed down the place pretty good so the framing was intact—barely. Charred—a write-off—but still standing.

"With fires you always have to be careful entering a building. You watch for ceiling beams or floor joists that are burnt out and could collapse on you. Some of the flooring had already burnt through but the joists seemed to be hanging on. It was a small place anyway so it didn't take much searching to find old Wild Bill. Sure enough, he was lying dead on the couch." The memory of it stopped him. He shook his head, trying to rid himself of the image.

"At least, what was left of him was lying on the couch. There was still some flesh on him, just hanging off the bones. Tom grabbed him by the heels while I reached under to carry him by what was left of his shoulders. But he was so charred his ribcage crumbled in my hands. My body went into involuntary reaction—couldn't help it. I puked right there. Took me a few minutes to pull myself together again."

"How did that go down with your Fire Chief?"

"Like I said, Lonnie understands this shit. He's been doing it longer than any of us."

"No recriminations?"

"Nope, just sent me home. Like he always says, 'Hey, we're all just volunteers here.' When we debriefed back at the firehall, I asked for the counsellor's phone number. I didn't know how the hell I was going to get that image out of my head."

"Sounds like the same shit war veterans have to cope with—PTSD."

"Yep. You think about it, you dream about it, it comes at you in the most awkward moments. You can be sitting over a candlelit dinner with your wife when something she says— totally unrelated—can trigger the memory."

"Ever think about quitting the Fire Rescue crew?"

He smiled sadly. "Every day since then. Some guys do quit."

"Who could blame them?"

"Exactly. It's not like we get paid for putting ourselves in danger's way. We do this because we care about this community."

"What's the attrition rate on the crew? How many guys—"

He raised a finger to stop me as the radio burbled to life. I recognized Lonnie's distorted voice. "Located a middle-aged man and his teenage son a hundred metres or so from the first summit. The man has a bad leg break from a fall. A little weak from shock. Son okay. Over."

Don reached for the mike. "You want to radio the hospital or should I? Over."

"Alert the ER. Just use the phone. We'll bring the boat straight to the hospital beach. We'll be there in ten minutes, max. Over."

He signed off, then picked up the phone and dialled. "It's Don. Can you give me Dr. Cameron please? Thanks. No, *don't* put me on hold! I'm on Fire Rescue call-out today. This is an emergency."

After explaining the nature of the injury to the doctor he hung up. Smiling, he turned to me. "Looks like your new handle should be Eagle Eyes. That speck of fire you spotted yesterday evening; looks like they found them pretty close to where you saw it."

"Glad I won't have to be a boat anchor."

Don laughed through the GQ smile. "Not yet, anyway."

"Think I should head over to the ER? Rosanna will probably be there anyway."

"Well you can head over if you want, but the nursing staff will probably kick you out. With Lonnie's crew it'll be pretty crowded in that little ER. If you want to hang out with the protestors that's your business."

"I'll need to know what happened eventually."

"You'll find out soon enough. Probably have to wait for the RCMP press release."

"That could take a week. What are you thinking?"

He sighed. "Another goddamn high-rise rat from the city. Thinks he can waltz off into the bush and has no clue how to do it right."

"Don't you sell camping gear to tourists? You must have some idea who it is. I mean, there can't be that many of them out there at this time of year."

"You're right. We get a trickle after Labour Day. And there were a couple of guys came in here buying stuff the past week. But I have to say again—protocol. Even if I knew which one it was, I'm not supposed to say 'til the cops issue their release."

"Come on...."

He laughed. "Hey, I don't know you that well yet. I'm sure I will, but...."

"Any comment at all? Off the record."

"Off the record? I get pretty fed up with having to go out twenty times a year to pick somebody up off a trail, or off the lake. Not because I don't care. Because too often it's people's stupidity that puts them there. They risk their own lives and then they risk ours. I don't mind if it's a legitimate accident; that can't always be prevented."

"Fair enough." I reached out to shake his hand. "Hey, thanks Don. It's been a slice."

"You're welcome. Be seeing you."

"Be seeing you." I had to wonder if Don knew the pop culture reference to the classic British cult TV series *The Prisoner*. I doubted it. He looked more like a *Law & Order* fan. The place dreamed up by writer-actor Patrick McGoohan was a village of another kind—an exotic prison for retired spies. Though in the end, one village is much like the next—a single theme, with endless variations. A social microcosm. This village was no prison but clearly it had its dangers. But right now I had other things on my mind....

I popped the clutch so hard on the station wagon the tires screeched, causing a couple of turned heads from passersby. I wanted to get there in time for a photo op—catching the Search and Rescue crew hitting the hospital beach—about the closest I'd ever get to a D-Day landing. As I turned off the highway onto the hospital lane, I could see the faithful pickup trucks still parked with their banners. They looked a little worse for the weather but were holding up. There was a handful of protestors with their picket signs milling about the hospital parking lot. They were mostly chatting with one another and smoking but had obeyed Rosanna's injunction not to block access. I couldn't see Rosanna or Marie-Louise. I knew I had very little time so I rolled to a stop, threw the gearbox into neutral and pulled the hand brake. I grabbed the camera from the passenger seat and hit the ground running. As I turned the corner by the helipad I could see the rescue boat slicing its foamy arc around the point. I'd just get there in time.

The distance between the rear entrance of the ER and the beach was only about fifty metres. I stopped short at about twenty-five metres and lifted the camera's viewfinder to my eye, fiddling with its dials so I was ready to fire away. The rescue boat had cleared the point and was starting to decelerate toward the beach. I could see Lonnie at the bow, three other men in safety vests, and one other person—probably the teenage son. A sixth person was strapped to a backboard, which was tilted upward slightly in the boat. As the boat hit the gravel shallows, Lonnie leapt out and pulled it by a rope closer to shore. Right on cue, the other emergency team members jumped out in their rubber boots and two of them grabbed each side of the backboard. Lonnie held it at the man's feet for extra support and they moved briskly up the slope to the hospital. The fourth crew member had his arm around the adolescent male, steadying him as they got out of the boat. It was indeed a kind of D-Day landing in miniature—minus the machine-gun fire and bombs.

I was already snapping, using my telephoto to get close-ups. The man strapped to the backboard was cocooned in a blanket so it was hard to make out who he was. As they got closer to the ER entrance Lonnie waved me off with one arm.

"Roy, you gotta stay back. Can't allow you inside either. Not yet."

They were inside the hospital so fast I barely had time to snap off a half-dozen shots. I replaced the lens cover and walked toward where the protestors were hanging out. Maybe they'd know where Rosanna was. A young woman with a head sprouting long blonde dreadlocks tied off with brightly coloured strips of cloth pointed me toward the x-ray lab.

In my rush to get to the back of the hospital in time to get shots of the Search and Rescue crew I hadn't noticed Rosanna and Marie-Louise seated on the steps outside the lab. Marie-Louise was as usual puffing on a hand-rollie, her basket-weaving materials laid across her lap in the hollow of a baggy peasant skirt. Rosanna smiled when she saw me.

"Hey, Roy, how's it going? I heard you helped with the rescue."

"Well, 'helped' would be an exaggeration. I managed to talk Lonnie Harrison into letting me go up in the plane with Jack. Got a fleeting glimpse of a campfire near the first summit."

"Always nice to meet a humble man," chuckled Marie-Louise, working a long strip of cedar between her well-worn thumbs.

"It's kept me busy the past twenty-four hours," I said. "How goes the battle here?"

Rosanna sighed. "It's good news/bad news all over again. PHA has been mostly stonewalling. They're getting flooded with letters though, so we're keeping up the pressure. The bad news is they're not backing down on the ER hours."

"And the good news?"

"They've agreed to another town hall meeting."

"When?"

"In about two weeks. I'm arranging for Eldorado Hall again."

I laughed. "Two weeks? That's a lifetime around here. I've only been here two weeks and I can't believe how busy I've been."

"A lot can happen in two weeks, alright," Rosanna agreed. "But it gives us more time to lobby the government in Victoria, put out press releases and generally pressure them."

"Make the government look bad in the media, you mean. 'Victoria Pulls Plug on Life Support in Remote Village.'"

"Thanks, I might just use that." She pulled a notepad from her purse and was writing.

"How's it going with Bob Williams and his budgetary strategy?"

"He's working on it. It's a big job. Mayor Miller's helping."

"Let's hope he can pull it together in two weeks then."

"Let's hope." Her expression was anything but hopeful. "Mayor Miller is working his political contacts to try and get a meeting with the Minister of Health."

"If that fails we could always get Moonglow to set up a crystal circle and call down fire from the heavens," joked Marie-Louise. Rosanna giggled, poking her playfully.

Just then we heard the double doors of the lab clicking open. We turned to see Tom exiting. He had a conspiratorial smile on. He wore the same jean jacket as always, yet strangely enough it was always clean and neat.

"I've got a little bit of news," he said, hooking his thumbs in his jean pockets. "But you all have to promise me you won't tell *anyone* where you heard this. And I mean *no one*." For someone whose voice was typically soft and mellifluous, there was an uncharacteristic edge to his words. He looked at each of us. We all nodded vigorously in agreement to the pact of silence.

"Good. You'll never guess who they brought into the ER today."

"Sorry, Tom," I said. "I never guess. Not a good habit for a journalist to get into. I can tell you it's a father and his teenage son."

"It's Wade Detwiler—the PHA suit and tie that was at the meeting in Eldorado Hall! And his 16-year-old son Ryan."

Tom's breathlessness echoed around the circle. Rosanna broke the silence. "Are they okay? I mean, how bad were they hurt?"

"Detwiler had a fall on the rock scree coming back down from the summit. He's got an open fracture on his left leg. He bled a lot but wasn't in any mortal danger—luckily he didn't hit any major arteries. But with the bone exposed, there'll be substantial risk of infection. They've got him on an antibiotic

IV now. His son wasn't hurt. But Detwiler was in no condition to walk back down to the lakeshore. They'll probably ship them both out today by medevac helicopter to the Hannaville hospital. Detwiler will need an orthopaedic surgeon to fix that leg, and soon."

"And how is it you know this, when they've only just brought him in?" I asked. "I won't be able to officially get his name 'til the police report comes out. That alone could take two weeks."

"I lease a room here in the hospital for my clients. Sometimes I get referrals from the physiotherapist, Rosie Huntingdon. I was just finishing up a client when they brought Detwiler and his son in. Normally I don't poke my nose in unless it's one of my clients, but the nurse at reception knew I'd been part of the hospital protest. She called me over on the way out and made me lean close enough to whisper. I'm under threat of death if it gets around that she told me. She says she could lose her job."

Rosanna stood up; at full height she was about two inches taller than Tom. She clapped her hands together gleefully, then spun around in a pirouette. "This is great!"

Tom looked perplexed, even a little shocked. "What do you mean, 'great'? A man was just seriously injured!"

Rosanna looked sheepish. "I'm sorry, Tom. I didn't mean it that way. I just meant, now we have a leverage point! I mean, besides the budget."

"What do you mean?" Tom asked.

"Well, think about it—here's a guy who's just had his life—and the life of his son—saved. If it weren't for our rescue guys—and a fully functioning ER—who knows what would've happened to them? Once he's recovered from surgery, we try to set up a meeting with Detwiler. Ask him to use his influence at the executive level of the ministry."

"Brilliant," chuckled Marie-Louise, still working her cedar bark.

"Yeah," I objected, "but how are you going to do that? Somehow I doubt he's going to want to talk to you, of all people."

"I'll figure something out." She was pacing on the landing now, a finger to her chin.

"Go see him at the Hannaville Regional Hospital," suggested Marie-Louise. "Just go as concerned friends visiting."

"I could threaten to make the story of his rescue public," I offered. "That could seriously embarrass him."

Tom was shaking his head. "I don't know.... We've gotta be careful we don't cross any ethical lines here. He *is* a recovering patient...."

"Look, Tom," I said. "Would you be willing to put yourself in place of Detwiler on the incident report written up by Lonnie?"

"What?"

"We offer Detwiler a deal—we don't release his name in the story of the rescue, spare him the public embarrassment and a possible reprimand from his superiors. Instead we say it was *you* who was rescued. If you want to get picky, we *did* kind of rescue you."

"Well, the truth is, I was never lost in the first place. The other fact is, you can't expect Lonnie to falsify an official report. Even if we could convince him to do it, he'd be putting his job as Fire Chief on the line."

"I agree, Tom," said Rosanna. "I seriously doubt Detwiler will want to talk to anyone in the news media, local or not. My hope would be that Detwiler's rescue will make him more reasonable. What Roy's suggesting would only be a last resort—one I'd prefer not to use."

"True," said Marie-Louise. "But let's not forget—we're fighting for our lives here. And the life of this community."

Chapter Nine

The next day Rosanna called me at home on my newly installed phone—oh, luxury! After Vancouver it was odd to think of something so basic being suddenly so precious. It made me realize how dependent we are on the apparatus of civilization—and how easily we fall apart without it. She'd arranged for a small delegation to visit Detwiler in the regional hospital facility in Hannaville. Basically just she and another woman from the village.

"So Detwiler's out of surgery then?" I asked.

"Yeah, in emergency cases they usually try to get it done within the first twenty-four hours. Especially with an open wound that could easily go septic. I checked with the admitting desk. They said he's in recovery, heavily sedated. Should be checked out by late tomorrow."

"So today's the day then. He'll be on a flight home by tomorrow afternoon."

"You have to promise me, if I let you come, you'll let us do all the talking. You're there strictly as a record-keeper."

"You want me to record it?"

"If you can do it discreetly. I don't want him to think we're trying to trap him. Besides, it would be pretty sleazy, visiting him in hospital to do that."

"I can take a pocket recorder. But what if he won't play?"

She let the line go quiet, then sighed deeply. "I really hate thuggish tactics, I really do. But Marie-Louise is right—we're fighting for our lives here."

"What's your plan then?"

"I'm bringing along an LOL we all know and love. Her name is Elizabeth Johnson."

"Wait—LOL?"

She laughed. "Oh, sorry—little old lady."

"Why her?"

"The Johnson family has been here in the village practically since the first lots were staked out in the 1890s. Her husband is a logger. Nearly killed in a tree-falling accident. If it hadn't been for the ER, he *would've* been dead."

I had to smile. "So, a soft instead of hard blackmail." Wrong thing to say. The line went quiet. "I'm sorry, shouldn't have said that...."

"Damn right you shouldn't. Call it 'soft blackmail' if you want, but this is about how government decisions affect people's lives, right here on the ground. Guys like Detwiler sit in a plush office in Victoria and seldom see that. It's all just numbers on a balance sheet to them."

"You're preaching to the choir."

She continued as if she hadn't heard me. "Besides, if there's any time in his life he'd be suggestible, it's now. Elizabeth is just insurance."

"Fair enough. But you'll hold my 'blackmail' in reserve, just in case?" I said it so she could "hear" the quotes around the word.

"Maybe. The main thing is, we have some kind of record, if he does agree to anything."

It was a hundred-and-fifty-kilometre drive from Eldorado to Hannaville, following the southward flow of Glacier River, then turning west. The Kootenay River flowed south from Newcombe through a system of hydro dams, spilling southward at the pulp mill town of Renfrew, where the river meandered toward the US border. This province's multitude of microclimates and its geographical variety never ceased to amaze me. By the time we passed Renfrew, the evergreen-thick mountainsides of the valley had thinned out to a more sparse tree cover on the ridges. The highway had been carved out at an elevation considerably higher than the river valley on the east side. Looking down at the river I could see small islands of sand breaking up the flow, whereas on Sapphire Lake sand was a rare commodity.

Rosanna insisted on driving her two-door Honda Civic, one that looked a few years older than Jane's. It was amazing her long legs could fit into it. The 1980s and '90s Civics were to this generation what Volkswagen Beetles were to a previous generation—cheap, reliable, and almost unkillable transportation. I gave up the front passenger seat to Elizabeth, who needed help to lower herself into the seat. It would be hard to hear the conversation from the cramped back seat. As it turned out I needn't have worried. Rosanna offered a few pleasantries to Elizabeth, who politely responded but seemed disinclined to talk much. She'd made some comment about hating to have to use a cane even though she was eighty-three. "And they can put me in a box before I'll use one of those damn walkers," she insisted. Mostly she watched the houses dispersed across the hillsides as they blurred past. Rosanna was tapping the steering wheel softly with a forefinger, probably thinking about what to say to Detwiler.

When we pulled up outside the main hospital entrance, Rosanna quickly got out to open the car door for Elizabeth and helped her shakily to her feet. I snapped the seat forward and climbed out to help as quickly as possible. I took Rosanna's place at Elizabeth's side, allowing her to go park the car. Elizabeth hung onto my arm, balancing herself with a cane in her other hand. A stiff wind could have blown her away—she was all of about five feet tall and very frail. She had the typical little old lady's head of white hair, curled at the hairdresser's and kept fairly short. I helped Elizabeth carefully over the curb. She stumbled a little as if one leg were heavier to lift than the other. "Damn!" she muttered. "Goddamn mini-strokes." She turned a pair of pale, piercing blue eyes on me. "When I think of the things I've done in my life, to be so *weak.*"

"I understand," I said softly, though it was at best a compassionate lie.

"Do you? You're still young. Don't think for a second because I'm old that this—" she pointed to her head—"is as weak as my body now."

I smiled as we made our way toward the automatic doors. "I don't think that at all."

"I remember when I was about your age—how old are you?"

"I'm forty-four."

"My, my. Still a youngster. To think I was that age forty years ago. When I found out my brother-in-law had been cheating on my sister Florence, I chased him down the street with a Wear-Ever frying pan. And don't you dare think I didn't!"

I couldn't help but chuckle. "I believe you." The picture it created in my mind was too funny. I wanted to add, "You wouldn't catch me pissing you off," but thought better of it.

Rosanna had caught up as we passed through the double glass doors. "The recovery ward is on the third floor. I checked this morning. Elizabeth, do you want me to get you a wheelchair?"

Elizabeth threw her a withering glare with her watery blues. I leaned in close to Rosanna, whispering, "I wouldn't go there if I were you."

As if shielding Elizabeth from the messy details, she too kept her voice low. "Listen, Roy. I want you to stay at the back of the room. Just let me and Elizabeth do the talking. I mean it. *Promise* me."

"Okay, okay already. Just give me a signal when you want me."

"I will, don't worry."

We'd reached the elevator and both steadied Elizabeth, who muttered irritably again about her weakness. "I need to be within three metres or less for the recorder to pick up," I reminded Rosanna.

"I don't care. Stay back. If he recognizes you're a reporter we won't get word one in. If I need you, I'll signal you. Promise me."

I held up my hands in surrender. "I promise."

We matched our pace to Elizabeth's, which meant moving at a crawl. It was almost painful to slow down that much. It made me realize how differently younger and older people move. By contrast, my own life seemed set on an express track—to where exactly, I had no idea. How odd that when all of life is ahead of us, we rush as if our time has run out. Yet when we're old and near the end, we move as if all of time must wait for *us*, in part because we no longer have any choice. It was hard to imagine my body forcing me to move at a pace not of my choosing. Walking with Elizabeth was a meditation on mortality—one I probably needed. It made me think of how hard it must be for her instead of obsessing about where *I* had to be.

My health was still good but hospitals always made me queasy. It wasn't the antiseptic hospital smells. I'd had to have a couple of minor operations as a boy. Being of what my mother called "an artistic temperament," I had a heightened sensitivity—not just to pain but the whole experience of being in a strange institutional environment when you're small and everything feels vastly out of scale. For most children it's frightening enough but to a sensitive boy it was excruciating. I cried and cried before going into the operating room, no matter what soothing noises the nurses made. It was as if some past life memory of death under a surgeon's knife was haunting me. I remember trying to pull off the gas mask they used for anesthesia, as if I were being smothered. Now, decades later, I shuddered. The memory lived in my body somewhere, making me as uneasy as if it had happened yesterday.

The recovery ward had four beds, all partitioned with curtains. Only two of the beds had patients. Rosanna tipped her head at me—a signal to hang back while she and Elizabeth went to Detwiler's bedside. I made my way discreetly to the bed next to him and perched at the end of it. He was sitting up in bed reading a newspaper, his injured leg wrapped in gauze and propped up on pillows. Rosanna greeted him and seated Elizabeth in a visitor's chair by the bed. He looked at the two of them with a puzzled expression, his eyes still a little clouded from painkillers.

"Do I know you?"

"No, sir, probably not. My name is Rosanna Yale. Do you mind if I pull the curtain open?" He shook his head and she ran the curtain around its ring. "This is my friend Elizabeth Johnson." What must have been an innate respect for the elderly changed his diffident attitude. He put down the newspaper and reached out his hand toward Elizabeth. She grasped it lightly. "Pleased to meet you, Mrs. Johnson."

She smiled. "Elizabeth will do, thank you. Though when I was your age anyone who was married was referred to as Mister or Missus."

"And my friend Roy," Rosanna said as the curtain exposed me to view. I felt like Shadowcat, trying to pretend he was invisible when he was caught shredding furniture.

"Uh-huh," he said, offering only a cursory glance in my direction. If anything, his razor-thin facial features seemed even thinner than I remembered. He seemed unwilling to let go of his newspaper, as if his unknown visitors might be easily brushed off, allowing him to return to his reading.

"Mr. Detwiler—" Rosanna began.

"You can call me Wade." He smiled at her indulgently. "They told me at the desk that you were on the local Save Our Hospital committee or something. These pain meds make my brain fuzzy."

"Actually we're from Eldorado, not Hannaville. But first things first—how are you doing? I heard you had a pretty bad injury."

He patted his bandages lightly. "Pretty good considering what could have happened up there on the mountain. You guys are lucky to have such a crack Search and Rescue team."

Elizabeth nodded. "Damn straight." She tapped her cane on the floor for emphasis.

"And yes, we *are* here about our hospital ER," Rosanna continued.

He sighed and turned to look out the window briefly before turning his narrow gaze back on Rosanna. "Ah, yes, I remember now—the meeting in your hall. No rest for the wicked, eh? All in a day's work for a public servant, even on my day off." He smiled his thin smile at this attempt at a joke. "To answer your question, the orthopaedic surgeon says surgery went well. As you can see, they've got me on an antibiotic IV and I'll probably have to keep taking the stuff for weeks yet. I'm probably looking at three months of recovery, followed by another six months of rehab and physiotherapy."

"Most of a year, then. I'm so sorry," said Rosanna, her face flushing. Her voice faltered, as if she were losing her nerve. I could see the struggle going on behind her brow. The conversation was swallowed up in silence. Detwiler continued to examine her through his narrow glasses, as if scrutinizing a financial statement that refused to balance.

Elizabeth came to the rescue. "Makes me think of my late husband George. Took him that long to recover from his accident."

Detwiler's attitude recovered itself again upon hearing Elizabeth speak. "Oh? What happened to George?"

"George was a logger—a faller. Worked in the bush all his life. From the time he was twelve years old he could handle a chainsaw. His dad forced him to finish high school or he would've dropped out to work in the bush by age fifteen. A lot of his buddies never did finish school. But we made damn sure all three of our kids finished school and went on to college. Two boys and a girl. 'Quick of mind, quick of body,' I always used to tell our boys. Logging's a tough life, and dangerous."

Detwiler smiled patronizingly. "I'm sure." I got the impression that if it had been anyone else, he would have ended the visit.

"The thing is," Elizabeth continued, "you never know when your day is going to come, do you?" She looked him directly in the eye. "And you never know if that day will be your last, or if the good Lord'll spare you. Well, that day came for George. The irony is, they say the worst accidents happen close to home, not out in the bush. When you're off work, just mucking around. Maybe not paying the same attention you do on the job. Well, we had a little property just outside Eldorado we'd planned to retire to. Raw land when we bought it, lots of trees. Up on the bench above the village. We'd had it for years and years when George finally decided it was time to start clearing it to build. I think he was fifty at the time. He'd been falling trees one Saturday afternoon on the property. Remember, we're not talking a beginner, here. He'd been doing this since he was a kid. But things being what they are, some days anything can happen. And on this Saturday afternoon— oh my God, did it ever."

Detwiler watched her closely as she paused, turning away to gather courage. Detwiler had the grace not to prompt her. Finally she turned to look at him again.

"You make two cuts into a tree to fall it," she explained. "One in front and a back cut behind, different angles. Some of these guys are so good they can put a tree down within five feet of where you ask them to. He was doing the back cut and when the tree started to tip over, it bucked like a stallion. No warning. Not enough time for George to get out of the way. The butt of the tree hit him in the chest, smashing several ribs and puncturing a lung. If it had struck just a few inches higher on his chest—who knows? It probably would have stopped his heart."

At this she paused again. Even from a good distance away I could see the water rimming her eyes as she recalled the event. But she was a tough old bird and wasn't about to let her emotions get in the way of the story she'd come to tell. A single tear skated down one cheek but she brushed it away quickly as if it were an unwanted insect.

"You have to remember," she began, recovering a stumble in her voice, "George and I married young. I was only eighteen, he was twenty-one. We met in high school. High school sweethearts, just like they say. I was lucky. A lot of women in Eldorado had trouble with husbands who drink. Some of the gals got beaten up pretty bad. Some left the bastards, some didn't—or couldn't. It can get bad that way in logging towns. But George had no taste for the booze. He was a good man. He always treated me well. Never missed an anniversary."

"*Was* a good man, Mrs. Johnson—Elizabeth?" Detwiler's expression was focused.

"Oh, he didn't die then. We celebrated fifty-five years of marriage before he died of a heart attack. That was ten years ago. No, we had another twenty-five years together after that horrible day." The thought of it stopped her again.

"Do you mind telling us what happened, Elizabeth?" Rosanna asked.

"Yes, of course dear. I was coming to that. I just—choke up a little sometimes, that's all, when I think of how close I came to losing him. I drove up from the house with coffee and sandwiches when I found him lying there, gasping for air like a newborn calf. Couldn't even talk to me. Had to force myself not to scream. Remember, this is the late sixties, so lots of us didn't even have phones yet out here in the boonies. We'd only *just* got electricity. So it's not like I could just run to the nearest house and phone 911 like we can now.

"'Hang on George, for God's sake, hang on!' I told him. 'I'm going for help.' I ran to the closest house, on the acreage across the Lowery highway. It was the McTavish place, as I recall. They had two strapping teenage boys at the time, Mike and Sean. I told them to come quick and didn't have to say it twice. My eyes were probably wide as saucers.

"'We need to get him to hospital,' I told the boys. 'But we have to lift him into the truck very gently.' The boys got on either end of him while I slipped a wooden ladder beneath him. He was in shock, moaning, eyes rolling in his head. I'm no lumberjack but I'm not a wallflower either. The boys stayed in the back of the pickup with him. Driving to hospital I floored it—nearly didn't make the hairpin corner at the bottom of the hill. That would've been *two* of us dead. I was shaking so hard it was all I could do to keep my hands on the steering wheel. Once we got to hospital they wheeled out a gurney and took him into the ER. In those days they'd even tell wives to stay out of the ward 'til the crisis passed. Not that I wanted to get in the doctors' way. After about an hour, old Doctor John Ward came out, all bloodstained. They'd had to open up his chest and stick a tube into it to keep his lung from collapsing.

"That's when I finally lost it. Thought he was dead. Started weeping like a baby. Doctor Ward had a real fine bedside manner. 'He'll make it, but only if I can get him to a better hospital,' he told me. 'We need a plane.' In those days, Jack Wingarde's father Walter used to run a floatplane on the lake. I told him to get Walter down there. He used to tie up his plane at a dock in Elkville, so it'd only take a few minutes for him to fly over. The hospital had a VHF radio they used and of course Walter had one at home and in the plane. He was used to being called up on short notice for firefighting. He was there pretty fast. I don't remember how long now—it's so long ago. But there was barely room for two people in the plane, and Walter had to push down the passenger seat so they could load George up lying down. Then I had to watch him flying off south over the lake. Had no idea if I'd ever see him again alive. I just stood there, looking out across the lake, trying to hold a picture of him in my mind. As if somehow that might give him a better chance. I wondered if I'd be telling the grandkids their grand-papa was dead." She paused, drawing in a slow, deep breath.

"If you don't mind me asking, Elizabeth," said Detwiler, "what happened?"

"Oh, Walter got him to the Renfrew municipal airport. The hospital phoned ahead to arrange a transfer to a bigger plane. They had to fly him to Vancouver. There was no hospital in the Interior that had the facilities they needed. Doctor Ward gave me all the addresses and phone numbers of the specialists at Vancouver General. Our boys were working in northern BC, at least twelve hours' drive away. So my neighbour Dorothy kindly offered to drive me to the coast so I could be with George. We couldn't afford to fly on jets in those days and I don't know how I'd have made the eight-hour drive in the state I was in."

"And as you say, George lived another twenty-five years," said Detwiler. "I'm so glad for you. It must have been a terrifying experience."

"Well, it was. You see, Mr. Detwiler, when two people have been together as long as George and I were, you become two parts of the same person. I couldn't imagine life without him. Sure, you get on each other's nerves sometimes. There's days you ask yourself, 'How am I going to get through this day without killing you?' But the bond you have carries you through. It's deeper than you even realize.

"There were moments in that Vancouver hospital when George nearly didn't make it. The first forty-eight hours were the worst. His pulse would just stop. Every time it happened, a shock wave went through my whole body. Like a giant piece of me was being ripped away. Like a knife was cutting through me." She took a long pause, signalling the end of her story. "But you've just been through a terrifying experience yourself."

"Yes, I have. My son Ryan won't forget it anytime soon, and neither will I."

"Care to talk about it?" asked Elizabeth.

"I'm not one to talk about such things even to my wife, never mind strangers."

"Care to try?"

"Well … you've been so gracious, telling me your story." He looked away again out the window, finally turning back to her with a thin smile. "Two days in the outdoors was more than I bargained for. We were pretty well prepared—tent, sleeping bags, lighter, a little bit of food. Hell, I spent two hundred dollars on hiking boots! But I realize now I should've had a flare." He shook his head. "Stupid. The things you don't think of—the one little thing that could save your life. Anyway, it all started off so great—the ride across the lake in the fishing boat, the landing on White Sands Creek beach. Beautiful. You people are so lucky to live on that gorgeous lake.

"The weather started off warm and clear for an October day. We'd hiked all the way up the glacier trail. I was proud of myself, keeping up with Ryan. But we wanted to camp down on the beach that first night. So we started back down. I don't know if you've ever been on that trail, but there's places where there's lots of loose shale. We were coming back down. After resting at the first summit, we decided to press on. I was just a little ways down from the summit when I slipped on the scree and tumbled ass over teakettle down a slope. A sharp rock tore my leg open and I heard the crack as it twisted. Ryan came running after me. Even then I was shouting, 'Careful! Careful!' I didn't want him to get hurt too.

"It's funny what the body does when you get hurt. At first you get the sharp, stabbing pain. Then shock starts to set in and you can't feel a thing. For awhile, anyway. I'd managed to tumble into a bit of a hollow. Ryan came down and tried to help me up. But even with him supporting me I couldn't stand. Every time I tried a searing pain shot through me. My pants were ripped and bloody. It was starting to get dark so I told Ryan to set up the tent and start a fire. 'Not before I wrap that leg, Dad,' he told me. There's that sickening second when you suddenly realize: We need to be rescued. We're not getting off this mountain without help. I was proud of how Ryan handled everything—getting ice-cold water from a stream to wash out the wound. I thought they'd have heard my scream all the way across the lake. He wrapped a sleeping bag around me to try and quell the shivers. It wasn't until he got the fire going I was able to finally stop shuddering.

"By that time darkness had fallen. We'd planned to be out only one night, and back well before dark the second day. I remember hearing an airplane engine passing over us several times. Ryan tells me he also heard a boat motor. He wanted to run down the trail to the beach to yell for help, but it was too dark. I wouldn't let him. All I needed was for him to fall and get hurt, or worse. The second night was the hardest, wondering when or if the Search and Rescue guys would find us. But by first light next morning, we heard the boat again, so we knew they'd be coming up the trail to look for us. I've never been so overjoyed to see strangers in all my life." He stopped, turning to the window again.

"Ah, yes," said Elizabeth. "The kindness of strangers. They're good boys, our crew."

Rosanna broke his reverie softly. "Imagine if we had no Search and Rescue crew there."

He turned back toward her. "I hope you'll convey to them how grateful I am—we are."

She nodded. "Of course. But if I know Lonnie—our Fire Chief—he'll just shrug and say, 'All in a day's work.'"

"You have some fine people there, then."

"We think so."

He smiled his lipless smile. "And you want to remind me what could've happened if you had no ER."

"Or reduced ER hours."

The conversation stalled right there. Rosanna's will was clearly failing her in an agony of indecision. Detwiler was looking from Rosanna to Elizabeth, as if searching for clues to break the impasse. I decided it was my turn to speak. "Mr. Detwiler, I'm Roy Breen. Would you consent to me writing your story—"

His expression shifted to one of intense alarm. "You—I remember now—I saw you at the town hall meeting. You're a journalist!" It was spat out like an accusation. "You're here to grill me about the ER cutbacks!"

"Naturally I'll respect your wishes if you prefer to stay off record. But—"

He avoided my gaze, turning back to Rosanna and Elizabeth. "Ladies, I hate to say it, but this—*visit*—is over. Please leave—NOW."

"Honestly, this was *not* a setup," pleaded Rosanna. "We only hoped to appeal to your sense of fair play. You must understand what a fully functioning hospital means to a small community like ours...."

"Fair play? I'll have to take your word for that, though I'm not so sure about Mr. Breen here. But I still want you to leave."

"Mr. Detwiler," I hastily cut in, "in fairness, I was the one who spotted your distress fire the evening before Search and Rescue crews picked you and your son off the trail."

I could see this forced him to moderate his anger. "Well, then. I owe you thanks. I'm sorry to be so hasty. But the fact remains, I won't do interviews from my hospital bed. I appreciate your help with the search but this just smacks of opportunism to me."

"I'm sorry you feel that way," I said. "That wasn't my intention." I could see the pressure building on Rosanna's forehead, as if not knowing whether to intervene and derail this potentially disastrous conversation.

"What was your intention then, if not to get a front-page scoop?"

"I left that media circus behind when I left Vancouver. I work for a community newspaper now. That means I write about what concerns them."

Again he paused to consider this. "Maybe blurring the lines just a little between reportage and activism, wouldn't you say?"

"Maybe. But it's not like I'm doing it to make a pile of money."

But it was no use by this time. Detwiler had had enough and his ears were closing. He turned to Elizabeth and offered a weak, conciliatory smile. "It was a pleasure to meet you, Mrs. Johnson." With that he turned his attention to his newspaper, using it as a shield.

"And you," said Elizabeth. There was no point continuing.

As we left the ward I felt a sharp punch land on my shoulder. I winced and reflexively backed away. If Rosanna ever needed a career as a lightweight boxer, I'd be the first to give her a reference. "You fucking IDIOT! What did I tell you? What did I TELL you? You've blown it for us now. You've BLOWN it...."

"Rosanna, you don't know that.... I didn't mean—" But it was no use. She was steadying Elizabeth and refused to look at me. The discussion was over.

There was little conversation in the car on the way back to Eldorado.

Chapter Ten

I got little sleep that night. It's annoying how your brain can sometimes behave in such a predictably clichéd manner, like a B-movie on steroids. You know, the way a certain phrase or idiotic snatch of song will echo in your head like Chinese water torture. I don't know about your mind but mine is highly visual too, so I get both sound and picture on instant replay for hours at a time. Especially when I feel like I've said something incredibly stupid, or worse—actually *know* I've done something cringe-worthy. Over and over again, I heard Rosanna's words: "You fucking IDIOT! What did I tell you? You've BLOWN it for us now." I liked to think it was the fact that, unlike some, I at least had a functioning conscience. But too easily it tipped over into self-torture. I often wondered why that was. Maybe it was partly my miserable public school years in the sixties, when a licence to teach was just as often a licence to torture kids. I had far too many teachers in those years who'd vented their rage on me. I was no angel, that's for sure. Liked to provoke teachers with smart-ass remarks, but never really did anything seriously wrong. Then when I got home from school I'd get it double time. It was days like that I seriously contemplated running away from home. But then what kid hasn't?

Who knows? Maybe the way I was raised was a good thing after all, when I think of some of the narcissists and sociopaths our culture has spawned. It gave my conscience a voice—often far too loud and self-condemnatory. But at least it functioned to deflate my ego when it needed some air let out of it. Still, it took me the first thirty years of my adult life to build up *any* confidence. As I often told friends, I had to build self-esteem one brick at a time, starting from zero. Some of us have way too much confidence and some of us way too little. Checks and balances. "Everything in life is a trade-off," my old buddy Dave used to say. You choose this, you lose that. Last night by 4:00 a.m. I'd almost have traded off my conscience. Almost.

But what had I really done wrong? I was just doing what any decent journalist would do, I told myself as I thrashed around the bed. Due diligence and all that. I prided myself on my integrity. A decade and a half in the city hadn't jaded me yet. I wasn't the guy looking to dig up sleaze on some mayoral candidate I didn't happen to like. And I flatly refused to do celebrity gossip. Intelligent interviews, yes. But Lindsay Lohan's latest conviction for drunk driving? Please. At the *Vancouver Daily* I'd been censured more than once for writing stories that tilted in favour of protestors or union picketers. Although I believed in objectivity in journalism, I was still human and that meant I had certain sympathies. And all I wanted to do right now was write good stories for the *Echo* that might possibly have a positive effect. Still, it didn't matter what I told myself, Rosanna's voice kept resounding like a gong, a hammer pounding out the message: You fucked up, buddy, BIG time. Maybe I never should have gone along at all. What if that *was* their last hope for saving the hospital ER?

On top of all that, Shadowcat was dealing with his own existential crisis. The last few times I'd come home, it had taken some coaxing to get him out of the towel cupboard in the bathroom. I'd look at him and say, "Hey, your old man is home! Time to rock, dude!" In answer he'd barely lift his head from his paws. "Uh, what Dad?" His eyes were glazed—an unusual expression for him. Normally his emerald-alive eyes were sharp enough to carve meat. I admit, the first few times it didn't dawn on me that my feline companion was suffering from depression. I may score reasonably high on the IQ scale but my EQ (emotional quotient) is somewhat obtuse. After a reasonably settled existence his whole life had been uprooted and shifted across the province. He was free to roam the forest here, but unlike the cultivated streets of Vancouver, there were predators—coyotes, great horned owls, bald eagles. Shadowcat wasn't a fearful creature, but clearly he was depressed about the move. I was finally waking up to the fact that the creatures we share this planet with have their own emotional lives too.

By morning I was feeling pretty ragged. The only thing to do was get up and work. I had plenty of notes on the hospital crisis to type up. By noon I was still in my bathrobe and had managed to get an article sketched out for the next issue of the *Echo*. Shadowcat had coiled himself in my lap for comfort but had barely raised his head in an hour. I'd have to disturb him to get up and make lunch, which would probably sour his mood further. Staring out the sliding glass doors facing Mount Pyramid often helped. Its presence had a calming, meditative effect. At night it was a star-catcher, a moon-netter catching the lunar transit on its sharp peak. Then it struck me—call Jane. It was a risk, but what I knew of her gentle nature suggested that her presence might be just the ticket.

"How about if I invite Jane to dinner?" I asked Shadowcat. By the way his head jerked up from his paws for only about the second time that morning, I knew I'd struck gold. His eyes were suddenly awake, attentive. It was a resounding: "Yes, Dad! Good one!" Jane had given me her office phone number so I dialled it quickly before she'd be gone for lunch. After our initial greetings, her feminine EQ picked up on my dispirited tone of voice.

"Everything alright, Roy?"

"Not great, actually. Rosanna is pretty pissed with me right now. Thinks I might have blown it for her."

"Really? How could you do that? Do you have some inside track at PHA I don't know about?" she laughed. "'Cause if you do, I'd like to borrow your influence sometime."

"Good point. Listen, I don't want to talk about it on the phone. Can we get together? Dinner, maybe?"

"When, tonight?"

"Sure, if you're up for it."

"Why not? And I'll cook this time—it's my turn."

"You sure? I mean, you've already worked a full week. You must be tired. Being invited to dinner to cook doesn't make me much of a date."

"I'm fine. I'll see you at six. Bye for now."

"Shadowcat will be delighted."

She was already lifting my spirits. I knew I could take my story in tomorrow. I took the chance to drive down to the head of the lake, which had one of the very few sandy beaches in the area. Only weeks before, I'd stood on that beach for the first time. There was a giant, ancient cottonwood whose gnarled bough extended out over the sand, drooping garlands of leaves. I'd taken a photo there with that bough forming a perfect frame for the distant, glacial peaks to the south of Sapphire Lake. Again I was struck by the pristine clarity of the water here. Just to the east of where the road dead-ended at the beach entrance was the Owl Creek delta, a haven for local bird life and migrating waterfowl. Eagles could be seen drifting in relaxed spirals above the delta, ready to drop like a thunderbolt on unsuspecting trout. Owl sightings of course were much more rare. As I looked out over the water I could see a pair of loons, sharp profiles leaving a broad V in their wake. I'd been told that at the right time of year you could also see trumpeter swans here. Certain places have an almost mystical serenity about them, and this was one of them. It reminded me of the few times in my life I've been inside a cathedral—the stillness was palpable. Not empty at all but layered over with centuries of devotion and prayer. With sustained meditation, this place too had a way of seeping into your pores.

I made sure I was home well before six. When Jane showed up at the door Shadowcat performed one of his "flop down, roll around" happy dances for her. It was the perkiest I'd seen him in days. There was genuine delight in her face too. She had two grocery bags of food with her. I teased her about "bringing coals to Newcastle" but she was quick to remind me that, like most men, I suffered from Bachelor's Fridge syndrome. With my penchant for stir-fries, I liked to think I was a little above that. But when she opened the fridge to load in her dinner stock, I had to admit she was right: A bottle of concentrated lemon juice, soy sauce, a loaf of bread, a few eggs, some sandwich meat, and a half-empty veggie drawer were all that confronted her. In my dejection after yesterday's hospital visit, I'd forgotten it was time to restock. Just having Jane in my kitchen, chopping veggies and cooking, had a lifting effect on my spirit. I offered to help but she insisted, "This one is on me." I concentrated on making tea instead.

After dinner we retired to the living room. I explained to her what had happened at the hospital with Detwiler. She was thoughtful as she listened, with a patient look that waited to reel in all the facts before coming to a conclusion. It was one of the things I liked about her so much. Most people these days can't wait to give you their opinion before you even finish talking. Hell, I can be as bad as the next person for that. She sat holding a finger to her chin in a way that reminded me of a Vermeer portrait. Shadowcat lifted his head from his paws from time to time, as if listening for her thoughts.

"So you think you've failed Rosanna?" she asked.

"She certainly thinks so."

"But do *you*?"

"Well, yeah. Didn't sleep much last night."

"Pretty hard for a leopard to change its spots though."

"What do you mean?"

"You are what you are. In your case—a journalist. That's what you do. Doesn't the job get to be kind of a reflex after a few years of doing it?"

"Absolutely. You barely have to think about it after awhile. Your brain is constantly jotting down notes and questions become habitual."

"So you were just doing what came naturally. Asking questions. Doing your job."

"Yeah, but Rosanna warned me. She made me promise—"

"What? She made you promise not to pull the blackmail tactic about his rescue, which you didn't. You asked a standard journalistic question. You asked if he'd be willing to be interviewed—"

"I don't know...."

"Listen. Do you do your job to the best of your integrity?"

"Well, yeah...."

"Right. Like the Moss the Crawler story. Now, let me see.... I don't recall reading about that one in the *Echo*. Or anywhere else, for that matter. Yet you could've dished that one up. It would've made for funny reading. And an extra pay cheque from your Vancouver contacts. But you didn't. Why not?"

"Because I promised Rosanna. I knew it would make the whole hospital protest look stupid. If the West Coast media got hold of it, they'd have had a field day. 'Crazy Protestor Crawls to Save ER,' that kind of shit."

"Exactly. You could've milked that story, made money on it, yet you chose not to."

"That doesn't seem to have occurred to Rosanna."

"Maybe she needs reminding, just like you did."

"I'm not sure she's the forgiving type."

"You'll never know 'til you check it out."

"I've already apologized, to no avail. You're suggesting I grovel?"

She gave me a wry look. "Hardly. I'm sure you'll think of something. Meanwhile, I'm sure she must have other sticks in the fire."

"Yeah, she's got Bob Williams working on an alternate budget. Let's hope that doesn't take a year. Mayor Miller is working his contacts to get a meeting with the minister. And the aerial photos of the sacred circle around the hospital will be published in the *Echo*, the *Newcombe Daily News*, the *Renfrew Chronicle,* and the *Hannaville Bulletin*."

"How about the West Coast media? Wouldn't they be interested? You could spin it your own way. 'Mountain Village Struggles to Save ER.' That kind of thing."

"Ah, but this is local news stuff, strictly small-time. Why would they be interested? Most of them think the province ends just outside Hope."

"So do a little extra research. Find out what other hospitals are in line for similar cuts. For all you know, the Eldorado ER could be just the first of many across the whole province."

I slapped my knee. "Jane, you're a genius. I must be slipping in my old age." I was up off the couch, pacing. "I could call up my old editor Bob Lejean at the *Vancouver Daily*, see if he'd run the story. That would put extra pressure on PHA, spin them in a bad light in the media." I stopped pacing, struck by a dark thought.

"Would you stop pacing, please?" She patted the couch next to her. I took the invitation, moving a little closer to her this time. Shadowcat was on her lap now and gave me a look that said, "Don't even think about moving me."

"Somehow I doubt they'll care unless some of their hospitals are affected."

"You don't know that. It's worth a try. You know, 'Coming Soon to a Hospital Near You,' with a question mark, gets people thinking."

I slid an arm around her shoulder and leaned close. "You're brilliant, you know that?"

"Oh, I don't know. Just trying to help."

"It's been a long time since I met anyone like you."

She laughed. "I'll take that as a compliment. But I'm really not—"

I closed the gap between us, gently kissing her. She yielded with no resistance. When we finally pulled apart, her eyes were sparkling. A soft smile flickered over her lips. I leaned forward and again our lips met. We slipped into the timelessness that envelops lovers. The spell was momentarily broken when Shadowcat stood up on her lap, arched his back, and leapt onto the carpet. "Ick. Humans mating. I'm outta here."

It didn't take us long to slip back into the spell. As we kissed the only thing I could hear was the faint swish of wind in the treetops outside. And my heart, pounding.

Shadowcat made sure to perform his Captain Cat routine the next morning to impress Jane while we were still in bed. He exhibited exceptional form, with his tail in an especially graceful upward curve while he stood stock still, waiting to be admired. "Am I not handsome?"

"I'd say at least a nine out of ten," I told him.

He looked away from me as if to say, "Not a ten? Really!"

She understood immediately what Shadowcat was up to and leaned back on her elbows to pay closer attention. "I think he wants *me* to notice how handsome he is," she giggled. "Yes, you're quite the handsome dude, you are." He returned the compliment by plopping himself down across her feet. It was a statement: "You're mine too."

"I think he thinks he was once the Prince of Persia," I said.

"I'm sure he does," she laughed. "And who knows, maybe he was!"

Our domestic bliss had to be short-lived—it was a workday for both of us. Jane had to get back to the SGS office to work on another campaign for Cathy Reilly. I wanted to get to work yanking Bob Lejean's chain on the hospital story. At the door, Jane stood on her toes to kiss me goodbye. Her petite frame was graced by doll-like hands that lightly stroked my cheek and hair. I'd never seen such delicate feminine hands before. I felt something go "twang" in my chest. If I'd had a stethoscope to her chest I'm sure I'd have heard it there too, judging by her look.

At the *Echo* office, I got Lance and Donna quickly up to speed on the story before hitting the Internet to do some research. Unsurprisingly, the government news bureau in Victoria had very little. Buried deep in a back page there was the announcement about the planned cuts to Eldorado's hospital. That news release hadn't been updated in a week. It made oblique reference to the ministry CFO raising "the possibility of similar cuts to smaller regional health centres in the province," but without naming them. Usually that meant they were waiting for the right time to drop the hammer—if possible, as close to the actual event as possible to minimize news coverage. But my persistence—and a good search engine—paid off. Two community newspapers, the *Fort Langley Herald* and *Delta Times*, each had a story about planned cutbacks to their small hospitals. I had to hand it to the reporters. In the absence of official statements being released, I could only assume they had a whistleblower inside the ministry, or at the hospitals themselves. Maybe the ministry's PR department had banked on these suburban hospitals raising less of a fuss. If they thought no one would notice, they'd made a bad bet, just as they had in Eldorado.

All I had to do was do a copy and paste of the story I'd already written for the *Echo*, leading with the cutbacks to the Fort Langley and Delta hospitals. That done, I picked up the phone and dialled Bob at the *Vancouver Daily*. Finally after getting past the automated switchboard, his familiar voice came on the line, a Scotch-soaked Eeyore-like drawl. It was a voice that mostly disdained exclamation points in favour of the steady, concise line.

"Roy, good to hear your voice again so soon. How the hell are ya? I heard you were up in the Interior, the Kootenays."

"I'm good, Bob. Yeah, I landed in a little place called Eldorado."

"Where the hell is *that*? Never heard of it."

"West Kootenay. About a hundred clicks from Newcombe—the now famous Newcombe, since they made a couple of movies there. I'm guessing you know where *that* is."

"Yeah, of course, smartass. You able to get any work up there?"

"I'm writing for a little independent known as the *Mountain Echo*. Strictly small—local circulation. About 9,600 per issue. Good community paper, though."

"Never heard of it," he grunted. "How the mighty are fallen, from bustling city newsroom to backwoods rag." I could almost see my old newsroom crowded with desks and people bustling in all directions. Here in the *Echo* there were exactly four desks, only two in constant use. Three if you add mine, which was only occupied part-time. "To think, all this could have been yours," he concluded drily.

"No it couldn't, Bob. Not since the corporate takeover, not for me. Besides, why is a small community newspaper any less important to its readers than a big-city daily?"

I could hear his characteristic "hmmph" on the other end of the line. It was a wordless concession, his usual way of conceding the argument.

"I'm surprised *you're* still there. I'd have thought you'd be too ornery by now."

"Yeah, well. I'm too old to change, especially with a pension at stake. An old dog and all that. Young rebel like you can get away with starting over...."

"Ah, that's *middle-aged* rebel, Bob. You know I always prided myself on my accuracy."

"That you did. What can I do for ya?"

"I've got a story for you. The Provincial Health Authority is planning a cutback to the hospital ER that could have deep repercussions in this remote community. It's—"

"Hold it right there, Roy. How is this of any interest to my readers here in Vancouver?"

"I thought you might ask that. Turns out the PHA has been quietly planning cuts to other outlying hospitals—namely, Fort Langley and Delta. From what I recall, the *Daily* circulates that far at least. Unless that's been cut back too."

"Of course it does. Don't bullshit me. You *know* the *Daily* is distributed across the Lower Mainland and points east. So you're saying this is another 'thin edge of the wedge' government cutback story?"

"Yep. Got it in one."

"Don't try and be funny. Okay, but I can't promise anything. I'll do my best, but—"

"Yeah, I know the drill, Bob. It's all about space, and prioritizing stories."

"And it'll have to be in our C section, 'Around the Province.' I'll shoot for the next few days. Wednesday if you're lucky."

"Great! Works for me. I'll email the story today."

"Listen Roy, hoist a Scotch for me once in awhile, will ya?"

He was asking me not to forget him. "If you don't mind, I'll share a wee dram in your honour with my new editor, Lance Robertson. He doesn't know I know, but he keeps a bottle of Highland Park in his desk. I've seen it. And Bob—don't worry. You're unforgettable."

By the satisfied chuckle at the other end of the line I knew I'd managed to crack his newspaper veteran's crocodile hide.

I was at the Glacier Convenience store early every day anxiously scanning copies of the *Vancouver Daily* for my story. I felt like an anxious debutante scanning for pictures of her graduation. Finally on Wednesday, there it was—buried in the back pages of the C section. I read it breathlessly, even though I'd written the words myself. There's something oddly compelling about seeing your own words in print, even if you know them by heart.

HEALTH MINISTRY PLANS QUIET CUTBACKS TO HOSPITAL ER WARDS

The village of Eldorado is hardly a household name in BC. Yet the Provincial Health Authority has quietly announced cutbacks to basic ER services here and in the community hospitals of Fort Langley and Delta. These cuts will see emergency wards operating on a nine-to-five schedule, leaving patients out in the cold after hours. Regional Health Services CAO Todd Mucklebrough has declined to comment and no formal announcement of the Fort Langley and Delta cuts has been made yet.

While ambulances in the Lower Mainland can simply reroute patients to other regional hospitals with minimal risk, such is not the case with tiny Eldorado, a village of 796 people. Its neighbouring village, Elkville, population about 450, also relies on the Eldorado hospital. Both communities are at least 100 kilometres from other regional hospitals. Mountain roads here can be narrow, windy, and often treacherous in the winter months. For certain critical patients that puts them just outside the 'golden hour' that could mean the difference between life and death. Even with a medevac helicopter it can take longer than that to get to the Caledon hospital, the new BC Interior facility with state-of-the-art equipment and a large staff of specialists.

Yet in what some here see as a misguided attempt to save money, PHA has yet to back down. To its credit, the ministry had originally planned to remove x-ray equipment from the hospital lab. This decision was reversed after local protestors staffed a 24/7 watch on the lab to prevent ministry staff from removing the equipment.

"That equipment was purchased with money we raised from bake sales and other fundraisers," said Rosanna Yale, a spokesperson for the protestors. 'It belongs to this community. And without a 24/7 ER, many people here could lose their lives. This is about more than just balance sheets. It's about saving lives.'

Ms. Yale points to the region's long history of mining and logging. Just getting to the Eldorado hospital can be quite an ordeal for patients injured on the job out in the backcountry. Added to that are the annual visitors during the tourist season, many of whom lack experience in wilderness savvy. According to Eldorado Fire Chief Lonnie Harrison, the local Search and Rescue currently performs an average of twenty-five rescues per year, including attendance at car accidents. "Banker's hours at the ER could definitely hurt us," Harrison said.

Bob had edited my original story by about two hundred words. I'd originally included a few paragraphs from nurses and doctors at the hospital, commenting on the various situations that could place patients in extra jeopardy of life and limb if they didn't get proper care in time. But the story as is was fine—at least it would reach a far wider audience than the *Echo*, or any of the other West Kootenay newspapers. Hundreds of thousands compared to merely thousands. And most importantly—in the West Coast media where most of the government bureaucracy lives.

I wasn't sure if Rosanna read the *Daily* so I thought I'd head over to the hospital with a copy for her. If this didn't thaw the glacial ice, nothing would. I went straight to the landing outside the lab doors, where Marie-Louise had taken up residence with a lawn chair while she worked on her basket weaving. Normally hospital staff wouldn't have allowed anyone to put a chair so close to the lab doors but in her case, they deferred to her status as a local elder. Tom was there, gesturing while he drove home some point or other in his soft voice. She looked up at him occasionally from beneath a furrowed brow, concentration doing double duty.

I had a copy of the *Daily* in my hand and was waving it at them as I walked up. Tom stopped in mid-sentence and they both looked curious. "Great news! We've made the West Coast press," I said. "I've got the story right here."

Marie-Louise put down her basketry and leaned forward as I spread out the page with the story on her lap. Tom stood behind her, stooping for a better look. She was the first to comment. "You wrote that? That's a helluva story. I love that you got 'banker's hours' worked into Lonnie's comment," she chuckled.

"Knowing how much everyone loves bankers," I observed.

Tom had finished reading and straightened to his full height at her shoulder. I could sense a stiffening of his posture. It seemed an odd reaction to what should have been good news. But for all I knew I might have been misreading his body language.

"Have you seen Rosanna today?" I asked. "I'd like to share this with her." I didn't add that I was hoping this might exonerate me in her eyes.

"She's working for Rick at the Garden Path today," said Marie-Louise.

"I was starting to wonder if she slept out here on this porch," I said. "This protest must be damn hard on her income, all the time she's devoted to it."

"She's a good gal," agreed Marie-Louise.

"You've been here just as much as Rosanna," I pointed out. "How are you making out?"

She lifted the partially completed basket in her lap. "Oh, I don't need much. I'm just trying to get a bunch of these made for the Christmas craft fairs. That's where I make most of my money. I've got a few local shops that take them too."

Even half-finished, the tight weave of cedar strands gracefully interwoven with birch bark suggested a piece that would be as much artful as functional. "Christ, Marie-Louise, with work like this you could be selling it in Vancouver boutiques for hundreds of bucks apiece."

She shrugged. "Like I said, I don't need much. My landlord is sympathetic. He lives in Oregon and lets me rent the house for the cost of taxes. As long as I look after the place."

"You *really* think that story will make any difference?" Tom's usually soft voice had an edge. It had an effect like an explosion at a violin concerto.

I straightened up; I'd been closely inspecting the basket. "Well, it's worth a shot...."

"Sure, and I'm not faulting you in any way. It's a good article. But this government we're dealing with, you really think they'll bow to that kind of pressure?"

I could feel my shoulders lift slightly in a shrug. "I can't really answer that, Tom. It's just one more tool in the toolbox."

"How did you find out about the Fort Langley and Delta hospital ER cuts?"

"That was thanks to our intrepid local reporters at the *Fort Langley Herald* and *Delta Times*. They must've had an inside contact, either at the ministry or hospital staff who got wind of it."

"In other words, the government is trying to keep it as quiet as possible." His tone was darkening. "Whatever happened to transparency in government?"

Marie-Louise laughed. "If it ever existed."

"Where are you going with this, Tom?" I asked.

"We have to do something more drastic."

"What do you mean? Rosanna's got Bob Williams working on the alternate budget," I explained, hoping to ease his despair. "The sacred circle photo will probably be picked up by the coastal media now that my story's out there. The mayor is working on getting a meeting with the health minister. And Rosanna tells me we've got another town hall meeting coming up."

"When?"

"Next Tuesday night at the Eldorado Hall."

He was pacing. "Yeah that'll help." I had a sense of pressure building up inside him—that feeling of a storm about to break open. Marie-Louise was watching him discreetly while she worked. She was picking up on it too, probably well before I did. Finally Tom stopped pacing. He stood staring out at the swaying cedars on the mountainside.

"I think I'm going on hunger strike." The words resounded in our ears like hammer on anvil. I had the hollow sensation in my core of my heart sinking. This was all we needed right now—another crisis layered over top the one we already had. Marie-Louise had shown she could work through almost anything; her fingers had a will of their own. But they were still now.

"Oh, Tom...." she said. "Please...."

"Listen, if it was good enough for Bobby Sands, it's good enough for me. Good enough for us. What else is going to get their attention?"

Marie-Louise looked at me. "Bobby Sands?"

"Sands was an IRA commander, an Irish Republican who was jailed in 1980 in Northern Ireland," I explained. "When the British government withdrew special category status for convicted paramilitary prisoners he and his mates went on strike. That meant they could no longer claim political prisoner status, which came with certain benefits. It was PM Thatcher's way of playing hardball with the IRA, criminalizing the resistance. There'd already been a hunger strike in 1980 before the one led by Sands."

"So did they get what they wanted?" she asked.

"Things deteriorated pretty fast. The prisoners had gone so far as to smear shit on the walls of their cells in protest." Her nose wrinkled at the idea. "Even then, it took the Archbishop of Armagh's visit to make the public aware of how bad conditions were. The first hunger strike was ended by one of the IRA prisoners because after fifty-three days, some were in a coma and close to death. By the start of 1981 it was clear Thatcher wasn't bending. She wasn't called the Iron Lady for nothing. So Sands took up the second hunger strike, only this time the prisoners joined in staggered intervals, instead of all at once like the year before. Right in the middle of this an MP in a critical riding died, and Sands managed to get elected in his place."

"What happened to Sands?" asked Tom. "Was he able to get the concessions they were demanding?"

"He died after sixty-six days on hunger strike. The Iron Lady refused to budge, even saying, 'Sands chose to take his own life, a choice the IRA's bombing victims never got.' It was disingenuous—the IRA did their best to issue warnings well in advance so bomb locations could be cleared of civilians, though not always successfully. In the minds of the hunger strikers' families it earned Thatcher a place in the Tyrants Hall of Infamy alongside Cromwell and other English oppressors of the Irish throughout history."

Hearing this, Tom turned aside, his intense interest suddenly deflated. Marie-Louise was looking up at him. "Tom, you can't really think this is a good idea."

"Okay, so Bobby Sands isn't the greatest example. So what? If we lose our 24/7 ER a lot more people than me could be at risk for their lives."

"We *need* you in this community, Tom," she pleaded gently. "You have a skill, a way with your hands that's healing for people. Why put yourself at risk?"

"Like you didn't put yourself at risk, doing the Water Walk across Canada."

"True, but I had support then. And you can't compare it to a hunger strike."

"Are you saying you won't support me if I do this?"

"No, I'm not saying that. But even if Rosanna does think this is a good idea, which I doubt, how can we support you? Unless we put more people at risk by joining you in the hunger strike. Sure, we could give you moral support, keep you hydrated, but...."

It seemed a logical place for me to jump in. "Tom, think about it. When your buddy Moss did his protest crawl for the hospital, remember what Rosanna and I said? We worried that if this got out to the big media, it would make the community look ridiculous. Luckily, when you had that miscommunication with Juliette and we had to go find you—"

"Moss broke his crawl to come look for me," he finished. "And I'm grateful you all care enough to do something like that. But, just like everyone else, I have a right to my own body. If I want to give it in a cause I believe in, that's *my* choice."

Marie-Louise suddenly stood up out of her chair, a distressed look on her face. Her eyes were bloodshot, as if she were about to burst into tears. She was collecting her basketry materials, stuffing them into a large homemade shoulder bag. It was rare to see her unsettled like this. Normally she watched events unfold with a kind of serene bemusement, throwing in sage or wry commentary as needed. Clearly this had struck a deep nerve.

"Fine if you want to go and kill yourself, Tom. I don't want to be around to see it." With that she slung her bag over her shoulder, folded up her chair and began walking away. We watched her retreating back without speaking for a long time. He looked sadder than I'd ever seen him before, which was saying something. Tom at his best moments had a melancholy cast to his expression. But the firm set of his lips made his determination obvious. I wondered if he might burst into tears. It was time for another tactic.

"Tom, will you at least let me talk to Rosanna before you start?"

"You can do what you want, of course," he shrugged. "She won't be happy about it either. Once I make a decision I stick to it."

"Just let me talk to her; maybe there's something else we can do. We've got the town hall meeting with PHA coming up—"

He snorted. "Another fucking meeting. They must think we're all brain-dead hicks to believe anything they say. I've been through the mill with these bloody town hall meetings. Nothing but a dog-and-pony show if you ask me. I've seen them pull this shit since the seventies."

"Still, let me talk to Rosanna...."

"Talk all you want, that's your right. That's about the only right we have left. Now, if you'll excuse me, I have some preparations to make."

"Like convincing Juliette? How easy do you think that's going to be?"

He refused to answer. Now I was watching him walk away, hands in his jean pockets, a determined stride propelling him forward.

Chapter Eleven

The comforting smell of coffee wafted into me as I opened the door of the Garden Path. I could see Rick and Rosanna behind the counter, busily making sandwiches. The place was only about a third full. The Gossip Clutch held a half-dozen customers. The post-Labour Day lull was taking effect. It was more like sitting around a kitchen table with friends and family than sitting in a restaurant. But if you wanted privacy, the Clutch was definitely not the place to talk.

Rosanna had on her smiling server's face. It clouded slightly when she saw me. Still, I was a customer, so she forced a smile. "Hi Roy. What'll it be?"

"Just a double espresso today. I'm not hungry."

"Okay, just be a minute."

"Oh, and do you think you could take a break? I've got some important news." Like her, I had to force a smile. I gave it extra gusto for cover but this would probably betray my true feelings even more than a cursory one. She looked to Rick, who nodded. "It's not busy. I've got this covered. Make Roy his coffee and take your break."

I took a seat at a table well away from the Gossip Clutch and spread out the *Vancouver Daily*. Within five minutes Rosanna walked up with my espresso, set it down and pulled a chair out for herself. In her other hand was a cup of tea. Her expression was cool. I wasn't used to seeing her looking this remote. "What's that you've got there?"

"The good news."

She turned her head to look out the window at the wilting flower garden, shaking her head. "Not another bloody good news, bad news story, Roy. That's getting old."

I sighed. "Seems we're stuck with it in this life. Yin and yang and all that."

She turned to look me in the eye. "Okay, let's have it."

I turned the newspaper to face her, open to the page with my story, and tapped a fingertip on the headline. "There. Check that out."

As she read her expression brightened. I was struck by conflicting impulses. On the one hand, it made me feel good to see her get some good news. On the other, I felt guilty knowing that the bad news I was there to deliver might slap her back down again. I didn't know whether to draw out the happier moment for as long as possible or just stop delaying the inevitable.

"This is *great*, Roy!" She was looking warmly at me for the first time since the hospital visit with Detwiler. "How did you manage it? I didn't think the coastal media gave a damn about our troubles here in the boonies."

"They don't, usually—too much going on in their bailiwick. I managed to gently twist the arm of my former editor. Did a little beating the bushes—found out it's not just Eldorado that's facing major hospital cutbacks."

"That's brilliant! I love Lonnie's quote. Straight to the point, just like the man."

"You make a pretty decent quote yourself. Makes it sound like PHA is stealing candy from babies with that bake sale bit."

"So this story'll be read all over the province?"

Now it was my turn to play devil's advocate. "Well, kind of. All over the Lower Mainland for sure, and a few points east. And it *is* buried in the C section."

"Still, that's better than just local coverage!"

"True. The power centre of the government is at the coast, and most of BC's population. So they get to look bad in the eyes of a LOT more people. But it remains to be seen how much political pressure a newspaper story will bring to bear on PHA. In my experience, some days it does, other days it flops like a pancake. Any word yet on the alternate budget?"

She wasn't particularly enthused about this gambit, I could tell. "I met with Bob Williams yesterday. He's been working with Mayor Miller on it. They've gone through two drafts already. Figures the ministry's CFO should have it in his hands by now."

"Just in time for Tuesday's town hall meeting," I observed. "Good. Hopefully they'll have had time to read it by then. Is Detwiler involved in that, or are they just referring it up the chain of command?"

She stiffened a little at the mention of Detwiler and the memory of the hospital visit. "I don't really know. He's the CFO for our region, so at some point he *has* to see it. But who knows, now that he's on sick leave?"

"How about the ministerial meeting?"

"Mayor Miller's working on it but so far he's not getting very far. Victoria keeps stalling—the minister is busy this week, the minister is considering your request, etc. etc."

It was my turn to stare out the window at the slate-grey late autumn sky. She knew something was coming. "I take it you're going to tell me the bad news now?" ·

It took more gumption than I thought I possessed to look her in the eye. "I'm afraid it *is* bad—very bad. Tom wants to do a hunger strike."

She dropped her head into her hands and held it there, emitting what sounded like a choking sound. I felt a shock go through me. I knew it would be bad, but not this bad. I reached out to touch her arm lightly. "Sorry to be the bearer of bad news. I was just over at the hospital with the *Daily* when he told me."

Finally she looked up, wiping a tear from one eye. "I'm sorry too. It's just ... this whole fucking thing has been über stressful. I've hardly had a decent night's sleep since it all began. This shit is really wearing me down. And now this...."

Unlike so many valley types, for whom profanity was so common you stopped noticing after awhile, with Rosanna it always hit me like a brick. "Marie-Louise and I tried to talk him out of it, but no luck."

A tear skated down her cheek. She quickly brushed it away. This was not a woman who cried easily. "Juliette is going to be devastated."

"You don't think she can talk him out of it?"

"Well, they're awfully tight as couples go, but he's pretty determined once he makes up his mind."

"Yeah, I got that impression."

"You saw how she worried when she thought he was supposed to be home from fishing."

"What if you gals all gang up on him—you, Marie-Louise, Juliette...."

She threw open her hands helplessly. "We can try, sure, but...."

"Okay, what about Moss the Crawler then?"

"What? Who's calling him that?" I could hear the protective edge in her voice.

I did my best to sound apologetic. "Um, well, pretty much everyone. You know how it is around here. They don't call it the Gossip Clutch for nothing."

"Sorry, I hadn't heard that yet. This is my first shift in a week or so. I don't know about Moss...." She looked off into the distance beyond my left shoulder.

"You saw how he rallied to help out when we thought Tom was missing."

"True. But I've known Moss for a long time. He can be *very* unpredictable."

"What do you mean?"

"Well what if he decides to *join* Tom in the hunger strike as a show of solidarity? Brothers in arms and all that. It's too risky."

I decided to let this one go and just strike out for high ground. "He's certainly very loyal to his friends. If we can even just get Tom to *postpone* the hunger strike 'til after the town hall meeting, that would be great. You never know, PHA might have something for us...." I realized as I said it how pathetic, how hopeless my words were. An old news hound like Bob Lejean would have snorted to hear me say it. I was surprised at myself. But I hated to see a fighter like Rosanna on the ropes like that.

"And what if they don't?" she implored. "I'm not putting all my eggs in *that* basket. At best we might be postponing the inevitable with Tom *and* the ER."

"I'm afraid I don't know what else to suggest."

She reached across to lay a hand over mine. It shocked me so much I had to resist the urge to pull away. Clearly things were on the mend between us. "I know, I know. And I'm sorry I got so mad at you at the hospital. I know you're going way beyond the call of duty as a reporter. I appreciate it."

I shrugged. "Despite rumours to the contrary, we're all in this big boat together."

She wiped her cheeks and smiled. "Thanks Roy. I think I'll go with the ladies first. Moss can be our wild card."

"Yeah, he's that alright. Let me know what happens with the Ladies' Brigade."

She laughed. "I will. Meanwhile, please try to keep this under your hat."

"You already know I'm good for it." I avoided the words "I promise."

She smiled. "Yes I do."

It was Friday–deadline day at the *Echo*. Donna had been extremely gracious about my irregular hours in the office, although I *was* a stringer, not regular staff. Earlier in the week she'd handed me two other assignments for stories of local interest—an investigation into sanitary conditions at the local grocery store and yet another police report of a marijuana grow-op bust. The grow-op bust was pretty much a cookie-cutter story, being the top priority the local RCMP detachment had for policing in the valley. You could speed through the Lowery Pass on a crotch rocket doing 160 clicks an hour, van-dalize village shops and cars, and beat your wife to within an inch of her life. But the one sure way to get police attention was to cultivate a greenhouse full of Kootenay Bud. To be fair, police resources were stretched pretty thin, and the truth was that there was very little actual crime in the valley beyond the domestic kind. I had to wonder, though, if some RCMP district commander was racking up brownie points with his superiors in Ottawa by playing up the 'drug war.' Eldorado Mayor Larry Miller had been quoted in the *Echo* as saying, "If the grow-op industry here was ever shut down, the local economy would collapse." And he'd produced the numbers to prove it. Still, village council's pleas for more community policing had fallen on deaf ears. The RCMP bureaucracy, it seems, was as impervious to a reality check as any other bureaucracy.

The grocery store under investigation was Elkville's Zippy Grocery, owned by a Chinese man named Soo Li. Local shoppers had gotten sick of buying meat that went rotten within twenty-four hours of purchase and had called the federal inspection agency. It seems Li was in the habit of relabelling his meat packages, constantly pushing forward the "best before" date. Most of the time people were able to avoid the worst of it by asking sympathetic employees, who knew the real expiration dates and were happy to tell, provided no one told the boss. Normally Eldorado and Elkville were so far off the beaten track you'd be lucky to see a federal inspector once per decade, and most locals were happy to keep it that way. But recently someone had been hospitalized for food poisoning after eating a package of Zippy's ground beef. That had been the final straw. When I checked with hospital staff they told me it was far from the first time; they could recall nearly a dozen food poisoning cases over the past two years attributable to Zippy's meat. Some middle-management food inspector with the federal agency took it as an opportunity to boost his career prospects. He was now blazing through the Kootenays, leaving a trail of traumatized business owners scrambling to keep their licences.

A five-minute drive took me to Elkville, where I parked outside the store. One of the employees at the checkout pointed me toward the rear office when I inquired after Li. The office had a window facing onto the meat section, something I found amusingly ironic. He was bent over a sheaf of orders when I knocked. At first he paid no attention, finally jerking his head up in annoyance. But when he saw me, he hid his irritation in a mask of polite amiability and yanked open the door as if trying to pull it off its hinges.

"Yes? You want help?"

"I'm Roy Breen, with the *Mountain Echo*. Can I ask you a few questions?"

The obsequious smile vanished. "Questions? What kind questions?"

"I understand you've had a federal inspector here?"

He waved a hand vigorously at me. "No, no—don't want to talk!"

He tried to close the door but I put a hand out to stop it. "Mr. Li, either you can talk to me or I can make it up. Write whatever I want. Your choice." It was a bluff, of course. I'd never made up comments for a story in my life. But he didn't know that. I could see fear creep into his face. He eased open the door again.

"Okay. I talk, I talk. What you want to know?"

"Have you had the inspector's report yet?"

"Yes, yes, he give me this—" He handed me a pink form with a list that had about twenty items on it. At least half of them had been checked off by the inspector. I scanned it while he watched me. Among the items were: "Clean and fully disinfect meat locker"; "disinfect meat-wrapping equipment"; "arrange for vermin control"; and other such points. It was worse than most people suspected. I scribbled down some notes.

"How long did he give you to do all this?"

"One month! Only one month! How I going to do it only one month?" His animated gestures made it plain he was distressed. "Cost me money, this! Big money!"

"We've had reports from shoppers that you repackage your meat past its due date. Would you care to comment on that?"

"Who tell you that? No, no I don't!"

"I'm afraid I can't reveal my sources. But someone found an old date sticker underneath a newer one. And somebody just ended up in hospital with food poisoning. Why else do you think a federal inspector is here?"

"I not talk anymore! You write bad story on my business, I sue you!"

"Nobody wants to hurt your business, Mr. Li. All we want is safe food. Just do what the inspector says and everybody'll be happy."

That seemed to relieve him. "Yes, I do it, I do it! Busy now, please...."

"So I can write that you have a plan to do everything on the inspector's checklist on time?"

"Yes! Yes! You go now!"

The truth was, I didn't know whether Lance and Donna would want to publish the story at all. Big-time advertiser Li may not have been, but every dollar in a tiny community newspaper counted, after all. The irony of it was not lost on me. In this case, the real power of journalism wasn't in actual public embarrassment but the mere threat of it. It's an ethical conundrum I'd never quite managed to resolve so much as find a way to live with. And it galled me that too often I had to do the job federal inspectors had refused to do, thanks to the current political culture of cutbacks. Still, if it kept people like Li in line, it was worth it.

As I sat in the wagon jotting down some notes, it struck me: Eccentrics come in all shapes, sizes, and ethnicities. I had to chuckle. How anyone thought they could get away with selling rotten meat in a community this small was a mystery to me. Five minutes in the Gossip Clutch and everyone in town would know. But then, if Li had come from a Chinese city of several million, where it's easy to blend into the woodwork, he might have been foolish enough to believe he could pull the same trick here.

Still, it annoyed me to have to be dealing with such small-time stuff while the hospital protest simmered on a back burner. Worse, I was preoccupied with Tom's threat of a hunger strike. It couldn't be helped, of course—stories develop on their own timelines. And the Tuesday meeting with PHA was just days away. That knowledge didn't stop the pins and needles though. Rosanna had said she and Marie-Louise were heading up to Tom's place today to try to help Juliette talk him out of it. I was far more interested in the outcome of that attempt than I was about some Chinese grocer with a penchant for selling bad meat.

Back at the *Echo* office I settled into my desk to write the two stories. The grow-op bust was basically an editing job, cleaning up the prose from the RCMP's PR department. It was extremely rare to get an impromptu comment from any senior staff these days. After awhile you just didn't bother anymore, lazy as that might sound. You just got sick of getting the runaround and listening to PR staff parrot press releases. We'd clearly entered the age of scripted communications. Call it the

Misinformation Age, not the Information Age. I usually tried to do some Web research for added context. Comparing stats on grow-op busts with drunk-driving convictions. Quoting criminologists comparing alcohol-related crimes with the impact of the marijuana industry in BC. Most were quite clear that it was no contest—alcohol spawned far more violence and crime, if the statistics for domestic violence were factored into the equation. Unfortunately this was rarely done, and the stats weren't kept nearly as assiduously as for grow-op busts. Meanwhile one Kootenay mayor had been lambasted in the media for supporting a campaign to decriminalize marijuana. Media pundits branding him the "Pot Mayor" had cost him an election. It made me sick to my guts of working in this trade some days. How strange, to feel shame about your own profession—something you feel such passion for.

Donna was signalling me from her desk as the phone rang. "Pick up line two, I'm busy right now," she said. I slipped on the headset and pushed the button. An older man's voice came on the line, a little thin but steady. "Hello Mr. Breen? My name's James Kieslowski. I live just north of Eldorado. I'm calling to report that there will be a memorial for my partner of thirty-five years, Ron Northcote. He passed away late Monday night at age eighty-four after a long battle with cancer." There was a pause.

"Would you prefer to talk to Donna? I'm new here."

"No, you'll do." For someone so recently bereaved he sounded quite businesslike. "The memorial will be held at St. Andrew's Presbyterian Church in Minto on Sunday at 1:00 p.m. I just wanted to make sure you got the obituary in next week's paper."

"Sure, we can do that. But it'll be too late to announce the memorial service."

"That's fine. I have friends helping me activate a phone tree. I don't do email but friends are helping me with that too. Word gets out pretty fast in a small town like this. I'll come in on Monday to pay for the obituary."

"No problem. And I'm sorry for your loss, Mr. Kieslowski."

"Thank you, son."

After I hung up I explained what had happened to Donna. Her face fell in dismay. For a few moments, I thought she might cry. It caught me off guard—I was so used to hard-bitten city editors who seldom displayed even a flicker of emotion. "You know him?"

"Oh, he's well-known—and very well-liked—around here. You've never read anything by Northcote?"

"Uh, no. He was an author?"

"Local historian and memoirist. He was a teacher in the valley, taught at a school they used to have here for delinquent teenagers back in the sixties. Ron came into a school system that—at the time—was still pretty harsh."

"Oh, yeah, I know. I have the scars to prove it."

"Well, anyway, the kids just loved him as a teacher. The first rule he laid down was that he wouldn't allow any kids to be strapped in his school. Instead of punishing them, he tried to get to know them better, find out what made them tick. He had a way of making them feel needed when the rest of society was telling them they were useless delinquents. It was life changing for a lot of those kids. They became his friends. As adults they still visit—I mean visited—him. Not a mean bone in his body—a thorough gentleman in every sense of the word."

"What are his books about?"

"He wrote what is still so far the only history of Elkville, *Elkville Days*. You can find it at Glacier Convenience and other stores around the valley. He grew up in Elkville way back in the 1920s. There were still retired miners from the original boom days living in the old Elkville Hotel then. The Northcote family knew most of them. His mother used to cook for them once in awhile. Ron's father worked on the railroad. He wrote a book of his memories of train trips his dad took him on, *Rails on the Rock*."

"Anything else? You've piqued my curiosity."

"Books, you mean? Yes, he wrote a lovely memoir of his school days in Newcombe called *Wu Xi Stories*. His parents had bought a house in Newcombe next door to a Chinese market garden. Wu Xi was a local character who used to sell his vegetables to his white neighbours in the days before the big supermarkets. Xi was so trusted by Ron's mother she used to let him and his brother get vegetables from Xi every week on their own. And this was when anti-Chinese prejudice in BC was at its worst."

"I'll have to look for his books. I take it Northcote was gay?"

"Yes, he and his partner James Kieslowski met in university. Ron was quite a few years older. I think he was teaching at UBC at the time."

"Unusual for someone of that generation to come out of the closet."

"Well, yes and no. Not so much around here. Nobody bats an eyelid about it. They become like any other old couple after awhile."

Lance had been engrossed in his layout for next week's paper but decided to chime in. "Just like my sister Nicole said about the local culture—"

"Yeah, I remember," I said. "Norman Rockwell with dreadlocks."

And then it struck me. "Do you know if Tom Bombadil was a friend of Ron's?"

Lance nodded. "Probably. Like Donna said, Ron was very well-liked around here."

"Loved, I would say," added Donna. "I suspect at least half the village will be at his memorial, plus relatives."

"That's why they're having it up in Minto?"

"Yes, our little churches here are too small, and the minister there is ecumenical. James is an atheist but Ron came from an old Anglican Church family."

"Could you excuse me for a moment?" I said. "I need to call Tom's place."

I looked up the number and dialled. An unfamiliar woman's voice came on the line. She sounded very shaky, like she'd been crying. "Oui? Allo?"

It was Juliette. "Pardonnez-moi, madame, my French is not good. Could I speak to Tom please?"

"Oh, mais oui. I will get 'im for you." I could hear other voices—women's voices—in the background as Juliette handed over the phone.

"How's it going Tom?"

"So you're calling to talk me out of it too?"

"I take it Rosanna and Marie-Louise are there?"

His tone was clipped. "Yeah. Was that your idea?"

I dodged the question. "Tom, they're there because they care about you."

"All it's done is upset Juliette."

I wasn't going to point out to him that he'd already done a good job of that himself. "They'll look after her. And they're trying to look after you too. I think you should be grateful."

A pause while he considered this. "So why *are* you calling?"

"I hate to be the bearer of bad news—getting to be a bad habit of mine. But your friend Ron Northcote died early this week. They're having a memorial for him in Minto on Sunday."

The line went quiet. It was awkward but I didn't push. He'd obviously put a hand over the receiver to tell the women. "Sad news, Roy. Very sad. I wasn't that close to him, but like everybody else around here I liked him a lot. Served me tea a few times in his beautiful garden just outside town. He was always a gentleman."

"So I understand."

There was a heavy sigh. "I have to pay my respects. He was a fine man. So you'll all get what you want. I'll postpone the hunger strike. But only 'til after the meeting Tuesday night."

"Let's hope you won't have to do it at all. For all we know there could be good news."

"This coming from the bearer of *bad* news...."

"Touché, Tom. I'll probably see you at the memorial service. Take care."

"Thanks, Roy."

Jane and I spent Saturday afternoon hiking along the old rail trail at the head of Sapphire Lake. In places the vegetation had grown over it and volunteers had cut a tunnel through the greenery. Then it would open up a vista on the lake stretching to the south, with the glacial ridges pristine in the late autumn sun. Jane had packed a lunch and we found a trail leading down to the water. Someone had been there before, arranging driftwood in a circle for seating. Overhanging cedar boughs made it a kind of wild bower, sheltered yet open at the same time. The fall breeze had its first teeth but the temperature was still warm enough for comfort. After munching down our sandwiches, we sipped jasmine tea from a thermos cup. Jane then leaned back into me, settling in so comfortably you'd think we'd known each other for years. A flock of Canada Geese was cutting a V noisily through the sky, heading south. Somewhere in the fir and hemlock forest a squirrel made it known he was *very* upset that jays had raided his stash. It was bliss.

The memorial in Minto for Ron Northcote the next day was a kind of initiation into local culture. Though only here about a month, I'd already noticed that the balance of population swayed heavily toward those fifty and older. That meant that death notices were a regular feature on the Post Office window. There was a fairly steady supply of retirees moving in to augment the resident population of Aging Hippies and logging families, but barely enough young families to keep the school open from year to year. It made me wonder if Eldorado was on a fast track to becoming a ghost town like the tattered remnants of Silverado in the Lowery Pass.

St. Andrew's Presbyterian Church in Minto was packed to the doors. The Eldorado Women's Auxiliary had prepared a massive lunch to follow the ceremony. Living in the city, I'd forgotten that in some parts of the country, the old-fashioned potluck was alive and well. Graham Kenwood had set up an open mike at the front of the church hall for people to offer their tributes and memories of Northcote. There was a casual, family air to the proceedings. The minister, Reverend Andrew Morrison, looked more like a white-bearded, bespectacled Santa Claus than a church official. His only concession to formality was the clerical band on his shirt collar, with corduroy slacks and a tan-coloured cardigan. Morrison was a far cry from the fire-and-brimstone preachers I'd been forced to endure as a boy in Sunday school. There was a fat little minister in particular I remember, a Jamaican Pentecostal who practically levitated from the pulpit during his sermons. I wondered what Moss would have thought of his fellow countryman. By contrast, Morrison's voice was so soft it would have vanished without amplification. He kept the religious verbiage to a minimum. Instead he focused on Northcote's reputation for kindness, his much-admired history as a teacher and writer. In conversation after the tributes, I learned that Morrison had degrees in comparative mythology and anthropology. Apparently he was something of a poet too. Religion sure isn't what it used to be, thank God. I must be in the right place.

Once the family had said a few words and offered thanks to the community for its generosity, Morrison opened up the mike. One after another, neighbours and friends stepped up to offer poems, prayers, and the occasional funny anecdote. I could see Kieslowski in the front row, struggling to keep down tears. He was a handsome-looking man of about sixty-five, with close-cut hair and beard. It was clear he wasn't the demonstrative type. Occasionally someone would squeeze his shoulders in a bear hug. He was too lost in grief to reciprocate but offered polite thanks. Tom and Juliette were part of the lineup of people offering hugs to Kieslowski and the Northcote family. It was impossible not to be moved. I found myself tearing up and I never knew the man. There were times in the city when I wondered how long it would take anyone to find my body if I died alone. During the five years I rented a suite in Kitsilano I never once met my neighbours. I doubted that would be an issue here. At least, I hoped it wouldn't.

When Reverend Morrison asked for help folding and stacking tables and chairs, everyone pitched in. The hall was cleared in ten minutes. It was astonishing to watch. I grabbed a dust mop and ran it around the floor. Jane insisted on helping the ladies wash up. In less than an hour the place was as neat and clean as if it had never been used.

I spent Monday at the *Echo* office, cleaning out my email inbox and doing research. The Ontario Ministry of Health had experimented with restricting ER hours a few years previously, to disastrous effect. While not a problem in urban areas with multiple hospitals, predictably in rural areas it had led to several deaths. Even in the cities, ER staff had complained about the overload. A new provincial government was elected with a mandate to restore health services and had reversed the decision. They'd produced budgetary figures showing that the cutback hadn't saved them any money. In some hospital departments it had actually cost them more. This was just the kind of grist for the mill we might need here, so I copied the information. Bob Williams and Mayor Miller were probably well ahead on this score, but the more we had to bolster our case, the better.

It was production night at the *Echo*, so Jane would be coming in to do copy editing sometime after dinner. Lance and Donna would be at the office for the long haul—putting in an all-nighter if necessary to get the paper to press on time. To save me driving home Jane invited me to her place for dinner—cod *amandine* but with tilapia again instead of cod, since the collapse of the Maritime fishery in Eastern Canada. "Ah—a post-extinction menu, then," I joked, but neither of us laughed. We were both too preoccupied with the upcoming meeting with PHA. It was the first time we'd had a meal together that hadn't been animated by lively conversation. After helping her wash up the dishes we walked the two blocks to the *Echo* office. Lance was taking one of his frequent cigar breaks, puffing away on the landing outside the office. Jane went straight in to get the proof pages from Donna but I lingered with Lance.

"Still no news from PHA?" I asked.

"Nope. But you probably know that."

"I checked the PHA website about five times today. Nothing—not a goddamn thing. If they're going to make any changes, they're making us wait 'til the last minute."

He was wearing the bearded Cheshire cat grin. "Or they're waiting 'til *after* the meeting so they can claim a decision was made in response to public consultation." Politics always seemed to amuse him deeply, whereas I found it a constant source of irritation. I'd lost count of how many times I'd blown a gasket reading government press releases.

"Well, I think Rosanna and the gang would happily take that over no change in PHA's decision. As long as we get to keep our 24/7 ER who cares how we get there from here?"

He nodded, letting out a dense cloud of cigar smoke. "Good point."

"But I'm not holding my breath."

"Oh, yes you are!" he laughed. "I can see the tension in your face."

"Me and most of this village."

"Yeah, true. I wouldn't worry about it too much. No government decision is ever final. We found that out a few years ago when they threatened to close down our school."

"Why would they do that?"

He shrugged. "Falling enrolment, budgets, the usual stuff. The school is one of our few steady, reliable employers in Eldorado. Take that away, the whole edifice collapses."

"Obviously you won that battle, since the school is still open."

"My point exactly. It ain't over 'til it's over."

Chapter Twelve

One sure way to gauge the importance of any event in a small village is to count the cars outside the meeting hall. I knew this one would be big so I left the car outside the *Echo* office and walked the few blocks to Eldorado Hall. Sure enough, by the time I turned the corner of Fifth Street where the hall was located, there were no parking spaces left anywhere on the block. Some were having to park on the adjacent block. The hall had a maximum capacity of two hundred and as I squeezed in the double doors it was already at standing room only. It was the same cross-cultural mix of people I'd seen at the earlier meeting with PHA. Logging families tended to stick together, creating a kind of self-imposed segregation. The Aging Hippies and New Agers tended to scatter themselves according to whim. The elderly mostly sat with whatever family members were present. Class-consciousness isn't dead in Canada, it just falls out along different lines than traditional class structure.

Graham Kenwood was running a microphone cord back to the control desk he'd set up near the back of the hall. He smiled warmly at me as he passed. "*This* should be interesting," he said. "Hopefully not too much of a Monty Python episode."

"You got something against Monty Python?" I quipped.

"Only if someone pulls a Ministry of Silly Walks skit," he laughed.

"Now that would be priceless."

I made my way to the serving counter outside the kitchen, which was shuttered, and set up my laptop. It gave me a better viewpoint than sitting in a chair. I could see the usual suspects seated at the head table—the PHA's Chief Public Relations Officer Marla Frankenheim, Policy Analyst Josh Denton, and meeting moderator Mayor Larry Miller with his trademark balding head and ponytail. Wade Detwiler, unsurprisingly, was missing. Frankenheim had learned from her last encounter with irate citizens and had toned down her wardrobe considerably. Her bleached teeth still flashed and glittered in the light but there was less expensive jewellery. And this time she wore casual slacks and a sweater instead of a business suit. Denton, who'd been relegated to nonentity status at the last meeting, was far more outgoing this time. Whereas before he'd been perfectly happy to blend into the woodwork, now he was smiling openly at people. It was impossible to know whether that was due to him occupying Detwiler's job temporarily or because he had good news to deliver. If it was bad news I doubted he'd be stupid enough to gloat in an atmosphere this tense.

There was a fourth person at the head table I didn't recognize, a tall, thin man of retirement age. I walked up to Mayor Miller and asked to be introduced. It was Bob Williams, the retired Immigration Department manager who'd been working on the alternate budget. I congratulated him on his efforts, though I'd yet to see a balance sheet. Grey, intelligent eyes looked down at me through rimless lenses. He held out a spidery, knobbed hand.

"All part of my civic duty," he said flatly. "This hospital has saved my life more than once. I have a heart condition."

Mayor Miller waited the usual five minutes or more past the hour to allow for the stragglers emerging from the spell of Kootenay Time. The hall was definitely over capacity now. I looked around anxiously for the Fire Chief, who might have something to say about that. As it turned out, Lonnie Harrison was near the back of the hall, chatting with other crew members. Obviously he wasn't worried. It was another reason I was fast growing to love village life—the "don't sweat the small stuff" attitude.

There was a dull pop as Mayor Miller tapped the mike to make sure it was live. "Ah, folks, we'd like to get started now, if you could all please take your seats. I remind you that if you have any questions after the presentation, please address them to me as moderator. We'll try and get you all home in good time. First up will be Bob Williams, who as you may know has been working on an alternate budget he's submitted to PHA. Bob, you ready to start?"

Williams rose as Miller sat down. Graham had set up a projector for his PowerPoint presentation. Williams was clicking through pages with the remote, looking for the front page. "Folks, your mayor and I have been working on this budget for three weeks straight now. Early last week I got our second draft of it to the ministry's finance department. They said they'd look at it but couldn't promise when."

There were a few "boos" and "aaaaghhs" from the audience. "Stalling tactics," shouted one man. Miller rose, making a calming gesture with his palms. "Please, everybody, let Bob finish. We've worked very hard on this. You won't be disappointed."

"Won't matter if they won't look at it," someone muttered loudly. Miller chose to ignore him. Williams continued. "Now here you see on the first slide the official PHA budget for the annual operating costs of our ER. About $375,000, including wages, maintenance, the works." He clicked to a new slide. "There's the pie chart breakdown." Another click. "And this slide shows what they hope to save per year by cutting the ER hours back. The bar graph shows both current and future projected operating costs, with and without cutbacks. You'll note that they hope to realize annual savings of about $37,000. Now that sounds like a substantial savings, doesn't it?"

"What's a life worth, Bob?" someone shouted. "Thirty-seven grand? Cheap at twice the price!"

"You could buy *two* of your lives at that price, Bill," a man's voice answered the first one. The room erupted in laughter, easing the tension.

"Not if you add up *all* my nine lives," Bill shouted. "I've used up at least four of them and nobody's paid me a dime yet." It provoked another wave of laughter.

I made my way to the audio desk set up by Graham. "Who is that wag?" I asked.

"Bill Radford," he said, keeping his voice low. "You haven't met him yet? Our local contrarian on every issue. You should read his letters to the editor sometime," he chuckled. "Classic stuff. A bit loopy sometimes, but classic."

"Not dangerous loopy, I hope."

"Naw, he's harmless. His hobby is provoking people."

Williams wasn't easily ruffled. He waited for the ruckus to die down and continued as if nothing had happened. "Well, the PHA figures might *sound* like a substantial savings. But what happens if you calculate the figures the ministry left out?" He clicked to a new slide. "For example, the added workload and potential impact on other area hospitals? By comparing annual budgets for other hospitals in the West Kootenay—which you can see here—" A slide appeared showing annual operating budgets for ER wards in Hannaville, Minto, Lowery, and Newcombe. The two largest cities—Hannaville and Newcombe—had ER budgets well over a million dollars per year. Minto and Lowery—two villages of similar size to Eldorado and Elkville—both hovered near the $300,000 mark. I could see peoples' eyes beginning to glaze over. Williams had spent countless career hours making presentations to rooms full of bored staff, so he moved on quickly. "To make a long story short, I did an aggregate accounting for added visits to other ER wards across the region, added ambulance and air transport costs and additional staff costs. As you can see from this graph, added all together, the extra *costs* to the ministry will be closer to $50,000 annually. That means the PHA's plan to roll back ER hours in Eldorado will actually cost them $13,000 *more*."

"I could've told you that," Bill Radford interjected from a seat near the front.

"No you couldn't, Bill," someone shouted. "You'd be lucky to keep your chequebook balanced." This time I could see Mayor Miller and the PHA staff chuckling too.

"So these are the figures I've submitted to the ministry," Williams concluded. He turned to look at Denton and Frankenheim. "Although I haven't heard back yet. Let's hope these folks will have some comment on that." With that he clicked off the screen and sat down.

Mayor Miller stood and took the mike. "I hear plenty of comments," he grinned, "but are there any questions for Bob?"

"It isn't rocket science, even for a government official," one woman said.

After another minute or so of scanning the audience, Miller turned to the head table. "Okay, since I don't hear any questions, next up is Marla Frankenheim, Chief Public Relations Officer for PHA. Marla...." He reached across the table to hand her the mike.

Her wardrobe may have toned down but her demeanour was as bright as ever. A little nervous, but she compensated with that broad, bleached smile in a moonlike face. "Thank you, Mayor Miller. I don't have an official press release yet, but I *have* been authorized to tell you that the ministry has decided not to foreclose on x-ray lab equipment—"

"We knew that!" someone shouted.

"What are you talking about? We *own* that equipment," yelled another.

"Bloody thieves in Victoria!" someone said.

It was then I finally spotted Rosanna's lanky form as she rose from her seat. Marie-Louise, Moss, and Tom were seated beside her. "Folks, please. This isn't helping. We need to let Ms. Frankenheim have her say." It was hard to tell whether it was the tone of her voice or the fact that she was a hometown girl that did it, but it worked. A few women glared at her but the men were spellbound. A few winced as their wives elbowed them.

"Thank you," Marla continued. "I really don't have much more to say except that your lab services will continue as before. I'll be putting out an official press release this week to that effect. I appreciate your time tonight." She handed the mike back to Mayor Miller.

"And last but not least," Miller announced, "Policy Analyst Josh Denton is filling in for Southeast Region Chief Financial Officer Wade Detwiler, who was seriously injured last week hiking the glacier trail. But before we continue, might I ask for a round of applause for our Fire Rescue team?"

He didn't have to ask twice. The hall clattered loudly with the sound of applause. Many twisted in their chairs to find members of the crew and smile back at them. Lonnie and three other crew members, including Don Houghton, stood up to receive the applause. As it died down, Miller handed the mike to Denton.

Denton stood up with the mike. "Hello everyone. As your mayor has said, Mr. Detwiler is unable to be here tonight due to injury. Normally in such cases where staff is off on sick leave, his job here tonight would've been handed off to a Chief Financial Officer from another district."

"How is he?" it was Rosanna. The concern in her voice was genuine.

Denton searched for the face to match the voice; she waved, helping him locate her. "Mr. Detwiler is recovering nicely, thank you. It'll be a long recovery though. I'll be sure to tell him you asked." He paused, smiling. "Like I said, it's unusual for someone on staff to pursue a case like this when they're in recovery, but Wade—Mr. Detwiler—has taken a personal interest in your hospital. Before he was even out of the recovery ward he contacted the office and asked to see the budget Mr. Williams put together. I have to tell you he was *very* impressed by that document. Mr. Detwiler is by far one of our most qualified CFOs and he couldn't find fault with that budget."

"I'm sure he tried," someone shouted.

"For God's sake, shut up. That's his job," Rosanna said.

"As the lady said," Denton continued, "that's part of his job. But I have here a personal letter from Mr. Detwiler he wanted me to read to you tonight." He held up a sheaf of paper. "And I have to say, this too is *very* unusual. Normally he'd only communicate through official channels." He cleared his throat, steadying himself.

Dear Mayor Miller and Council, members of the Eldorado community.

First things first—please convey my deepest thanks to your Fire Chief, Mr. Lonnie Harrison, and his crew. If it weren't for their skilled efforts on my behalf, my son Ryan and I could have come to a very bad end. Eldorado and Elkville are lucky indeed to have the benefit of their services in such a rugged environment. I wish to also thank Dr. Cameron and his fabulous nursing staff at the Eldorado Health Centre, who gave Ryan and me first-rate care. I don't know what we would have done without them.

> Second, thanks are due Mayor Miller and Mr. Williams for their diligent effort at preparing the alternative budget submitted to the PHA. It's obvious that this was done with great skill and attention to detail. Some of my older colleagues remember Mr. Williams from their days in the Immigration Department and his advice was always valued. As Mr. Denton has no doubt told you, I asked to see the spreadsheets from my hospital bed. After checking and double-checking these figures, I have no qualms in stating that they are correct. Often it seems we in government working in our little silos can lose sight of the big picture, and you have certainly made us aware of that now.
>
> I am writing you for two reasons. The first I've already stated: To thank your volunteers and medical staff for very possibly saving our lives. The second is to let you know in advance of the official press release that—based on the figures compiled by your mayor and Mr. Williams—I have made the recommendation that the cutbacks to your ER NOT go forward. Once again I—

Denton's voice was drowned in an explosion of cheering. People were on their feet, waving ball caps and other hats in the air, hugging their neighbours, cheering, shouting. The hall sounded like thunder in a bottle, muffled and explosive at the same time. A couple of loggers at the back of the hall were dancing round each other do-si-do.

"Wait! WAIT!" It was Bill again. He was standing on his seat to gain height, waving his arms to calm the chaos. "How do we know it isn't a *trick*? He's making a *recommendation*." He turned to face Denton. "What does that mean? He recommends and Victoria ignores it?"

It had the effect of throwing a wet blanket over the crowd. They stopped in mid-embrace, mid-cheer, mouths open as if suddenly caught out in a lie or a shock. But Denton was smiling. "Folks, I understand how you might feel. This has put you through a lot of worry. Let me put your minds at rest. Mr. Detwiler is the Chief Financial Officer for your region. That means he is the top official where Southeast Region budgets are concerned. It would take someone from the cabinet in Victoria to overrule such a decision. But based on this budget, I can tell you with confidence that's *not* going to happen. You owe a debt of gratitude to Mr. Williams and Mayor Miller, who made sure every t was crossed and every i dotted. The official announcement will go out this week. In other words, your ER is saved!"

It was like someone had hit the "play" button after a movie scene had been paused—the cacophony erupted anew. There was the sound of chairs thudding to the floor as more people leapt to their feet in joy. I was typing furiously on my laptop. It was moments like this I was reminded yet again how hard it was to be an observer—not a participant—in these events. I had to restrain an urge to pump the air with my fists. And I had notes to finish writing.

When the blare of celebration had died down a little, Rosanna spoke up. "Everyone, I'd like you to please put your hands together for Bob Williams and Mayor Larry Miller!" She turned to face them as she raised her hands above her head to clap. The two men stood for their cheers. Both were beaming— Williams with his understated smile and Miller with a wide grin. "And," Rosanna continued, "I think we deserve a village celebration after tonight. I'm going to talk to Rick about opening up the Garden Path for a party. Rick, what do you say?"

Rick was near the back, and although privy to most of the town's gossip, usually preferred to keep quiet at public events. He stood, smiling. "Sure, why not?"

Bill Radford the Village Wag was on his feet again. "Let's make it a hospital-themed party—bare bum gowns and wheelchairs only!"

"Only if you clean up the mess," Rick shouted back.

"I not be showin' I black ass in public!" It was Moss, provoking more laughter.

Now it was Mayor Miller's turn to call for quiet, raising his arms over his head. "Ladies and gentlemen! While we're giving credit where credit is due, let's not forget our other volunteers—the people who faithfully held the vigil on our lab." He held up his hands to clap and the crowd echoed him. He pointed at Rosanna, Marie-Louise, Tom, and Moss, who stood as the crowd clapped. Gradually he calmed the applause. "Think what you like about protestors, but at heart they're volunteers who care very much about community." The loggers joined in reluctantly at first but more enthusiastically as their wives elbowed them in the ribs.

As the applause subsided, Miller added: "And I'd just like to add thanks to our very own community newspaper, the *Mountain Echo*, represented tonight by Mr. Roy Breen." Everyone in the room suddenly looked my way. It wasn't a feeling I was used to, so I waved the accolade away. "It's Donna and Lance you need to thank," I said when the noise died down. Applause tailed off briefly before surging loudly again. "They're the ones holding this newspaper together with spit and elbow grease."

"And you, too," said Rosanna. "You helped us a lot by getting that story into the *Vancouver Daily*. And for what you kept *out* of the media." There was a sly, co-conspirator's smile on her face. I was relieved that our falling out had been healed. I was less relieved that she'd tipped her hat to my unorthodox journalistic methods. Thankfully the crowd was too much in the spell of celebratory euphoria to catch the subtle inference in her comments.

I had to raise my voice almost to a shout. "All I can say is, this is one helluva community. I'm glad I came and I hope to be part of it."

Rosanna led the cheers, offering an ear-shattering wolf whistle—another of her many talents. I could see Jane making her way toward me. Her height meant she was shorter than most in the room so she threaded her way unobtrusively through the crowd. She was at my elbow, slipping her arm around my waist.

"You already are a part of it," she said. The look in her eyes told me she meant something more than just the community.

Rosanna arranged with Rick to hold the party at the Garden Path the following Saturday. To accommodate the older folks, the celebration was to be officially launched at three in the afternoon by Mayor Miller. I filed my story on the PHA decision at the *Echo* and told Donna and Lance about the party—one they wouldn't want to miss. It was likely to be remembered for a long time in the collective memory of Eldorado. The nature of a biweekly community newspaper's publishing schedule meant the story wouldn't be known to the rest of the world for another week. But if anything that only made it seem more right, that the citizens of Elkville and Eldorado should have their own private celebration first.

I found Jane and me a small table near where Graham had set up his trusty microphone. I needed a front row seat to get good pictures. As I walked up to order lunch and coffee, Rick smiled slyly. "It's a beautiful day in the neighbourhood," he said.

I recognized the Mr. Rogers reference, dated as it was already. "For sure. I think I could get used to village life."

He managed to work a shrug into the motion of buttering bread. "It has its ups and downs like anywhere."

"You're okay with having a party here during business hours? You're not worried about annoying your customers?"

"Nah. If they don't like it, too bad. Besides, most of them this time of year are locals anyway. I did draw the line at having wheelchairs in here though. As you can see, there isn't a lot of room for the traffic jam that would create." He grinned. "I'm okay with the bare bum hospital gowns though. We'll see if anyone's bold enough."

I laughed as the young woman working the espresso machine handed me a lemon tea and an espresso. Jane and I huddled over our drinks, happily chatting. The door swung open and Rosanna came in with a tall young man I hadn't seen before. She waved gaily in our direction. Close on her heels were Tom and Juliette—whose shy nature kept her mostly out of the public eye. Tom's customary look of sombre contemplation was replaced by a good-natured grin. Behind them were Donna and Lance, both beaming. Normally they seldom showed up together, since there was *always* work to do at the *Echo* office. But this was too good to pass up—the celebration a news event in itself. Then Bill Radford showed up, his curly grey hair partly concealed beneath one of those papery hospital caps. And over his T-shirt and jeans he wore a hospital gown, loosely tied at the back. A couple of his buddies who came in behind him had done the same.

"Aw, come on," Rosanna teased, "you too shy to expose a little butt, Bill?"

He actually blushed slightly, making an already reddish complexion even deeper. "Why, Rosanna, I didn't know you cared!"

She shrieked—a sound I never thought I'd hear from her. "Hardly! But you came up with the idea!"

"You come on over to my house one day and I'll give you a private showing," he said, turning his jean-clad backside suggestively in her direction. She waved him off, still blushing. Her tall boyfriend looked mildly amused but kept quiet. I could see them exchanging whispered words as the background hubbub got louder.

I hadn't met the rest of Village council yet but there were four of them—two men and two women—whose faces I recalled from the meeting Tuesday night. They were seated at a table near the mike, chatting with Mayor Miller. In a fitting concession to Kootenay Time, he started precisely at 3:10 p.m. The protocol seemed to be not less than five minutes and not more than fifteen minutes late. I had to smile—it was a nugget for the memoirs.

"Ladies and gentlemen, Garden Path patrons," began Miller, "if you'd please give me your attention for just a few minutes. I have a couple of things to say before the party begins. I promise I won't keep you long. Rick has promised everyone free coffee refills today so I remind you to please tip the servers generously."

"Gee, thanks Rick," Lance said. "The first refill is *always* free here." Another ripple of laughter. His bearded Cheshire grin was as contagious as Donna's thousand-watt smile.

"Just testing to see if you're all awake," Miller laughed.

"Village council and I decided at a specially convened meeting Thursday afternoon that we'd like to present some awards. Now, I know it's customary to present public-spirited citizens with a Freedom of the City award, usually in the form of a brass or gold key. But we're a small village here in Eldorado, so...." he turned to the table behind him, where a row of golden coffee mugs stood. He picked one up and held it high for all to see. "Instead of a Key to the Village, with the consent of Rick Offenbach we're presenting the Garden Path Golden Coffee Cup Award. On one side it reads: 'Freedom of the Village, Eldorado, BC, 2003.'" He rotated the cup in the vain hope the words could be read, then turned it around. "And on the other it has Rick's famous motto—famous as far

away as Elkville—'If you don't like the service here, go somewhere else.' Now that's what I call a dedication to customer
service." He was interrupted by a fresh outbreak of laughter.
Meanwhile Moss the Crawler slipped into the restaurant.
Seating was already at a premium so he leaned against a wall,
wearing a mildly stoned grin.

"And because we don't believe in putting anyone on a pedestal, our Freedom of the Village coffee mugs are NOT mounted
on a plaque, which actually makes them more functional. They
come with a lifetime of free coffees here at the Garden Path."

"That *doesn't* include espressos, Roy!" shouted Rick from
the kitchen.

"And the first award," continued Miller, "goes to Rosanna
Yale, who never let up in the campaign to reverse the PHA cutbacks. Rosanna?"

She was blushing as she stepped up to the mike, standing
several inches taller than the mayor. Cries of "Speech! Speech!"
were building, deepening the crimson of her cheeks.

"I hate making speeches," she began shakily. "I get so nervous. But I really have to share this award with Marie-Louise
Tremblay and Tom Bombadil—" She was interrupted by
Mayor Miller, who lifted two more golden mugs from the table
and whispered in her ear.

"Oh, Mayor Miller said they already thought of that!" More
laughter. "Would you guys please come up and get your—
mugs? I don't know how I would've done it without you."

Tom shyly made his way to the front and leaned into the
mike long enough to say a meek, "Thanks everyone, thanks,"
before melding back into the crowd. Marie-Louise had been
working on her ever-present cedar baskets and looked up in
surprise. She shambled up to the mike.

"I just want to say, uh—you guys have all been great.
Rosanna, Tom, and Moss—and Roy, who we're just getting to
know. I hope you all know how lucky you are to have such a
warrior woman as Rosanna in your village." She was momentarily drowned out by applause. "I also feel I should apologize
for the scene at the sacred circle with Moonglow." Those who
hadn't been there exchanged puzzled glances. Those who had
couldn't help chuckling. It had been another vignette to last a

lifetime. "I can only chalk it up to the frustration women feel at having almost no power in this society—"

"*Please*, not another rant about the patriarchy! We'll be here all day." It was Bill Radford, who had a laser instinct for comments guaranteed to get an audience laughing. I had to laugh despite myself. I made a mental note to learn more about him. Jane gave me a knowing look and whispered, "He has a point, she does ramble on...."

Marie-Louise grinned good-naturedly. "Okay, okay, I'll skip the lecture." She raised a knobby finger. "At least, 'til next time. Thanks Rosanna. Thanks Mayor Miller." She made her way back to her table.

Rosanna stood up again as a smattering of applause died down. "Everyone, I think there's someone else we've missed, and that wouldn't be fair." She looked across the room at Moss as if seeking his permission to continue. She covered the mike, asking in a lowered voice, "Are you sure?" He shrugged a grinning assent.

"Some of you maybe don't know it, but our friend Moss here did his bit to save our ER. But maybe I'll let him explain it."

Moss shambled his way through the crowd to the mike. "I tank Sista Rosanna, she's like I own daughter. When I study in seminary I learn all de great pilgrimages of de world. De Tibetans dey make pilgrimage to Lhasa to see Dalai Lama. Muslims, dey make pilgrimage to Mecca. Christians, dey walk de hard way to Santiago de Compostela."

A puzzled silence fell over the crowd, finally punctured by Bill Radford. "What's your point, Moss? Anyway, I thought you were a Rastafarian."

"Catholic, Protestant, Jew, Muslim, Rastaman—Jah spirit de same in all. Some, dey do penance, count de rosary, pray de Hail Mary."

"Or hail Mary Jane, in your case," Bill quipped, getting an instant laugh.

"Some, dey smoke holy herb in praise, some, dey make holy pilgrimage, yeah? I follow de saints, walkin' on burnin' knees to Newcombe to save de hospital. Sista Rosanna helped, kept I fed. Roy an' Jane too."

"You're saying you were prepared to crawl all the way to Newcombe on your knees?" Bill's tone was incredulous. His words parted the crowd like Moses at the Red Sea, with about half erupting in laughter, the other half unsure what to think. There was some tentative applause that died down quickly. It was a reminder that there were indeed divisions in the community.

Moss looked disappointed, a little hurt. "Ay, Babylon! Some of you t'ink I crazy, I know an' I don't care. But Sista Rosanna know I all dese years, know I be de *wise* fool. An dis wise fool, he carry de sins of de people, de sins of Babylon—de gover'ment. Look—I show you de scars." He reached down and pulled his pant leg up over one knee to the sound of a few gasps from the older ladies. The knee was cherry tomato red, the skin pocked and broken in a few places. He was carrying more water, judging by the slight swelling. He rolled up the other pant leg, standing with legs apart and bowed.

"Whaddya want, Moss, a medal?" Bill again. "You gonna nominate *yourself*? Best Citizen Crawler?" It got some laughs but also severe looks from Rosanna and Marie-Louise.

Rosanna stood up. "I'll nominate him. Like he said, Moss is an old family friend. And he *was* willing to do what he says." Mayor Miller was whispering in her ear. "Um, the mayor tells me we don't have enough mugs."

Moss let his pant legs down. "Ay, den! I be on de way. Dis fool know when he not wanted." He turned toward the door but Rosanna strode over to put a hand around his on the doorknob.

"Hold on a minute, Moss." She turned toward the kitchen. "Rick, you've got other special mugs from the Garden Path, don't you?" Rick nodded. "Would you mind offering one to Moss for his community spirit then—same deal as the rest, lifetime free coffee?"

Rick thought for a moment, drawing it out for effect. I could tell he was barely suppressing his trademark puckish grin. "Yeah, why not?" Rosanna turned back to Moss.

"Irie! Dat's gen'rous, tanks Rick," he agreed.

Rick strode forward with a black mug embossed in gold with the Garden Path motto and handed it to Moss. The two men gripped one another in a firm handshake. A cheer went up. When it died down, Mayor Miller was at the mike. "Now, due to conflict of interest, I have to hand over the proceedings to Councillor Catherine McLachlan."

A woman about forty, of slim stature and brown hair, stood up to the mike. "What Mayor Miller means is that because it was he and Bob Williams who wrote the alternate budget, he had to declare a conflict of interest in presenting the next awards. Without further ado, I'd like to call them both forward to receive their Freedom of the Village coffee mugs. It was, after all, their budget that clinched the deal with PHA!" She extended a handshake as each one accepted their golden mugs. McLachlan sat back down as Miller resumed his duties as MC.

"And last but not least," said Miller, "we have one final Freedom of the Village award to present. Unlike our other citizens here today, many of you don't know him yet, but I have a feeling you'll be getting to know him well in the years ahead. I call upon Roy Breen of the *Mountain Echo*."

Jane looked me in the eye and led the clapping vigorously. I could feel my heart rate rising. It was only about three steps to the mike from our table. "Listen—thanks, but this really isn't about me." I turned to Rosanna, gesturing toward her, Mayor Miller, and Bob Williams in turn. "These are the real heroes here today. But if I can offer my talents as a writer to help the cause, I'm more than happy to do so." As I spoke I could see that Zelda the Sarcastic Server had quietly slipped in. She stood near the door beside Moss, her serrated grin as inscrutable as ever, face framed in parentheses by her glossy, bobbed black hair. Her presence made me more nervous so I looked away. All eyes were on me but I wasn't finished yet—there was more to say. I paused, looking at Jane. I felt that old telltale flutter in my chest.

"You've all made me feel welcome here. I've only been here a month or so and yet I feel I've made more friends in that time than I did in *years* in the city."

"You're just trying to butter us up for more free coffee." It was Zelda's voice—friendly but not without its usual sharp edge. There were a few chuckles. I had to wonder if she and Rick—or maybe Bill Radford—had been a couple in a former life, thinking up zingers like that.

"I don't think anyone ever puts *anything* over on you, Zelda," I shot back with a laugh. I thought of thanking her for the early warning signal, but realized she probably wouldn't take kindly to me tipping her hand in public. "I'm serious, though. If what I've seen in this community in the past while is any indication, you people are lucky to be living here. Not just the gorgeous lake and mountains, but the human ecology too."

I paused to take in the sweep of faces around the room. "When I was in Vancouver there was an elderly gentleman who lived in a little house next to my apartment block. He used to go out for a walk every day. Always dressed neatly—always wore a hat and tie. And he was always polite—friendlier than most people in that neighbourhood. But he had no family. After he died it took five days before they found him. Five days. It sent a shiver down my spine." I paused long enough to let the story sink in. "So thank you, thank you all for showing me what community *really* means."

I sat back down while people clapped and cheered. From the Gossip Clutch I saw a familiar figure stride in my direction—the pilot Jack Wingarde. He clapped me on the shoulder and leaned down to be heard over the noise. "Welcome to Eldorado, Roy!"

"*There* you are! You're a part of this victory too, you should be getting—"

He straightened but kept a hand on my shoulder. "Oh, no you don't. I don't need any awards or REwards. I just do what I do, like almost anyone else in this village."

Mayor Miller was at the mike. "By now you're all probably wondering if we've forgotten our amazing Fire Chief Lonnie Harrison and his rescue crew. It's been suggested that their rescue of Mr. Detwiler had something to do with the favourable decision he passed along to the PHA brass. Well, not to worry—we've nominated Chief Harrison and his Search and Rescue crew for Eldorado Citizens of the Year."

Once the cheers had died down he continued. "But as we usually hand out that award at Eldorado May Days, we'll be doing a separate awards ceremony then. You all know Lonnie isn't much for making a fuss, so I phoned him Friday to let him know."

Jack looked down at me knowingly. It seems modesty was

contagious in this village. Men and women who quietly did what they had to do to keep the wheels from coming off the village wagon. Who knows—maybe it was in the drinking water? "So in conclusion," Miller continued, "please stay awhile and enjoy the food and drinks. Rick tells me he'll look the other way if you brought your own wine or beer. Though I don't know if the liquor inspector would, but thankfully he only gets up here once every few months. I won't say anything if you don't." This too was met with raucous cheers. "All we ask," Miller continued, "is that you drink responsibly and use one of our designated drivers to get home." Here he pointed at several people in the audience, who raised their coffee cups. "Rick has probably been up since six this morning so we need to let him go home eventually. After dinner he'll close the restaurant. From there you're welcome to go down to the beach, where I've asked the volunteer fire department to prepare and monitor a bonfire. And we'll have music for you too, courtesy of Rosanna, a bunch of other folks, and me."

The ceremony over, Rick and his staff moved quickly to push three small tables together for the dinner buffet. Graham had the mike broken down and packed in under five minutes. "No Ministry of Silly Walks today then," he quipped in my direction with a grin.

"The day is young yet," I shot back. Turning to Jane, I lowered my voice. "Did you know Rosanna was a musician?"

"No, I didn't. But then a lot of people here have hidden depths." She paused, looking straight into my eyes. "Like you, apparently."

"What do you mean?"

"Do you really fear you'll die alone?"

"Where do you get that idea?"

"Oh, that little story you told about the old fella next door to your apartment."

"I guess ultimately we *all* die alone."

She smiled. "Well, if you want to get philosophical about it. But it's not entirely true." She put her hand across the table; I took it in mine. "People still somehow manage to reach across their solitudes and connect," she said.

There wasn't much more to say.

Lowery Park at the foot of Eldorado's main street looked out on a vista that would make postcard manufacturers drool. The evening sun fell orange across the mountaintops and spilled across the waters of Sapphire Lake, a slight breeze riffling flecks of scarlet into the deep distance. The roseate glow of sunset was daubed as if by a painter's brush on the glacial mountaintops, contrasted by the darkening tones of evergreen-lush slopes. It was hard to believe that this lake wasn't a mecca for artists all over the world. The receding mountain ridges were an object lesson in colour theory, gradually diminishing in hue from blue-black to pale blue-grey in the far north, each ridge just paler than the one before it.

A marquee tent had been set up on the small triangle of grass offered by Lowery Park, hung with battery-powered lanterns. Graham had been busy—a PA system and mixing board had already been set up beneath one corner of it and musicians were checking their instruments. After the smorgasbord at the Garden Path, Jane and I had wandered down to enjoy the view. The ground fell away sharply from the park to the lakeshore; a path of carefully laid stones led to the beach. Tall, gnarled cottonwoods with massive trunks luxuriated in having their "feet," as Jane called them, in the pristine water. She told me their new leaves in springtime practically glowed—spear-tips of luminescent green light. It wasn't a beach for sunning oneself on—there was no sand here, only gravel and boulders. The beach pathway clung to the remnants of soil and roots on the bank that led to the park above. Fir, hemlock, cedar and even the odd rogue apple tree flung their sheltering greenery over the path. Like the lake surface on a still day, it was a haven for deep reflection.

I reached for Jane's hand as we made our way carefully down the path to the beach. She clung to my grip as I walked the six metres or so to the waterline. I squeezed her fingers gently, glad of her touch. When we reached the water, I let go of her hand, dropped to a squat, and stared out over the painterly scene. She stood beside me, just as lost in reverie. There was a presence here in the land, a palpable energy. Its beauty was so stunning the only praise for it was silence. As I'd learned to do from my old man growing up in the north, I cupped my hands to scoop a drink of the icy clear water. It was so fresh and clean it sent a shock of energy through my whole body. This was *living* water—one of the last lakes uncontaminated by humanity, filtered clear by three hundred metres of mountain granite. On impulse, I scooped another handful and dipped into it to daub my forehead and the place on my jacket over my heart. Like a priest dabbing holy water over a reverent congregation, I wetted my fingertips again and flicked water droplets over first one, then the other shoulder.

Jane watched the impromptu ritual quietly. When I was done, she spoke. "Where did you learn to do that?"

I straightened to standing and put my arm around her shoulders. "I didn't. It just—happened."

"It looks vaguely Indian in nature. Ritualistic."

"Maybe. I guess I just made it up."

Her face was absorbing the gradually fading sunset glow. "It's very touching."

"Call it a covenant. A covenant of wonder with this beautiful place. A promise never to desecrate it in any way."

"And protect it?"

"Absolutely."

We stood a few more minutes bathed in the immensity of lake and mountains. We could hear more voices arriving in Lowery Park just above us. Someone was testing the mike while somebody else tuned a guitar. I looked at Jane and said, "Shall we go?" Without a word we turned to walk the short distance back to the park. As our view rose above the level of the lawn we could see the grass filling up with lawn chairs. Some were turned to face the music tent but most had been turned to face the fabulous sunset. There was only room for fewer than 100 people but the street would allow more seating. It wasn't like anyone would be blocking traffic on a Saturday night in Eldorado. There's only one traffic light in town anyway. These were the makings of a block party to rival anything seen in New Orleans.

Mayor Miller was the one who had been tuning his guitar. As he fiddled with tuning pegs and dials on his amplifier, Moss the Crawler was pressing some point home, his hands busily working the air as usual. As we walked up we could also see Rosanna standing at a mike while Graham adjusted it for her.

She blushed as we came up.

"I don't do this very often. Please don't get the idea I think I'm some kind of diva."

"I can hardly wait to hear you!" Jane answered.

Moss was hectoring Mayor Miller as he calmly continued with his setup. "Promise I, Mista Mayor, do some Bob Marley, Lee Perry tonight."

"No problem, Moss. And it's Larry. Call me Larry."

I chimed in. "And some *blues*. Gotta play some blues. Please."

Miller grinned. "Oh, don't worry, we've got something special planned for that. When I was on the road with my band we always opened and closed with a blues set."

As the evening faded indigo-black over the mountains I nudged Jane toward the edge of the park closest to the beach trail. But before we could get there, I felt a tap on my shoulder. Turning, I recognized the wavy auburn hair of Deb. She was smiling warmly. "I just wanted to thank you for your help with the hospital," she said.

"You need to thank Rosanna, Tom, and Marie-Louise. They all got the Freedom of the Village Golden Coffee Cup Award this afternoon. And Moss."

Jane nudged me. "So did *you*."

"Oh, I know, I heard all about it," said Deb. "I was working afternoon shift so I couldn't make it. I'll definitely talk to them too. Welcome to Eldorado, Roy." To my surprise, she threw a hug around my shoulders. It wasn't something I was used to from strangers. "Well, bye for now." With that she made her way toward the marquee to talk to Rosanna.

When the band started, it was a revelation. I hadn't expected anything better than garage band quality or worse. But Miller was obviously a seasoned musician. And with him was a full complement—including Tom on drums, Dr. Cameron on keyboards, and a hairy, bearded young bassist I didn't recognize. With his headband and tie-dye shirt it seemed he was a second-generation hippie—the kind seen more and more in the south Glacier Valley as these kids grew up. Retro they may be in the city but here they're part of the native ecology now.

Miller's voice wasn't likely to topple Mick Jagger or Michael Bublé from the charts anytime soon, but his voice had a rough charm. When the band performed the Stones' "Let it Bleed," he reminded me of Keith Richards' forays into vocals. Rosanna was hanging back, waiting for her moment, but joined lustily in the chorus of "Honky Tonk Women," ratcheting up the vocals several notches. Moss was standing near the marquee, nodding heartily in approval. As more beer and wine was consumed, chairs were folded up and put aside to make room for dancing. Soon the sweet musk of marijuana wafted over the swaying, dancing crowd. When Rosanna stepped up for her solo spot, her first notes momentarily froze the audience. Launching into "Chain, Chain, Chain" it was as if she were the blonde, white sister of Aretha Franklin. After a gust of wild applause the audience recovered enough to keep dancing. She followed with "Wade in the Water," finishing an all-too-brief set with a foot-stomping, hip-swaying version of "Take Me to the River" that went on for a full ten glorious minutes. When the delirious cheering died down, sending a red-cheeked Rosanna offstage, Miller stepped up to the mike.

"Our last song of the first set may be a little obscure, but some of you younger folks—meaning those over forty and younger than sixty—may recall it from the glory days of Glam Rock. It was written by Ian Hunter and it's called "Walkin' With a Mountain," something I think we can all relate to living here in the Valhallas." The first few bars sounded more like the intro to "Johnny B. Goode" but then, so many songs from the early seventies cribbed from Chuck Berry. I vaguely recalled the song from Hunter's Glam Rock band Mott the Hoople. It was an appropriate choice, with its reference to "mountain trains," although the Canadian Pacific Railway had long since abandoned their Glacier Valley tracks. In true valley tradition, the rail lines had been taken up by the community and transformed into hiking, biking and ski trails. Out here nothing much goes to waste.

As the last strains of the boisterous rocker died out, it seemed to be the cue for the volunteer fire department to torch up the bonfire. Jane and I walked back down to the beach to join the group gathering around the flames. We were joined by Graham, who was taking a break from the mixing board between sets. He had a beer in his hand but was nursing it. Someone threw a stick into the fire. A cloud of sparks shot up into the night sky, which was clear and crisp, with stars spilled like glittering pinpricks over the mountains. Lonnie was there, keeping a large fire extinguisher close by. He nodded acknowledgement at me with a smile. It was the closest he ever came to the warm and fuzzies. Don Houghton was also in the group, flashing his effortless GQ grin.

"Looks like you passed the Eldorado initiation test," he quipped.

"No, he hasn't—not yet," Lonnie shot back. "We haven't made him do the January Polar Bear Swim yet."

"Good luck with that one," I laughed.

And Moss was there, his eyes red and soft-lidded already from his intake of pot. With his grey-flecked dreads and blissful expression he reminded me of an oversized teddy bear. He came over to us, waving a water bottle in one hand, and draped his arms around our shoulders. I could feel Jane flinch slightly as he squeezed and shook us in congratulation. "I an' I—everyone in dis village done fine, yeah? Never did tank you for helpin' track down Brotha Tom."

"Hey, it was nothing. You did most of the work. You knew his favourite fishing holes."

"I tink you could get to like dis place, Brotha Roy. Dis be natural livin', I say. Crazy baldheads dey make fun of us dat come here—draft dodgers, hippies, Rastas. But I an' I just natural folk, yeah?"

"Sure, Moss." Slipping into his Rasta accent, I added: "Some, dey smoke holy herb in praise, some dey make holy pilgrimage, yeah?"

This was met with his belly laugh and a resounding slap on my back. "O, Roy be clever, Roy be quick!"

"Sorry, Moss, you were saying…."

"I be tellin' de story from way back now. Back in de day, I an' I generation just reactin' to all de crazy Vietnam shit. Ay, Babylon politricks! De cities polluted, de rivers polluted, de skies. Brethren an' sistren stuck an' dyin' in de ghetto. Jah revolution! De revolution babies just wanted some natural livin', close to de Motha, de Earth everlivin'. An' I found dis here."

"I can understand that."

Marie-Louise had wandered up, exhaling tobacco smoke as usual. "You got it, Moss." She watched him with a mixture of amusement and fondness, as for one of her own children, the one who can't help acting up in class. "I propose a toast," she continued, holding up a wine glass. "To this amazing place, our Mother—the lake, the mountains—to the Valhallas!"

Wine glasses and beer bottles were raised all around us. "To the Valhallas!"

With ganja being Moss's substance of choice, he had only a water bottle to raise. "Irie! To natural livin'!" His words were echoed by the crowd.

But I could never have predicted what happened next. Moss was stripping off his clothes with the fury of a man on fire, down to his boxer shorts. Jane's hand reflexed to her mouth in amusement as she stepped well back. Graham was smiling. Next thing we knew Moss was running over the stones and into the lake, splashing and shrieking like a kid in a pool on a hot July afternoon. "C'mon! C'mon everybody," he shouted. "Polar Bear Swim in November! Why wait for January! C'mon in!"

Don Houghton moved quickly toward the waterline. "Moss! Get the hell outta there, you idiot! That water is probably below zero this time of year! You'll catch your death!"

"Irie! Clean, cold—natural livin'!" Moss was shouting. But by the third time he said it, his teeth were starting to clatter. Yet he had no inclination to get out of the water. Some were laughing, others looked worried. A couple had started stripping down to join him, but Lonnie warned them off sternly with a wave of a fingertip. Moss chanted and capered like a leprechaun, then slipped and fell in the shallow water. There was an involuntary reaction of alarm in the campfire circle. Lonnie and Don strode briskly into the shallow water and hoisted him out by his armpits, hauling him back to the fire. He was giggling uncontrollably. In another crowd, the laughs would have been *at* him. Here, the laughs were *with* him. Jane and I just watched quietly.

"Nice one, Moss," muttered Lonnie. "As if my guys don't have enough to do rescuing city boys from the glacier trail…. Don, go get a blanket from the emergency kit, will ya?"

I felt a gentle poke on my arm and turned to see Graham. "So it's the Ministry of Silly Walks after all," he said, laughing.

Once Moss had dried off he struggled back into his clothes. As the flames warmed him he grew steadily more drowsy, gradually falling asleep against a log close to the bonfire. Jane and I found ourselves entranced by the star-washed sky. Once again the only appropriate praise was silence, a reverential meditation that held many of us in its grip.

"I have a surprise for you," I finally whispered to Jane.

"Oh, what's that?"

"You'll have to walk up to the *Echo* office with me to see."

Without a word we turned from the bonfire and made our way up Eldorado's main street—past the Garden Path, past the Post Office, finally to the humble building that sheltered the *Mountain Echo*. My old wagon was parked out front.

"Right here," I said, opening the passenger-side door. Already I was getting into the habit of not locking my car like everyone else in the village. I could see the curiosity on Jane's face.

"Hey Shadowcat. Shadowcat!" I shouted into the car. A sleek black head poked out from under the car seat. In response I got a "Yeah, whaddya want?" look from him as he slowly stirred from the self-induced trance he adopted whenever I put him in the car, blue-green eyes half lidded, almost sickly.

"This is the surprise—you brought him to the party!" Jane exclaimed. She bent down over the seat and stroked his head. He closed his eyes the way cats do when bliss is approaching. He had that put-upon look he always gives me when I announce another road trip. But Jane's ministrations were definitely helping. He looked up at her adoringly as if she were Mama Cat.

"Oh, poor thing," she said. "He obviously hates the car." My universal translator picked up Shadowcat's thoughts again: "Yeah, you put me in this damn box on wheels again. And I don't even know what for."

"It's a party, dude," I said to him. "We saved our emergency ward!"

He looked away from Jane long enough to offer a doleful stare. "You humans have a weird way of celebrating—torturing cats."

"I hope you brought him a treat," Jane said.

"You bet I did," I said, reaching into the glove box for a can opener. Within minutes he was gratefully slurping away at a can of tuna. "I just thought the celebration would never be complete without him."

She gave me a soft look. "Absolutely."

We made our way back down to the bonfire on the beach as we heard the music starting up again. Mayor Miller was back at the mike introducing the next set with another medley of fast-paced rockers. After wearing down the crowd, the band slipped into a set of slower numbers. Finally Miller announced the last song of the evening.

"I decided to save the best for last. I'd like to play a song I wrote called "Mountain Blues." It's based on an old blues classic, "Catfish Blues." This is dedicated to Rosanna and everyone who helped save our ER. Hope you like it." He chose a down-tempo arrangement that had couples swaying gently to the beat. "Well, if I were a mountain, mama / I said, standin' above Sapphire Lake / I'd save all I can, sweet water to taste / and if the man come to take it away / I'd be your rock, mama / and nothin' could make me sway / I got the mountain, oh I got the mountain blues, mama / and nothing,' no nothin' gonna take me away...."

Acknowledgements

An undying debt of gratitude is owed to Anne Champagne, who copy edited the manuscript and rescued the book's timeline. Further thanks are due my early readers of the story, Ernest Hekkanen and Gary Wright, for their valuable insights.

Permissions

Hell's Angels
Words and Music by Roy Harper.
Lyrics cannot be copied or used without permission.
Reprinted by Permission of Roy Harper and Science Friction.

PHOTO: JUSCHA GRUNTHER

Sean Arthur Joyce, better known in the Kootenays as Art Joyce, has published two books of regional history and in 2014 published *Laying the Children's Ghosts to Rest: Canada's Home Children in the West* (Hagios Press).

Joyce's poems and essays on poetics have appeared in Canadian, American, and British literary journals. In 2016 his poetics treatise, "A New Romanticism for the 21st Century," appeared in the peer-reviewed journal *Canadian Poetry* from the University of Western Ontario. His poetry has appeared in several anthologies, both Canadian and international, most recently in the Corbel Stone Press Contemporary Poetry series (UK 2017), Nanaimo Public Library anthology and *Fire & Sky*, a fundraiser for victims of the Ft. McMurray, Alberta firestorm of 2016.

New Orphic Publishers of Nelson, BC, Canada has published three collections of his poetry: *The Charlatans of Paradise, Star Seeds,* and *The Price of Transcendence.*

In 2016 he produced his second poetry video, *Dead Crow: Prologue,* with music soundtrack composed by Noel Fudge and video production by Isaac Carter of ICandyFilms. A live version of the performance toured the Kootenays in Fall 2016.

Mountain Blues is his first novel.